Emissaries to the stars . . .

From somewhere deep in space came the radio signal that Earth had long awaited; there *was* intelligent life out there, and it was prepared to be friendly. For the eleven people on board the starship *Open Palm,* that signal was the beginning of the greatest adventure of their lives. Some expect to be able to come home and tell their grandchildren about it; others, older, expect that the *Open Palm* will be their tomb, for the journey is to take many years.

And what will happen under the pressure of those years of isolation? No one knows. It has never been done before. They are pioneers, committed to a way of life that is as unexplored as the stars themselves.

MARATHON

For Mark

who accidentally lit the fuse

MARATHON

A parabola in time

D. Alexander Smith

'Aiming at the stars,' both literally and figuratively, is a problem to occupy generations, so that no matter how much progress one makes, there is always the thrill of just beginning.

—Robert H. Goddard, in a
letter to H. G. Wells, 1932

**REACH FOR THE STARS
NOT THE BOMB**
—Found on the back of a
subway seat, Boston,
Massachusetts, United
States of America,
July 6, 1976

Ship's Manifest, Starship-1 *Open Palm*.

Captain. Aaron Michael Erickson.
First Officer. Helen Marie Delgiorno.
Pilot. Walter Tai-Ching Jones.
Engineer. Willem Kees van Gelder. ("Casey")
Medic. Heidi Diane Spitzer.
Life Support. Thomas Edgar Rawlins.
Xenopsychiatry. Yvette Heloise Renaud.
Xenopsychology. Harold Nelson Bennett.
Xenosociology. Olga Katerina Belovsky. ("Katy")
Translator. Samuka Lin Tanakaruna.
Emissary. Patrick Henry Michaelson.

Liftoff: 083423   18 November 2058

MARATHON

D. ALEXANDER SMITH

SF
ace books
A Division of Charter Communications Inc.
A GROSSET & DUNLAP COMPANY
51 Madison Avenue
New York, New York 10010

MARATHON

Copyright © 1982 by David Alexander Smith

An ACE Book

First Ace printing: July 1982
Published Simultaneously in Canada

2 4 6 8 0 9 7 5 3 1
Manufactured in the United States of America

1.

I am ashamed to say, I dye my hair. I hate the process, but I must appear, if not immortal, at least ageless. Though I am human and must die, to my crew I must be immutable: forever old, forever tired, forever strong.

My hands have become arthritic, but I do not let that show either.

Today we are halfway there: even though none of us celebrates liftoff anniversary, we all cheered today. Four hours of relief, while the ship swung around. We now begin deceleration.

After three and a half sub-years of full gravity, weightlessness was a novelty to most of the crew, but for me it was like coming home. We bolted down what we could, but much was disarrayed nevertheless. No matter. Time we have enough of.

They were afraid of weightlessness in the early years. So were my paying customers. Of course they remembered it from training, but that's not the same thing as living it. Casey and Heidi were out of sight for a couple of hours. When next I saw him, Casey's grin kept slipping out the sides of his mouth. It was touching; I only wish we could have it more often. It seemed so helpful to the crew's spirits.

The latest alien transmissions have been scenes from *djan* reunions. You who read this log, if it ever returns to beautiful Earth, have by now seen them too. Strange: the shout sent from ten light-years away will take another four years after I write these words to reach you, so far behind us.

On the screen, the aliens look so much like us. Oh, at first we all saw just the differences. But as I watched (in my spare time, of course), their behavior began to make sense. We don't yet understand all the Cygnan rules of behavior, but we know that rules exist. We have found neighbors, and they are much like us. By that I am comforted. Things must be getting better.

Both Mr. Bennett and Ms. Renaud see many examples of convergent *social* evolution, much like the convergent physical evolution of the tasmanian wolf of Australia, the doglike marsupial of that continent. If so, it will help. We can trust only if we understand. Back on the ground, Australia's species remained unique only because they were isolated from the mainland, uncontaminated. Will we lose our uniqueness to these new people?

The crew seem to have weathered the first three and a half years remarkably well. The young ones are all so passionate, in a hurry, full of that same fire and zeal that I think I once had. I would not want those feelings back; do I even mourn their passing?

First Officer Delgiorno is handling the crew well, if roughly. It seems to be working; young people are impetuous yet resilient. I have always questioned Helen's methods, but seldom quarreled with her results. She says a little friction helps keep us sharp; occasional sparks prevent a major explosion. She has been right so far, and I must trust her judgment.

Was Earth wise when it picked us as crew?

We are all, in one way or another, outcasts. We are widowers, widows, single people. Few of us have strong ties with Earth; what ties we have are withering away. Those candidates who were tightly bound to their society stayed behind. My passengers have borne the strains of loneliness well.

Despite the signs of success, I worry. I grow old. Being this close to so many has tired me. The captain, aside from being the central figure of authority, is also a father figure, at one with his ship. This is a strong ship that holds the cold vacuum of space from us, and I must be a strong captain to hold the inner cold away also. I touch the pebble in my pocket and wonder. I cannot be weak, or I doubt myself, and if I let others know my doubts, they will share them.

Sometimes I fear that I may not live to see the end of our journey, and the thought terrifies me. Not the fear of death, not my own death, no. But my ship: without me, there will be

no heart left in this ship, and I fear that she will die. She is
steel and titanium and genius, she runs with the same force
that powers the stars, and she cradles my soul. If I die, she
must also.

I have written too much. I am a vain old man, who believes
that his passing will be a monumental occasion. I should
know better. Give me strength to carry my burden. Give us
fair winds. Let my beautiful ship sail the currents of the
vacuum of space. Let our journey end in a safe harbor in a
foreign, alien land.

First Officer's Log, 7/4/62

Midpoint Day is finally here. I took advantage of the
opportunity to arrange a party. As usual, TCJ was a boister-
ous troublemaker. He has lots of free-fall experience and he
used his advantage over most of the others (although he got a
surprise from me!), throwing several of the crew around in
his playfulness. He is immature (I've said that before, but it's
still true) and too full of energy. Plus, between the extra time
he's got and the strain of breaking up with Heidi, he's piling
up frustration like a pressure cooker. If I don't find some way
to vent that steam safely, he will be the death of us all.

The Dreamer hasn't been enough. He needs to let out his
energy on a real live body. Lovely. I don't see how anyone
could keep up the act for several years. Back home they
might call that duty.

He loves to shake up Renaud. God knows she's not my
favorite person, but when I see the mauling he gives her, even
I feel slightly sympathetic. A middle-aged spinster with
neurotic tendencies is just *not* going to be able to cope with
someone like Tai-Ching Jones. He relishes that, of course,
and plays on it unmercifully: he doesn't like shrinks and he
especially doesn't like her. He'd love to pick on Harold, but
Harold gives as good as he gets, and Walt bruises easily.
Beating up on helpless Yvette is more fun.

We obviously made a mistake in choosing her, but there's
nothing to be done now. She was supposed to be a member of
the command structure; instead, she's one of the ones I have

to juggle: a psychiatrist who cannot cope with herself, let alone others.

I will speak to Kees and see if he can put a muzzle on his friend. Friend! Master might be a better term. I wish that Dutch bastard would for once take a stand rather than be pushed all over the place just to preserve the 'proprieties'.

Enough of this cheerful garbage. I'm just too damn tired; today was a long day, and talking into the empty air like this isn't my idea of self-expression. Things aren't as bad as it seems; I'm just blowing off my own frustrations. We're halfway there. Maybe it'll be easier from now on.

2062:4:7:2234:56.275

Please allow me to introduce myself, I'm a man of wealth and taste.

The evidence suggests that discovering oneself is a time-consuming and incoherent process. Although no practical benefit arrives from such introspection, comprehending the process may prove helpful when attempting to analyze human behavior. Such analysis is necessary if this entity is to pass unnoticed.

2062:4:7:2234:56.630

7 April 2062. Psychiatrist's log.

Midpoint Day means so little to me: simply, the easy half of my job is over. That is all I have won in three and a half years. The major developments of the day were the increasing deviance of Bennett and my own personality problem with Tai-Ching Jones.

Bennett is irascible, and intelligent, and highly specialized. His outlook upon the rest of us is mostly contemptuous. He regards us as imbeciles, and he scarcely bothers any more to hide his condescension. Fortunately his job keeps him busy.

He cannot broaden his outlook with the rest of us—he is confined to the Cygnans and their psychologies. I suppose this is part of what has made him so renowned in the field—

this ability to immerse himself in whatever psychology he is investigating. Certainly his studies of the aborigines and Eskimos reveal a sensitivity and a bond of friendship not displayed here.

"Now let's be quite clear about this," he will say, "to understand the Cygnans, we must go inside their minds. Accept; not judge. Participate; not chronicle."

He is up to something. I am frightened.

He must be handled with kid gloves, and the best way is the way we have followed for some time. Total immersion in his subject will mitigate his harmless eccentricities where they won't grate on other people's nerves. Bennett is too self-centered to understand how irritating he is.

Tai-Ching Jones is just about at the other end of the spectrum from Bennett. Where he looks up to the captain as to a father, Tai-Ching Jones treats Bennett as a sibling—constant bickering, constant stress. Bennett just thinks Tai-Ching Jones is a young loudmouth. Which he is—but telling him so doesn't make him any easier to live with.

Tai-Ching Jones particularly affects me. No matter how impassively I sit, no matter how much I try to turn the conversion away, he can hurt me. He's a presumptuous ass, but I'm proud that I don't hate him. I cannot flee him, for that also would only aggravate the problem. Thank God he isn't a practical joker, but if I ever let on that I can't stand practical jokes he will become one.

I must retain my objectivity. If I got angry, he would just laugh and come back for more. And it would also ruin my effectiveness.

I don't like these developments. We may be in for rough times ahead. Whenever I see Bennett, chills run up and down my spine. Rats' blood . . . .

In the long run, Tai-Ching Jones doesn't bother me as much as Bennett does. What Tai-Ching Jones needs, I guess, is some physical release. Rawlins would be the only one of the crew who could do the job. I will have to see if I can get them interested in karate, or judo, or some such. Van Gelder might be big enough to handle Tai-Ching Jones, but he is too pacifist even to think of fighting for enjoyment. And considering that Spitzer has bounced from one bed to another, Walt might rip Kees' head off. No, Rawlins is better; he's tough enough to know how to goad Tai-Ching Jones, then careful enough to work it off safely.

No change in the status of the rest of the crew. I suppose that only two, no three (counting myself) problem children in a crew of eleven is not too much, after three and a half years' confinement together. The Tai-Ching Jones/Spitzer conflict is being defused, thank goodness.

I'm sixty-three years old and I'm tired. Even with no outward manifestations, I fear the spectre of lunacy. Under every shadow, behind every grimace, lies my fear of Ganymede.

Translator's Log, Midpoint Day, 7 April 2062.

Our faithful steel steed gallops onward, ever onward, tirelessly. You have run half your race, dear friend, bear us on to safety at the other end.

It is spring now. Fujiyama must be beautiful, trees just beginning to blossom.

> Under the mountain
> Flowers spring skyward daily
> Life begins anew

> My candle burns at both its ends,
> It will not last the night.
> But, ah, my foes, and oh!
> My friends,
> It gives a lovely light!

The first is mine, a Tanakaruna original. The second belongs to an American poet, a Miss Edna St. Vincent Millay. And, I think, we are both right. Life is frantic at its beginning. The trees explode forth with buds. They reach their glory through the summer in the sun. Then, as the summer ends, they fade into wrinkled brown, and silently drop to the ground, to become the food for the next cycle. Life begets life.

The young ones on ship, do they understand that life is a flame, and that the most comforting warmth comes, not from the initial flash of ignition, nor from the glow of flames, but from stately burning embers, whose light lasts into the night?

I am old, but I have never been a flame to be extinguished. I am an ember of a slowly burning leaf. It is good to be an ember. It is good to burn slowly.

An old woman may easily hope, for death will not take from me my 'best' years. Every year lived is the best year, because every year I live is another miracle from the universe. Imagine, that I, small in my kimono, can sit, and think, and love.

Tears fall on paper
They are absorbed, and are gone.
But the words remain.

What a gift thought is, what a gift language! How personal it is, and how beautiful, that we can share our hearts and minds. I can hand my thoughts to the future, as Miss Millay sent hers winging down the ages, and her dead hand stirs me again.

How could the universe be, if not for man?

I cannot explain that thought, but I know it is true. The younger ones, they say there is no god, but how could there be a creation without a god? A god of the trees, a god of the rocks, a god of the birds, a god of men. How could there be saintliness and purity without god?

And how could he not be imbued with love? I am human, yet there is nothing which I hate. There is no evil, only misunderstanding.

Do I believe that?

Do the Cygnans?

I am tired. I will sleep, and what matter if that sleep last six hours, eight hours, twelve hours, or forever? I have lived on the Earth, I have felt the grass, without me the world would have been different. The differences might be subtle, but I am a part of the world, as much a part of the world as a bird or a mouse, and I was a part of the world at the beginning, and I will be a part of the world long after I am dead. I will nourish trees with my nitrogen.

I hope they grow tall and straight.

Walter Tai-Ching Jones, Pilot of the spaceship *Open Palm,* twisted and tossed in the grip of a dream. Phantom shapes fled before him, spun around him.

He was eight years old, at one of the nearly endless functions to which he was often whisked. He was uncomfortable in his jacket and shining shoes, in which he could see reflections of the glare of the lights, the glitter of the diplomats. Gaiety and tobacco smoke swirled with the adults.

Boys: some yellow, some white. A birthday party for one of his acquaintances—a "working" party, an excuse for the adults to convene, slander, plant rumors, swap secrets, make deals. Business as usual—under the table. While the boys rollicked and yelled, the men (his father among them), drifted off among the cocktails, playing their deadly polite games.

The highlight of the celebration was the spaceship race. Nine boys entered, each with his own model spaceship carved out of a single block of balsa, an elastic-driven propellor through the center. Nine ships, each with two tiny hooks, to be set on a line, to race the length of the hall, an expanse larger than the imagination of a child.

Graceful and sleek, his own ship was his pride and joy, the product of his own weeks of labor, unassisted by his father. The *Open Palm,* his own face painted into the tiny window. In the finals, ready to win.

He set his little ship tenderly on the track, and looked briefly at his only remaining obstacle, the other boy . . . was that really van Gelder? No matter. This ship was his beauty, he would fly the length of the course straight and true and faster than the other. He began to wind the elastic band that held his tiny ship.

And wind it, and wind it.

And wind it again.

Each time he wound, the propellor slipped off the end of his finger and snapped back. Though he glared in helpless fury at his hand, the propellor slipped back, and back, and back.

Now the scene dissolved. The elastic was miraculously winding up, tighter and tighter. Tight enough—stop winding. But the propellor kept turning, turning, tightening the elastic band. He looked at van Gelder, who was smiling, and he looked for his father, who was absent, and he watched in fury as the band grew tauter, tauter . . . till finally it snapped.

Snapped! and he was inside his ship, on the bridge of the *Open Palm* with van Gelder beside him at the engineer's console, and the ship was running her utterly straight course to 61 Cygni.

Snapped! and suddenly the *Open Palm* roared away from under him, veering wrenchingly to port, spilling him out of his seat. He cried out, tried to stumble back to his seat before the ship got utterly off course, but the G force was too great. As he flailed on the floor, he stared spellbound at van Gelder, but that crazy Dutchman sat quietly, calmly, saying, "it's all right, this is just a planned maneuver," and smiling, smiling benignly.

Now he was in his seat, madly calculating, slapping rows of switches. No effect—either from the ship or from his friends, she was gone, out from under him, he could not control her. He jerked himself out of the seat and lurched down the heaving corridors. Tragedy had struck the ship, but no one responded. Then he saw someone: Spitzer, beautiful blonde Heidi, sweet Heidi, she would understand, but she too smiled, smiled, and smiled.

He screamed but no one noticed, he cried in pain but no one turned, he writhed in agony, and he watched himself as Renaud, a demonic grin on her face and a dagger in her hand, crept up behind him, plunged it in his back, splashing blood on the walls, the dagger, her hand, her grinning teeth . . .

He awoke in a scream.

He shook, he did not know for how long he shook, but it was long enough for them to come pounding down the corridors, he heard them come, down the deck, out of doors, till the pounding became a beat on his door. He wished they would go away. Finally he could deny their existence no longer, and he thrust the door open.

Sweating, haggard, he peered into their faces, Spitzer and Renaud and Erickson and Delgiorno, concern written on their stupid faces in grease pencil. He hated them, he despised himself, he knew it was wrong and foolish, the grip of the dream was so strong he could not but hate them, and he snarled, "Sorry!"

"Are you all right?" "Were you hurt?" "Anything I can do to help?" Moonfaced, they peered at him. It took all his self-control not to shout out and slam the door. "No. Nightmare. Sorry to wake everybody. Go back sleep." He shut the door as quickly as he could, for he wanted to be free. He leaned on the door and closed his eyes, sweat trickling down his arms into the pillow he clutched in one hand, down his side down his legs. His mouth agape, he panted until a measure of sanity returned, until he was sure that he could open his eyes without terror filling them.

There was his bed, rumpled and torn. He wiped sweat and saliva from his mouth and flung himself back onto it.

2.

Regard the spaceship *Open Palm* as she sweeps gracefully toward 61 Cygni. It is dark out here, with only the stars for company, here in interstellar space, where the atoms are thin, dark and silent. No medium transmits sounds. The dramas of the heavens are played in pantomime.

But the human ear cannot accept perfect silence, and the human mind must imagine demons in the unremitting darkness. Inside their steel cocoons, amidst the comforting electronic illusions of control, the spacemen have peopled their heavens with myths as real as the myths which originally populated the constellations. It is so quiet between the planets you can hear the dead voices of the poets, or the mariners. That is why no ship is ever named *Odysseus*, nor *Argonaut*, nor *Flying Dutchman*. Regardless of whether or not they exist, there is no point in angering the gods and the ghosts.

Regard, then, the spaceship *Open Palm*, sweeping ever onward. It is dark here, black as a velvet curtain, yet also blindingly brilliant, here in this gap in Creation. No obstructing matter, no receding haze, no luminous nebular swirl, no comfortable horizon for the eye to settle upon. We are far, far closer to the glorious stars than on tame Earth; they shine, like pearls, in magnificent panoply.

And across the entire panorama of these same stars runs the blazing band of the Milky Way, the ring that is our perception of our galaxy, a phosphorescence of terrifying power. Too numerous to count, too small to isolate, the stars of the Milky Way come at us like a wave, a great limpid belt about the heavens, drowning us in distance, color, light.

It is a sight which catches you, at the first porthole you inadvertently glance past. They call it 'the gape', and it gets everybody, the first time. You think it won't, you'll be along in just a minute fellas, and then . . . and fifteen minutes later, some crew hand comes by and suggests that it's lunch time, and you turn back, and shake your head, and say thanks, I'll be right along, and yank yourself back to an interior reality gone empty bland, and walk away disoriented, turning back over your shoulder for just one more glimpse.

Having no convenient referents, the eye swiftly becomes swallowed, one moment thinking the blackness is infinite, the next convinced that it is but an arm's length away. The sensation can be so strong as to be tactile. They have a name for that sensation, too, not a pleasant name.

The twitch, they call it. It begins in your extremities and works its way toward the center of your body, reinforcing itself. To the disciplined mind the sensation of an arm or leg moving of its own volition, as if controlled by a spastic deity, while the endless black skies smash down through the walls of the ship into the fibres of your bowels—that sensation is, well, disturbing.

They test very thoroughly for that one; it is the one automatic, irrevocable ticket back to the ground. This crew has been through it many times before—in flight, in simulation, and under drugs. They all passed, or they wouldn't be here.

In the center of this great vastness lies the spaceship *Open Palm* itself. Though the ship speeds onward at a large fraction of the speed of light, her motion is imperceptible here, swallowed by the great distances she must cross. To the external observer, the ship appears motionless and mute, the sole actor on an empty stage, suspended in eternity, destined perhaps to be ever here, till the cosmic fires burn out and time itself crumbles into entropy and dust.

So it seems to her crew, on the inside looking out, that the ship has always hung thus. For this crew, reality ends just outside the windows. The chronometers (one for subjective time, one for objective) and the inertial guidance computers churn out their daily numeric propaganda, but to the crew the figures are of little comfort.

How, they ask, can the advance of those digital readouts bear any relation to reality, when it is always night outside, when the sky never changes, when the sun never rises and the moon is a cloudy memory, when day and night become conventions and not constraints; when a man may wake on

Monday morning, work a sixteen hour shift, and go to sleep on Thursday, when the measure of progress must be judged by the yardstick of the soul.

To Walter Tai-Ching Jones, the pilot, there is no sense of achievement beyond the numbers; for his job is to make sure that the status quo remains inside the plastic womb of the ship while the computers call the silent minuet. To Tai-Ching Jones, as to Yvette Renaud, or Harold Bennett, the fabric of space (so tantalizingly close) is as immutable as it was to Aristotle.

On she speeds, to a destiny that none can know and few can even hazily imagine, yet the background against which she moves never changes. From the outside, the *Open Palm* is in stasis, frozen, enambered, as dwarfed as a mote of dust floating in the fetid air of an abandoned palace.

Yet without the numbers to divide the darkness, the ship would be truly lost, tracking through a wilderness in hopes of being found. And if for some reason the rendezvous is missed, or the crew incapacitated, she would pass in an instant from oasis to coffin, sailing forever into the darkness, to be opened by some future unimaginable historians, of some other planet and culture, peering with indescribable eyes into the still-functioning interior, making detailed scholarly notes of the relic, perhaps finding a skeleton in a jumpsuit and speculating on the vanished race . . . .

This is not a thought the crew confronts pleasantly.

Like a tiny jewel this beautiful ship floats on an invisible sea of ether. There is no scale; she could be a tiny toy, instead of a behemoth. From a distance she is a silver needle arrowed across the sky.

On closer inspection she loses much of her grace, becoming instead an awkward cousin of the sleek, streamlined atmospheric-entry spaceships. For this is a creature of space, a lumpy shishkabob. Uniting the ship is a slender, multiply-reinforced elevator shaft, which runs the entire four hundred meters of her.

At the base of this spine are the giant thrusters, three of them, the perpetually red-hot drivers and brakes of the ship. Some days ago they briefly rested, but now they roar (silently) with the fires of the stars. Above the thrusters is a cadmium-carbon shield which forms the base of a lattice grid of supporting struts. Through this lattice run, like blood vessels, the feeder pipes of hydrogen and reaction mass, a full two hundred and fifty meters. Like the slave Aesop, who began the army's march nearly buried under the weight of its provisions, but who ended the trek strolling and whistling, so did the ship begin its journey laboring to lift the fuel she will burn and discard along the way; she will return to Earth virtually empty.

After the reaction mass come the honeycombs of the storage section, then the bio-converter, the labs, the Dreamer, the lounge and the Alien Reception Area, the crew's quarters, and finally the bridge. From the outside it is hard to tell where one section ends and another begins, for the *Open Palm* covers her secrets with a coat of white enamel. Were you close enough to read the writing on her surfaces, you would see cryptic notations and numbers, complex directions, arrows, diagrams, and a network of television cameras, which sweep the entire accessible surface of the ship, as well as a number of shy, small black machines sucking their way along the beast's flanks.

But the picture is still disoriented, for the tip of the needle, the bridge, points not toward the destination, but back to home. The ship is decelerating, beginning the long glide downhill which will bring it to a stop at the rendezvous point, and the powerful emissions of the thrusters are applying one long, continuous braking effort to the ship.

For she has been designed never to rest, always to thrust, either faster or slower, both to cut the journey to its theoretical minimum time and to provide the gravity necessary to cater to the human passengers. For as Einstein correctly postulated, to a man in an elevator there is no difference between the force of gravity and the force of constant acceleration. So now *up* is toward home, and *down* is toward the end of the trip. The little radar eye which up to now had pointed toward their goal now looks back to vanished Earth; the big eye, which had followed the waning of the planets,

now quests ahead into the void, listening to the voices from
that other world.

Regard then the *Open Palm*, suspended thus in space. Note
the bulges of the engines, the long abdomen of the reaction
mass tanks, the more articulated bulges in the forward section, finally the nodule of the bridge. To understand this
universe, and the eleven people trapped in it, one must travel
from within the *Open Palm*. Her secrets are inside.

From an indefinable distance, the *Open Palm* is a lumpy,
off-white arrow, with its cargo wrapped around the shaft,
vital modules surrounding an elevator spine. The engines
cooled somewhat when briefly shut down for Midpoint, but
with the rekindling of the forward drive they have returned to
a glowing, serene red.

They face the destination; her bridge looks backwards
towards home, now merely a typical yellow star. From a
distance we approach the ship, and she swells in our vision,
becoming more and more defined, taking on new features
and exposing new wrinkles to our sight; the flaking of non-
essential paint, the fine grittiness of interstellar debris which
has relentlessly fallen upon the ship since the journey started.

We continue methodically closer, and antennae glitter
with starlight. At two thousand meters the ship is large,
swelling in our vision and dominating the view in front; we
can see the ship's insignia—an extended hand—painted carefully over the metal plates and rivets, in a position where she
can be seen only by the crew's collective mind's eye. Larger
and larger the ship grows, more and more dominating, until
in an instant the ship is no longer an object in the sky, she has
become the ground, and we are falling, falling down to her
forbidding exterior, falling toward this overwhelming
mass . . .

Until we magically pass through the hull, impervious,
catching a glimpse of tubes and wires under her skin; and the
stars, only moments before appallingly close, are now
merely small lights winking, at a fraction of their former
power, through multiple layers of quartz windows.

In this empty room of instruments, there is light, water vapor, and the sense of life. Mankind has left his mark. But the instrument room is empty; none of its builders are here.

Instead there are a battery of dials, digital readouts, instruments, and television monitors. For here is the firing line for the engineer; it is here that Kees van Gelder comes, both to work and to think. For here, amidst all this machinery, van Gelder can find a universe wherein everything is as it should be, where life can be restrained, evil impulses effectively countered. It brings van Gelder professional and spiritual satisfaction to ride this great beast, the greatest his race has known, and to know that he is its master, if not its equal.

Travel now out of the instrument room and into the tiny elevator, up a thin tube which is all that connects the great horses which drive the ship from the fragile humans who ride it. Between the walls of this elevator and the vacuum of space, only two meters away in any direction, lie a network of pressure hulls, wires, and pipes.

For fifty meters the elevator spine is braced solely by a trellis of gray wires. Then for three hundred meters more the elevator shaft is cocooned by ocean-size tanks of water. For the *Open Palm* is a steam engine; she burns water.

Using computer-controlled magnetic pinchbottles, the great engines remove the hydrogen, heat it to greater and greater heights under ever-increasing pressure, until the hydrogen gives up the struggle and fuses into more compact helium.

Pressure. Heat. Then more pressure, more heat, stress and power and violence crushed in the magnetic hands of the ship's furnace, till matter itself surrenders. Hell in a magnetic bottle, watched in red light by van Gelder.

But heat by itself is not enough; to thrust a ship as massive as the *Open Palm* requires reaction mass many times heavier than the ship itself. And the cheapest mass available is water; so tank after tank, enveloping the elevator shaft.

Finally the great water tanks give way to the ship's storage section. Here are things which the *Open Palm* cannot produce; hence to the members of her crew, here are treasures beyond price. Here is the hardware of the ship's computer, containing bank after bank of information, reel after reel of microfilm, a substantial fraction of the history of the race.

Art, music, technology, literature, philosophy are all here, both for the members of the crew (at work and at play), and for the silent judges on 61 Cygni to whom a never-ending stream of the archives of humanity is directed.

Also included are delicacies or rareties which cannot be simulated—food, perfume, wine, antiques. The Ritz can synthesize or simulate a large menu of foods, but for this crew nothing has been spared. Had a crew member asked for space for his security blanket, it would have been found, though the engineers would groan and the psychologists frown.

Immediately above the storage area comes the bio-converter, the heart of the life support system. Thanks to advances in test-tube biology, this tiny sailing universe has achieved the ecologists' dream of a completely closed system. Waste is converted back into simpler compounds, which are in turn synthesized into food as needed.

Unbreakable glass rings a small laboratory. Behind the glass, in every direction, it is morning green, the sweet light green of springtime, the green of bloom, always morning in springtime, always moist, always growing. Water, carbon dioxide (generously contributed by *homo sapiens*) and minerals meet, swirl, and are ingested by a myriad of algae. Whenever Rawlins steps into this room, he thinks, *home*.

Here too is the meat farm. Inside a nutrient tank, a slab of beef pulses with electric wires, commanding biologically "grow, grow, grow . . . grow, grow, grow . . . ." So a steer long since dead on Earth still produces beef and a sheep, whose wool graces a sweater and whose brains and eyes have long since been feasted upon by some connoisseur back on the home planet, still provides sustenance for the crew of the *Open Palm*.

It is eerie to watch this slice of meat growing, an undead piece of flesh biologically simpler than lower-order ferns, with the bubbling red water circulating merrily about it, and the wires running to some Frankensteinian panel. Perhaps that is why no one comes to watch, and only Rawlins occasionally stops in, to chop away several pounds' worth of sirloin.

Perhaps the feeling is the same one which the first men felt, as the first fire danced into the smoky night. For the meat is grown by a process known once as cancer—a controlled cancer, just as the fusion which powers this ship is a controlled implosion, the electricity a controlled thunderbolt, the human body a controlled erosion.

Beyond the meat farm is the synthesizer, used to create or recreate plastic or polyester for packages, covers, placemats, cups and the like. Easier to remake than to clean, they are thrown into the ship's oubliettes, to return eventually to the bioconverter, where the ravenous little algae break it all back into the primeval mush of the ship's ecology.

Directly above the converter sleeps Rawlins, the life support officer. Above his bed hangs a complex monitor, ready to shriek out danger at the first indication of deviation in the ventilation, heating or disposal systems which are interlinked with the converter. Every night Rawlins gazes up from his bed at this device, thankful that it has not yet rung.

Opposite Rawlins' quarters is the crew's lounge, an almost opulently furnished cubicle which attractively disguises its inherent cramp. Nevertheless, it is a far more cleverly designed, far more comfortable place than the typical apartment in Under New York, Luna Central, or the cheaper vacation rooms in the Antarctic.

It has been carefully furnished, both with imported replicas of works of art, and with the crew's special offerings. In none of these scenes is the sky the center of attention; none of the sculpted figures gazes up. The crew prefer, off duty, to be reminded of tame, sweet Earth, not the harsh realities of space. But on one wall, alone against the stolid white, there is a giant rendering of the Earth from space—billowy clouds swirling around the beautiful deep blue which characterizes the planet. It is a picture into which one can gaze, and forget the journey, and rub one's eyes, and look upon the lovely place from which man came.

Beyond this level are the work/play facilities: the library, with its set of microfilm readers and its display screens for

incoming transmissions; the Alien Reception Room where
the latest 'news' is picked over after breakfast. News means
Cygnans; by common consent the crew have limited incoming information from Earth to a few periodicals and occasional sports and entertainment broadcasts. Recreation and
laboratory areas (for tinkering in a lab is recreation for most
of the travelers) are on the same level, along with the rumpus
room (so named ever since a celebrated incident in which the
pilot was the central character). In actuality it is a quiet study,
in which silence is the rule, if not the practice.

The Alien Reception Room resembles a cross between
a newspaper office and a television studio, clustered with
masses of recording and processing equipment, vocowriters,
and even books and papers for such scribbles as the crew find
conducive to thought. On the silver screen the latest transmission is received and taped, usually to four or five viewers.
Above the screen sits a little sign stating, "THIS PROGRAM
RECOMMENDED ONLY FOR MATURE ADULTS." Various comments
have been pencilled in beneath it.

In a quiet room, all its own, comes the Dreamer. The crew
seldom talk of the Dreamer, or their experiences in it, and, at
first glance, the flaccid heap of rubberized clothing seems
unremarkable. But when a crew member puts it on, the *Open
Palm* will slip away, and any fantasy—any time, any
place—can appear. Dreams, but more real than dreams;
living fantasies. If the Dreamer imagines a fight, the suit will
bunch and deliver the equivalent of a blow. If the Dreamer
commands a scene, that scene appears—more crisp than eyes
could see because it transmits impulses through the skin to
the retinal nerve.

Real pain, real joy. For an hour, Arabian nights—or
nightmares.

He who dreams may control his own actions; the computer
controls everything else. For an hour the computer will
deliver an adventure tailored to work out the psychic kinks
built up since the last Dream. *When you take your turn in the
barrel,* say the crew, *you never know what you'll get.*

Some wish they never saw the insides of the suit, never had
to pull down the goggles, never saw the featureless gray that

begins and ends every Dream. Others yearn for their next visit. When the hour ends, the golden computer voice booms in your ears, the scene dissolves, and for a few moments withdrawal ravages your soul. You pull off the goggles, blinking at the ceiling lights. For a moment you crave the Dream. Anyone would.

But they have an iron rule: no more than once a week, no less than once a month. And that rule is enforced, oh is it ever enforced.

Close the door, back to your cabin.

The next three levels are crews' quarters. Each room can sleep two people; the ship's designers were realists. And above them lies only the bridge and the engineering rooms.

First of all is the EVA center—rarely used, but potentially vital. Robots, spacesuits, communication devices, and a complete auxiliary control are here. Every crew member has a spacesuit hung in his or her cabin, positioned so that it can be found and donned in the dark, from a dead sleep, in less than four minutes. The crew have practiced putting on the suits so many times that it can be done in semiconsciousness, without thought. And to make sure, Delgiorno occasionally drops in unannounced when an occupant is asleep, to test anew. Nobody complains (very much) at the intrusion; they know the reason behind it.

Everyone knows how to reach emergency control, how long it takes to get there, and what should be done first. As a further control, buried in each crew member's memory is a complete knowledge of necessary procedures to follow in the event of disaster. Each has a keyword which will unlock — cascade — little compartments in his subconscious. And for these devices, van Gelder and Delgiorno both rest a little easier; van Gelder decided what information had to go into the memory, and Delgiorno put it there.

Delgiorno put in a little bit more, too, but no one knows about that yet.

But the room does not reflect these grim facts; it is as ornamental and sympathetic as a machine shop. Next door is the bridge.

If the *Open Palm* has a life and a soul, it resides here—in a

small, oddly shaped room furnished only with three padded
couches and a gaggle of gauges, here in its brain.

A brain must have eyes; here are eight television screens,
each showing a strikingly real image.

Here, for instance, is a view from the precarious ledge
over the thrusters; adjacent may be a section of the hull
outside the converter, a quarter of a kilometer away. On a
third the picture shifts and jerks as a service robot trundles
awkwardly along the hide of the ship's elevator shaft, waving
its waldoes in front of it. A pair of inverted gloves reinforce
the illusion: should Tai-Ching Jones insert his hands into the
gloves, he can perform tasks on the other side of the ship.

Above all the screens, like the eye of heaven, is a computer
display, now flashing out a series of equations, now cutting
to a monitor view, now listing a detailed inventory of the
storage area. More such terminals, hooked into the ship's
brain, and scattered through the ship, provide information
relevant to the various crew members.

If Tai-Ching Jones wishes to think in solitude, he comes
here. He has programmed the Beast (as it is known) to play
chess on the screen when there are no malfunctions occur-
ring. But the Beast does not talk, except on the monitor in
Tai-Ching Jones' quarters—he programmed it to, and he has
keyed the program to talk back only if addressed with ''Hi,
beast,'' in his own voice.

3.

Humming to himself, Rawlins dressed for Spitzer's birthday party. Heidi would approve of this costume (turban, pantaloons, scimitar) and after all, it was her party.

As his fingers worked, his mind, set to neutral, idled.

Perhaps rumination might even be more effective than concentration—when you were stuck in a dead end. At the very least, being stumped was better than being bored out of your gourd the way Walt was.

When he had signed up for this voyage, Rawlins had little or no idea what to expect—and those few ideas he brought with him had been proven totally wrong. He had expected the academics to be friendly and helpful—*boy were you naive*. When that failed, he had taken to showing up at Movie transmissions and lectures. *Appreciative audience, right*? He was ignored.

In frustration, he had decided to start studying something on his own. Show the superior bastards—especially Bennett—that they didn't know everything. Having nothing better to do, he had decided to think big: see if he could track growth and decline of the weaver *djan* from its emergence to the present. None of the others had shown much interest, and besides none of the soft scientists would spend so much time on old numbers.

It was a good task for him: little reading, little writing. Lots of painstaking data collection and correlation. Sift out the chaff and find the nuggets of usable numbers.

Using computer analysis, Rawlins had scanned records. The machine would cull or interpolate statistics from available sources, develop least-squares fits, and print out both an abstract of its conclusions and the backup data from which they had been derived. Rawlins was thankful that he had computer help—four man-years of work compressed into a month or so.

Sometimes Rawlins wondered why he kept at it.

Even with the computer's assistance, it had seemed a boring effort. If he'd known how much grunt work it would have taken, Rawlins conceded to himself, he'd never have started. More than once he had been prepared to abandon it, to walk away as he had done so often in the past. But it seemed a shame to waste those detailed printouts, each one adding its piece to the puzzle, as if the computer hadn't wanted him to quit.

Gradually a pattern began to emerge; the numbers started making sense. Like a repairman tuning a recalcitrant video unit, he rescreened his data. This time the correlations were stronger. Amazing, really; the numbers *by themselves* held a powerful internal logic. Even if you had no idea what a widget was, you could tell when a particular widget statistic was out of line.

And this was analysis on a grand scale: it wasn't miniscule microbes or cells, it was whole populations he was testing. Raw numbers at first, they soon started to talk to him in a language all their own.

A man who finds himself in a dark cave is for the moment effectively blind, for he can see nothing. Afraid to move for fear of encountering some invisible danger, he will stand still. But if he strikes even a tiny light, he can see shadows. He has a starting point for investigation. As he wanders throughout the cave, one step at a time, the intrepid explorer learns. Each flicker of light tells him more, each shadow carries more meaning than the last.

Bit by bit, the explorer builds up a complete coherent perception of what had been unknown darkness. Eventually he can even close his eyes, or extinguish his light, and walk confidently, guided only by his accumulated knowledge.

So did Rawlins peruse his numbers, sift his printouts, and explore Cygnan history.

After a while, he began taking pleasure in the research for its own sake. Forgotten was his desire to show up the others; for the first time since grade school, learning was fun by itself. And, as the pace of his progress slowed, the scope of his inquiry broadened. He wasn't tracking just one *djan*, he was tracking total population shifts. There hadn't been enough time to do everything before liftoff, so he was working in relatively unexplored territory. Most of the time that meant fumbling around with no idea what you were doing—or even what you *should* be doing. Like trying to understand a game by first having to figure out the rules. Progress was slow. But satisfactory.

Now most of the research was over. And, irony of ironies, he confronted a problem he never expected: he seemed unable to reconcile what data he had. The statistics almost added up. *Almost*: he couldn't quite make them fit. And like van Gelder, Rawlins could never feel comfortable until the pieces meshed.

Ecological rule one: a planet is a closed system. Births minus deaths equals population growth. Right?

Except in this case it didn't. His figures were off by eight million Cygnans. Not good, but in a basic population of one billion, pretty close. *Close enough for government work, right?* He smiled at his reflection. Straightening his scimitar, he headed for the door. And stopped.

"Oh hell," he said aloud, "you win, machine. Let's try once more." He took off his turban, sat down at the terminal.

Population one billion, give or take five million. Well documented.

Average life span—he punched some buttons—yes, fifty Cygnan years was a solid average. Average deaths from old age must be twenty million per Cygnan year.

Age to adulthood, roughly twenty Cygnan years. Say six hundred million adults, three hundred million females.

Roughly twenty-five years of fertility. Each female bears one or two litters in that time. Say one point two litters. So three hundred divided by twenty-five, times one point two: say fourteen million litters a year.

Average litter eight, so say twelve million births a year. Versus twenty million deaths is eight million a year gap.

Dead end. The same damn dead end. Maybe the average female had two litters per career.

He leaned back in his chair, away from the computer terminal. *Any ideas, genius?* No, none.

Well, he'd solve it tomorrow. Once again he started for the elevator, pushed the button.

Its doors were closing when it hit him, with the force of a sledgehammer:

Fourteen times eight weren't twelve—they were *one hundred* and twelve.

Idiot!

One twelve minus twenty isn't eight short—it's *ninety-two over*.

Somewhere, ninety-two million Cygnan deaths a year were unaccounted for. *Where are they going?*

The party would have to wait. He elbowed his way through the elevator's closing doors, ran to the computer terminal and jumped back into the seat. Fingers dancing, heart pounding, he keyed up the computer. The screen flicked greenly to life.

READY.
Emigrant.

This was the name of the storage files and program routines for his studies. Bennett was always poking into other people' business and disingenuously ignoring their outrage and pointed remarks. Rawlins had no intention of letting Harold know he was encroaching into squishy science, so he'd keyed it with a password.

VERIFIED.
Flyway.
   OPEN.
Query.
   SET.
Cygnan death statistics, old age.
Confirm or deny: fifteen times ten-seventh births?
   CONFIRM.
Old age, accident, disease total 42 x 10-sixth?
   CONFIRM.
Explain gap.
   NADVAYAG.

Nadvayag? He grabbed for the Cygnan Dictionary
Tanakaruna had compiled. Quickly he flipped to the entry.

> "*Nadvayag.* 'Killing the unpersons.' Cygnan infants are
> born after only eight weeks of gestation; they spend the next
> sixteen weeks in the mother's pouch. During the pouch
> period, the brain is first formed, so a Cygnan infant's first
> consciousness is not of himself but of his siblings. Formed at
> birth, this *djan* bond remains the strongest throughout a
> Cygnan's life. No Cygnan would pollute his *djan* by engag-
> ing in *hro* with a *djan*-brother.
>
> "Prior to the last hundred or so Cygnan years, lack of
> hygiene resulted in frequent womb-deaths (see *dvadudja*).
> Now, however, *dvadudja* is rare. However, some *dudja* are
> deformed, mentally deficient or otherwise incapable of be-
> coming active Cygnan adults. *Nadvayag* is the infrequent
> process of culling these few before their name-day
> (*eldbra*)."

*Infrequent? Says who? A month ago I'd have agreed with
you, Sam. Not today. But let's check.*

Cygnan estimates of nadvayag?
FIVE TIMES TEN-SIXTH.

If the machine was telling the truth, *nadvayag* was *fourteen times* more common than Cygnans let on.

Confirm or deny: Cygnan birth minus accident minus old age
equals seven times ten-seventh?
CONFIRM.
Confirm or deny: Cygnan nadvayag statistics claim five
times ten-sixth?
CONFIRM.
Statistics conflict.
CONFIRM.
Justify. Repeat.
NADVAYAG.

"Oh my god," whispered Rawlins.

Probability?
    95% CONFIDENCE INTERVAL 6.5 TO 7.5 TIMES TEN-
    SEVENTH.
Are you sure?

    He had no idea why he typed that.

    95% CONFIDENCE INTERVAL 6.5 TO 7.5 TIMES TEN-SEVENTH.
Justify.
    SEE DATA.

    The writer began shucking paper into the output tray.
There was a lot of it. Rawlins was depressed and angry. He
looked at the first page without really seeing it.
    What does a man do, wondered Rawlins, *when he holds
seventy million deaths in his hands?*
    The page of computer printout slipped from his fingers and
slalomed through the air to the floor.
    Got to see the captain, he thought. *Oh damn, there's that
stupid party of Heidi's going on.*
    He hurried to the elevator.

4.

Music, winking candlelight, and festivity, strung about a utilitarian hall: a party in the lounge.

Costumes: the special exaggerations of formality. For a time, perhaps, the fetters of daily existence forgotten. Amber and gold lights flickered off shining silver walls and white plastic floors.

Walter Tai-Ching Jones, immaculate in black satin drawn up to a simple collar, with black slippers and a queue. Beneath olive and black his eyes glittered satanically. He was elegant and he knew it.

Yvette Renaud, dressed in the habit of a nun. Emphasizing simplicity, emphasizing chastity, hating herself but knowing that the picture so conjured was real. For her, this party is something of a confrontation. As Bennett talked, she nodded wearily.

At one of the smaller tables, now pushed into the corner, van Gelder clopped his wooden shoes against the impersonal plastic. He was listening with half his mind. The other half was nowhere. Somehow it felt pleasant.

Across the table from him was the ship's medic, Heidi Spitzer. Mimicking a famous namesake, she was dressed in dirndl, voluminous skirt and apron. Her hair, normally a bun, was carefully braided with flowers. But it was not a child's voice speaking.

"Maybe they're just afraid," she was saying. "I suppose that if one is the dominant sex for millennia one naturally begins to think of oneself as somehow superior, and when that is not the case one is upset. Men seem to have trouble adjusting to the idea that a woman can be an equal—don't you think so, Kees?"

"Um," he hmmed.

"Kees, you're not paying attention. I was saying that I think most men find the idea of a woman who is an equal (if not a superior) both disconcerting and challenging. Don't

28

you agree?''

"In some sense, I suppose—"

"After all, men, more than women, have to have the obvious trappings of status and position. They have to be dominant. Don't you think so?''

"I don't," he shyly, unwilling.

"Well, perhaps," she went on, "but then you're the exception and not the general rule.'' She craned her neck to see where Tai-Ching Jones was. "I think that the development of a truly equal society is a hallmark of civilization. After all, Harold was telling me some of the details of the Cygnans' social systems and they don't have a trace of sexual discrimination. No wonder they couldn't understand a lot of the literature we sent them.''

Kees had no stomach for argument. Not right now. The party was pleasant. The candlelight had a relaxing quality to it after the merciless extremes of space and engine room. The sound of her voice was soothing by itself.

"Are we all set?''

"Shh, shh, she'll hear.''

"Careful, get them all lit, OK? Ready?''

Spitzer looked up, saw the winking candles reflected in the silver of the tabletop and the sparkle of their eyes. Yvette, Tom, Samuka, Helen. "Oh, danke, danke, it is lovely.''

"Make a wish!''

"Blow out the candles; quick, they're burning up!'' Happy childlike voices; perhaps it was the dark. The voices would have been incongruous in the colder light of profession.

"All right, all right, I will blow them out.'' She took an exaggerated deep breath, then blew.

"Congratulations! All of them! Your wish will come true, Heidi.''

"Ah, good. Let me tell you all, it was—''

"No, don't or it won't come true. Keep it a secret. Somebody get the lights, please.'' Even in darkness, the speaker was unmistakable—only Delgiorno could make a disembodied voice in darkness a specific command. Belovsky jumped, then ran to the switch. Fluorescent light returned, bluish-cold and disillusioning. Erickson put his sunglasses back on.

"Take a look at the design."

A bent old doctor with braids leaning over a swan and putting a stethoscope to its neck, and the caption, 'Say quack, please.' Heidi laughed. "Oh, that is good, I like that."

"It is an insult." They turned.

There was Bennett, dressed incongruously in impeccable black tie and tuxedo—*damn it, when did he come in?* wondered Delgiorno, *I didn't see him earlier. And why hasn't he got on a costume like the rest of us?*—standing almost at attention. "Who did this?"

"I did," she said. "I think it's cute."

"You did. You think it's cute. How touching."

Bennett walked serenely over to the cake, looked down at the design. "How nice. Just a little joke. Blackface, maybe. Like painting a Hitler mustache on the opposition political candidate. Wop. Spic. Kike. Swan. They're all derogative, and they always have been." He looked at Delgiorno. "You should know better, First Officer."

"Stop a second, Kees, there's Walter. Hello, Walter!" Spitzer stood on tiptoe and waved.

"Hello, Heidi. Hi, Casey. Are you enjoying the party?"

"Stop looking like you've just swallowed a slice of lemon peel, Walter. Or perhaps it pains you to be nice to me?"

"Captain, could I talk to you a moment, privately?" asked Rawlins.

In the bright lights of the party Erickson's sunglasses made him seem expressionless and blind. "What is it?"

Now that he had the captain's full attention Rawlins felt his courage oozing down to his toes. "Captain, what I'm about to tell you is going to sound remarkable—"

"Tom, in the three and a half years you've been on this bucket you've been one of the most level-headed ones. Something has upset you. Now what is it?"

"I was doing emigration studies. Movements of large

segments of the population when a *djastraban* was depleted. Trying to track guilds through the generations—''

''And?''

''Things didn't add up.''

''Tom, I'm a big boy. Stop hinting and tell me.''

Rawlins began speaking quickly, almost as if by rote. ''Base population is one billion. Average lifespan fifty years. This means an adult population of six hundred million.'' He was ticking the points off on his fingers. ''That checks with census figures. Over approximately twenty-five fertile years the average female has one or two litters with an average birth between seven and ten. Say one point two litters at eight births each. Got that?''

The sunglasses nodded.

''That's one hundred twelve million births. Population is stable, so the same number of deaths. Twenty million in old age—one billion divided by fifty. And after a lot of work I've established that the absolute maximum from disease and accident is twenty-two million.'' He had come to the end of his fingers. Now he shrugged. ''There's a seventy million person hole.''

''Are you saying what I think you're saying?'' Erickson's voice was intent.

''Somehow—without telling anybody—somehow the Cygnans kill seventy million of each other every year.''

There was a silence. Erickson's head was turned away. It was impossible to know what he was thinking.

Finally he spoke. ''How could this happen?''

''Computer says *nadvayag.*''

''We've heard about *nadvayag.* I thought it wasn't important.''

''Captain, the numbers don't lie. Either the Cygnans don't know the real truth, or they're lying. Take your pick.''

''Why,'' asked Erickson, '' didn't Earth tell us?''

''Probably wasn't time before liftoff, or maybe Earth knows by now and isn't telling us. Actually, I think maybe Sam knows already.''

Erickson nodded. ''Get her over here.''

She came, rustling her kimono. Erickson gave her the

details. "It could be that post-birth abortion, couldn't it?"

"Yes" she said quietly. "It's called *nadvayag*—killing the unpersons."

"Sam," said Rawlins, "six out of ten births die—by *nadvayag*."

"Yes, that could be. I wondered about that."

"Why didn't you say anything?" asked Erickson.

"Captain, they think differently. When a young Cygnan is born, it's less than seven centimeters long. Before it has any consciousness of itself, it is aware of its *djan* members. Until it is named, it is an unperson. It has no existence. It has no rights. Why should the Cygnans keep track of *nadvayag*? Do we count pigeons squashed under cars?"

"Sam, it's not the same," said Erickson quietly.

"Captain, you may think me too sympathetic to the Cygnans. I'm not. When your young are born live so early and so small, birth does not begin the personhood. Personhood is conveyed at *eldbra*. It is a crucial ceremony. Read the literature." Her arms moved inside the kimono. "It's just not the same," she finished. Though small, she commanded respect.

"If they think that way about their own people," Erickson asked, "could they think the same way about us?"

Rawlins expected quick indignation, but instead she seemed disturbed. "No one knows, Captain," Tanakaruna finally said.

"Think about it," he commanded, without rancor.

She had already turned away and was walking toward the elevators. The kimono seemed large on her, and her steps were slow and tentative.

Seventy million a year. Seventy million a year. Seventy million a year. What sort of beings are we going to meet?

No birth control. Routine mass killing—if Tom's right. And this is Harold's Utopia. Wonder what he'll say when he discovers this.

Goddam bitch. "Did you check out fuel impurities, Casey?"

"Yes, I went over the consumption profile. Whatever the impurity was, it's gone now."

"Performance back to normal?"

"Less than 0.005% RMS away from norm."

"That's good."

"Aren't you going to wish me a happy birthday, Walter?"

"Happy birthday, Heidi. I hope the coming year treats you kindly."

"Don't snicker, Walter—it doesn't become you."

Van Gelder always felt uncomfortable in such situations. "Please stop, both of you."

Spitzer put her hand on his arm. "Look, Kees, I know that you and Walter are friends, although," she looked Tai-Ching Jones in the eyes, "I fail to appreciate why." That was Heidi.

"Casey, you have to be crazy to get involved with a chick like her. You don't know what you're getting into." That was Walt.

Typically, van Gelder wished he was somewhere else. "Please, friends, not here. Walter, you joined us. Don't cause trouble."

"OK, Casey, but it's hard. I don't like getting sniped at, and I guess some people think I behave badly."

"I've got to get another drink."

"How many have you had, Walt?"

"Not enough," he growled. *Leave me alone, Casey. I've had enough of your brotherly solicitous concern, especially when Heidi's around.* "Anybody else want a refill? No? OK, back in a minute."

"Please, Heidi, don't irritate him."

"He deserves it, Kees, he's so stuck up and so egotistical."

"If he's all that, why did you love him?"

"Ha! I never loved him. I slept with him before I knew what he was really like. Oh, you're back, Walter."

"Tell you what, Casey, let's slip away and play some backgammon."

"No thanks, Walter, I'd prefer to stay."

"You're sure now?" he said almost desperately. "Please?" He reached forward to take hold of van Gelder's arm, and some of his drink spilled. "Sorry," he said, and clumsily tried to wipe off the liquor with a napkin.

He's drunk, realized van Gelder, *whining drunk and self-pitying.* "OK, Walter," he said gently, disengaging Tai-Ching's hand from his drink and setting it gingerly on the table. "Come on, let's go." With his other hand van Gelder took hold of Tai-Ching Jones' shoulder and pointed him toward the door.

"Nighty night, Walter," said Spitzer sweetly. "Unpleasant dreams."

Tai-Ching Jones started to turn, but van Gelder held his arm. "Let me go, dammit," he grunted, wrenching it loose and turning to Spitzer. "I don't care about you any more," he said carefully, drunkenness slurring the edges of his words, "but I won't stand for you screwing up Kees. Germans have been fucking over Dutchmen for all of their history."

Before he knew what he had done van Gelder hit him, crashingly, in the chest.

Tai-Ching Jones fell like a marionnette, head cracking against the deckplate. Van Gelder jumped on him, trying to pummel his friend on any exposed surface, but hitting mostly shoulders and chest. "You stinking, *verdomm'*, do not say such things, you foul scum!"

Strong hands pulled him to his feet. He swung around, tears forming in his eyes. Through the blur he saw Rawlins' face, set in determination.

"You stupid fool. What the hell brought that on?"

But van Gelder could only shake his head and sob.

They helped Tai-Ching Jones up. His black hair spilled down into his face; his cap had been knocked off and lay wilted on the floor. Now he looked ridiculous in his costume, childish and hurt.

"Jesus, Casey, why did you do that?" he asked, wonderingly. Then, as it did when he was drunk, his emotion shifted lighteningly. "I was trying to *help* you, you blockheaded Dutchman, don't you know what I was doing? Don't you know what she's like?"

Whether to hit or simply touch, he reached for van Gelder, but Delgiorno had taken the precaution of doubling one arm behind his back, and he was rewarded with a shooting pain up through his shoulder. "All right, Pilot," she said in a voice of iron. "And you too, Engineer. Tom, take the Engineer to his quarters and keep him there until he's in proper condition. And when he is, have him brought to my cabin. I want to find out what happened here. And as for you, my friend," she wrenched Tai-Ching Jones' arm up to get his attention, "you're going to your cabin and I'm going to get your side of the story. If you have one. Sorry for the interruption, everybody. Go back to enjoying the party." She gave a brief curtsey, still holding Tai-Ching Jones' wrist. "March."

5.

Destiny[1]

A fable[2]

In the province of Vleta, two hundred and sixty-one tohru[3] to the southeast of Eopla, would be found[4] the Havna djan. In this province had the Havna dwelled, passing from hand to hand throughout forty generations.[5] Never had a Havna refused the land.

Unto the forty-first generation was born a djan in which was Derna. When that spring arrived at which the old one responded to the call to pass on the land, unto her was the land given. The Havna saw twas justest that Derna assume the land and she did accept the station of havna unto herself.

Some time after the old one died, Derna deserted the Havna. Came then a day when she was not found at the market, nor at work upon the land, nor upon any journey that any of the farm knew of. Many days passed in this manner. Others of her djan carried responsibility for the maintenance of the farm and the upholding of the Havna. None knew whither had gone Derna.

One thought she had been killed by brigands; another, that she had injured herself in some way, for the journey between farms and town was rough, the hillsides treacherous, travelers few. None knew; none sought the answer.

Came a day when a local merchant mentioned that, a day after her disappearance, he had seen her on the road to Eopla, bedecked like a pilgrim. Then did one venture to say that perhaps she had abandoned the Havna. Others did not believe this and demanded tiost[6] upon him that spaketh thus, until finally the merchant was called, and told what he had seen. And finally they believed, and with heavy hearts, chose they a successor from amongst their midst to assume the Havna. To lessen the burden, and in honor of him who had been

chosen, they promised support for his hroi[7]. And he became
the Havna, and the line was continued.

True the accusation was. Derna had deserted the Havna.
More proof, if it had been needed, was found some days
later, for buyers for the farm appeared, asking if the Havna
were no more.[8]

Derna's plea was that she was not competent to manage the
farm, and that she had no further obligations to the djan after
the death of the old Havna. No favors had been conferred
upon her at the attainment of her Havna, nor had she asked
any of her djans. In truth, the farm had been poorly managed,
in spite of the forty generations before, and under the new
Havna it prospered and grew in honor amongst the telling of
the people of Vleta.

Came then Derna to Eopla, haven of the exiles. Named
herself Erdna, eodja.[9] She became an appeaser.[10] In this she
prospered, and grew wealthy, and possessed of many things,
many she did not need, acquired only to ignore or utilize less
than that for which they had intended. Said it was that some
of those who worked with her were actually servants, that she
did not her own chores.

Held the new Havna and the djan a fnaeld[11] for Derna,
deeming the name never to be given to their children, or their
children's children, unto the fortieth generation, that being
the number previously unsullied.

So this continued for many years, until the winter which
was most cruel amongst the past thirty. Suffered the farm that
winter, more because the new Havna had reached the point
where the sunlight fades from the eyes and dusk settles upon
the mind. Yet heard he not the call to pass on to the forty-
second Havna the farm and the Havna. And the djan of his
loins did not assume the Havna until four years later, when he
died, and by that time the name of the farm had grown faint in
men's voices, and the produce of the farm sere and small, and
bitter to the taste.

As she must, learned Derna of the difficulties of the farm,
for her knowledge spread wide. Ever alert she was to whispered problems to which she might apply her talents and reap
the rewards of such perception.[12] Still remained in her the

vestiges of responsibility, though badly worn these many years. The forty-second Havna was a capable successor, so the trees said,[13] and well the farm would prosper if it could recover from the neglect of the previous four years.

Came a time when she made the journey back to the Havna, to offer a loan. The Havna recognized her, and the elders from her djan did also, but she did not acknowledge herself, and thus they were able to remain while she spoke before them. Stood she amidst their number and asked them, "are ye not in need of funds? Are ye not strong? Can ye not restore to the Havna the lustre of its name?"

Muttering was there when she said this, and one of the elders spake, saying "who is this speaks thus of honor?"[14]

But she did not respond, and continued, offering a loan full twenty percent beyond that needed to restore the Havna.[15] Heard they the offer in full, though it galled them to do so, for the custom demanded that an offer by a stranger be heard to completion.

Finally, when she was done, they asked if she had said all that she offered. And she agreed 'twas so.

Then rose up he among them who had become tladja to speak for all. Began he, "name thee I Derna, cast out from amongst us under these past summers, who did defile the name of Havna from forty generations and abandon the line to die and decay. Our answer is this: we would rather you give it double than this."[16]

And called they all from among the shadows and agreed with him, and began they to speak of other things. Hearing their judgment, she left, returned to Eopla, lived the remainder of her days upon the Earth in the isolation which she had chosen. And when the days of her misery had run, died Derna.

Gave the Havna to save the farm, to perpetuate the line. In vain, for they could not afford the costs of planting, nor work the land sufficiently, nor yield crops enough to provide for the winter and the year beyond.

Passed in this way from the province of Vleta the Havna, after the forty-first generation. Dispersed they into other provinces, never spake amongst each other again, took new names and new professions, becoming finally part of another's lineage and name.[17]

Footnotes to the story. By Tanakaruna.

1. Cygnans seldom give stories titles, except purely de-scriptive ones, such as humans give to technical papers. The 'title', if it can be called that, of this story is, roughly translated, 'A possible effect of exclusion upon a young Cygnan djan member, with implications into the justice of the *ostracos*'. I have given it the title which comes closest in meaning to the spirit (not translateable) of the Cygnan title.

2. Stories are classified into a number of types: this one is a mata, which translates basically to fable. "Instructive (past)-possibility" is closest in direct translation. I think fable conveys the sense.

3. I have not italicized Cygnan words, and have translated numbers and other simple conventions (e.g., time) into Terrestrial equivalents. A tohru is roughly 1.35 kilome-ters; the word comes from the double root to (large) and hru (step). Apparently a tohru was the original size of farms under early Cygnan feudalism (see the discussions on Cygnan history for a better description of the impor-tance of tohru on political and economic development). Basically, one square tohru was the area one farmer djan could reasonably manage.

4. Cygnan language has no verbs. Instead, nouns and ad-jectives and suffixes which inflect time into five seg-ments: far-future, near-future, present, near-past, far-past. It is highly context-dependent and stylized. Thus "the boy threw the ball" might be rendered present-boy near-past-arm, near-past-ball, near-future-ball, new-future-distance. I am told that this is comparable to a computer state transition diagram, linking possible states via instantaneous connections. English, in con-

trast, is a flow-chart language, progressing logically
from point to point, with no turning back. (Again I must
rely on my computer friends for the accuracy of this
analogy.) English emphasizes the process of moving;
Cygnan, the states which result from that movement.
My translation has tried, through syntax, to capture the
flow of this inflection.

5. It is probably worth mentioning that Cygnan passage
   does not follow any common Terrestrial norms. Of
   course, primogeniture (the most common Terran
   method) is utterly meaningless in a Cygnan society. As
   might be expected, the passage from djan to offspring
   djan is decided communally by the recipients. What
   might not be expected, it is considered dishonorable, or
   at least neutral, to be the one chosen. Upon selection by
   the previous landholder that the time for transfer has
   occurred (a time at which it becomes the obligation of
   the recipient to support the former owner), the receiving
   djan decides which child among them shall become
   owner. Because of the obligation (and stigma) he assumes, the owner customarily may request one favor
   (either immediate or delayed) from each of his fellow
   djans. Note also that the honorific Havna passes to the
   head of the household each generation, and that he
   becomes known as Havna, the embodiment of the
   group.

6. Pronounced tee-ohst, a mild punishment (metaphori-
   cally, somewhat stronger than a wrist-slapping). Cygnans very seldom threaten, and the entire passage is an
   attempt to illustrate the seriousness of the accusation. Of
   course, to human eyes, it helps to highlight the seriousness of the crime.

7. Hroi; the plural of hro (sexual love). A general term
   applied to one's spouse and offspring. Since the raising
   of children is more of an onus than an accolade, the offer
   to relieve a Cygnan of his mate and children is an

extreme inducement. Some Cygnan scholars (revisionists, chiefly) believe that the reader is supposed to
read between the lines here: the good djan who accepted
the Havna (against his will, they feel) is being offered as
a foil for the wayward Derna. It is difficult for a human
commentator to make a meaningful interjection, except
that there is, at least to my ears, an odd haggling note to
the entire discussion which suggests (to me, anyhow)
that the revisionists may well be correct.

8. A public sale of anything is rare; advertising is almost
non-existent. The implication is that Derna told
townsfolk that the farm was no longer tended. If so, this
would be a compounding of her crime, since it reveals to
others beyond the circle of the djan her desertion. To
Cygnans, truth comes in rings corresponding with djan
levels. What is a truth at the lowest, broadest level, may
not carry a density of truth sufficient to qualify it for the
next level. The highest truths are shared with one's
djan—one's pouch brothers.

There is no Cygnan word meaning absolute truth. In
Cygnan, ''to thine own self be true'' is both untranslate-
able and false.

A Cygnan proverb asks, *is it true for the djan?* Here
Derna has expanded the ring of truth: in so doing, she has
cheapened it, in effect adding insult to injury.

9. Eodja. The direct translation is 'only child'. One Cygnan litter in twenty thousand (roughly) contains only one
living offspring. Eodja are wily and clever; also un-
trustworthy.

10. The Terran word would be mediator. In Cygnan, the
word implies that the negotiating parties have failed
because one from outside the appropriate dja-level circle
must be brought in to resolve the difficulty. The disdain
conveyed by the chosen translation word is evident in the
original context.

11. The annullment ceremony, at which ostracos is invoked. The casting out of the name amongst the offspring is unnecessary, in fact, somewhat theatrical, and indicates the anger felt by the other members of the djan: they were acting in accordance with their deepest convictions and not merely in satisfaction of the law.

12. It is instructive to reread the preceding sentence in light of the Cygnan's extremely strong sense of privacy (privacy of the group, not of the individual). In this context, the sentence sounds much like the approbation of a law enforcement officer commenting upon the acumen of a drug pusher who knows just where his markets are and who caters to them very adeptly.

13. Cygnans love gossip, but only if both the source and the object can be mentioned without attribution. It is an elaborate guessing-game, with the storyteller presenting the information in the form of an allegory or a legend out of the past, and supplying clues in the form of puns or allusions which may only be understood by members of the local community. It is yet another example of the way in which the Cygnans attempt to divide their society horizontally into subsets with levels of truth.

14. Asking her to identify herself. Normally used to suggest that the speaker is dishonorable; in this instance clearly an attempt to tell her that they wished to hear no more.

15. Since Derna offers more than is needed, she is flaunting her wealth upon them, and confronting them with the success she has enjoyed since leaving the Havna. The period of solitude has not changed the error of her thinking.

16. The tladja (speaks for the guild of record-keepers) returns Derna's offering by saying that, rather than borrowing the money, he wants to have her give it to him, and not just 120%, but double the amount necessary.

There is not really a word for 'give' in Cygnan; there is a word that means 'receive a gift'; in spirit it is akin to 'grovel'. And since the amount asked is again as much as that needed, the net effect of the entire response is something along the lines of, 'I would sooner waste twice as much money obtained dishonorably than touch your offer'.

17. Although not explicitly mentioned, the story (and it is much prized for the simplicity of the conflict and the clarity of its message) has a moral. The moral is that Derna's desertion of her duty must inevitably lead to disaster for her and for the group. They have a saying in Cygnan: 'the stain of the individual cannot be washed from the group'.

Another interesting storytelling point is that, from the moment that Derna is introduced, she is called by name, while all the others are called through their djan name and addressed through their function in relation to the group. She must look to herself for status and place; the others are part of a group. So from the introduction of Derna the reader has a suspicion that she is a loner who will break from the group.

A second important result of the story is the uniform praise which commentators bestow for the expression of Cygnan law. The law is upheld even to the point of the destruction of the Havna; the only equivalent to this that I can recollect among human experience is the saying, 'it is better to die on one's feet than live on one's knees'.

6.

Even a few days later, Erickson could not understand what had triggered van Gelder's anger. Kees was normally the mildest, meekest person on board. What could Tai-Ching Jones possibly have done?

Equally baffling was Delgiorno's handling of the situation. After pulling them apart, she had roundly chastised both combatants without turning a hair. Yet she had greeted them both cheerfully the next morning. Erickson was not sure which was more unsettling, her frightening anger or the apparent ease with which she controlled it. Forced to conjure up anger, Erickson would have felt ridiculous. Forced to endure such a thrashing, he would have felt humiliated, a humiliation from which it would have taken him days to recover.

Now she wanted to talk to him about personnel problems: so, now he sat waiting for her arrival, trying to look dignified. His dark glasses helped, but he wished that such institutionalized gossip could have been part of someone else's job.

Perhaps it's age; there was a time when I was as full of fire as she is.

Erickson had had the good fortune to be born with no strong emotions, nor any great desire to be with people. It sometimes amused him.

In an abstracted way, he knew he was missing something, the way a color-blind man might feel that there was something to all this discussion about shade and hue. People thought him colorless and cold; in all honesty, he could not blame them. But he had long ago given up trying to be disturbed. Like many of the men who had gone into space, he had null spots in places where most people had emotions. But he lived joys they never knew.

How, for instance, could one describe the calm ecstasy of lying on one's back, at the top of a rise, in the middle of the endless grass of Nebraska, on a starry night? He could reach up and touch the stars; they belonged to him alone. Of course, other people saw the same stars; city people walked under them every night. But the city folk never really saw the stars; city lights drowned their sharp crisp light in a warm glowing haze. No, the city folk did not own the heavens: *he* did. He lay in the warm grass with the endless wind blowing over him, and let their magic names roll in his head and onto the breeze.

Wolf, Alpha Centauri, Deneb, Procyon, Sirius. He would name them, aloud, there in the deep blackness of the night, on the familiar hill.

That was a long time ago. Before he had to be responsible for other people.

A long time ago, but the pull of it had brought him here, to the ship. To *his* ship. He had made a vow, a long time ago, the kind of vow you make when you are young and the future is expanding upon you like the swelling of a great wave.

"You guys belong to me," he remembered saying aloud. He spread his arms to encompass the stars. How old had he been? Fifteen? That was the kind of thing you did when you were fifteen, if you were one of the first children of the twenty-first century. "You're mine, all of you," he said.

"I can't visit all of you, or even get to many of you. But nobody else has ever been to the stars at all. I'm going to be among the first."

When he thought about it now, he realized that there had probably been half a hundred—half a million?—adolescents who had made a similar vow. Well, they hadn't made it. He had. Foolish though he might have been, he had stuck with it.

When he had first lain down, the sun had been setting. To his right, the horizon, bright white-blue daylight, turned red, then glowing yellow as the sun set through it, then orange, yellow, lime green, azure, indigo, blending the colors as it sank into the night.

Then, to his left, another light, colder, weaker than the last. A full moon, amber in the evening, swimming up out of the ground, so close it seemed oversize, rising through a curtain of colored haze, then gradually bleached as it rose, till it hung in the sky, gleaming white as a skull.

Slowly the limpid moon lifted itself from the ground, serene and confident as a lover, distant and untouchable as a succubus. Orb of dreams, in a bed of stars.

Stars.

Stars beyond number, stars beyond counting, stars beyond seeing. If he concentrated on one part of the sky long enough, more and more appeared. As the night wore on, his eyes became more sensitive; even more stars. By the time morning came, the bright stars were too painful to view directly. When toward dawn the light began to seep into the sky, at first his eyes hurt, but they reluctantly adjusted. He could feel the pupils shrink.

He rubbed his eyes.

Dawn. Once again, as they always did, the stars were surrendering the sky to another ordinary day. But not yet. He stood up for a closer look, then abruptly sat down in surprise.

There was a pebble in his shoe.

He pulled off the shoe, shook it until the pebble fell out. He rolled it in his hand, feeling that he had been made to look slightly foolish by that little piece of rock. "Feet of clay, eh?" And then, with a kind of testing roll of his shoulders, he hefted it in his hand, imagining it to be of greater weight. With a theatrical heave, he hurled it skyward.

In the instant of doing it, he felt deflated; to lie on one's back and utter airy words was all well and good—a long way from the goal. Easy words. It would take a lot of work; it would take many years. It would take selflessness and strength to match the desire that fired him. He would need something tangible to help him through the lean times, the hard times, the times of incomprehension, the times of disappointment. He would have to find some way always to remember what his goal was.

He got down on his hands and knees and began feeling carefully, methodically, in the now-damp grasses.

He worked hard in school, calculating that special scholastic achievement would get him a ship. His prize exceeded his expectations: first manned expedition to Uranus. Farther than manned vehicles had ever gone before, several light-hours.

Technically the ship carried a crew of five; but for all the companionship Erickson's four passengers provided, he might as well have been alone. He was chauffeur, cook, conductor and tour guide, all rolled into one. Get them there, get them home. Watch the computers. Nothing to do as long as no problems developed. Babysitting.

For that, they made me captain, he thought sardonically.

Before that trip began, Erickson had thought he knew loneliness; he had thought himself completely self-contained. Yet out amidst the endless silence, he found himself longing for a human voice. His riders spoke a language he could barely understand. Oh, he had the basic special relativity, a scattering of physics, and some chemistry. He even knew something about Doppler shifts, and spectral classes, and stellar evolution. But his knowledge paled before theirs, and as they occasionally reminded him, the journey was not a sightseeing expedition, and there was just no time to explain the subjects in sufficient detail.

Translation: *go away boy, you bother me.*

Could it have been boredom in the afterglow of his triumph? He had attained his dream. He was where he wanted to be; alone with the stars, farther away from home than any man before him, farther than the wildest imagination of da Vinci. In the midst of an expanding universe: *praise then creation unfinished,* Erickson remembered thinking.

With so much time, and so little companionship, Erickson began to till new ground. For the first time in his life, he read fiction. He played endless music. Bach mostly; he liked the complex mathematics of Bach. Even that finally paled throughout the long hours of routine. It was a time when he was at his most introspective—still, he admitted to himself, not very.

He had all he ever wanted: stars, peace, a ship, solitude, and a sense of satisfaction. But Odysseus had had these things, too, and a goddess to boot. And the ancient Greek had thrown it all up, just to go home.

Like Odysseus, Erickson felt the lack of—of what? Obstacle, he decided: challenge, purpose, and drive. By piloting standards, Uranus was a milk run. And once the ship sank into planetary orbit, the scientists plunged into their work like contented ferrets, burrowing into the new secrets of the universe. He was totally idle. Useless. Nothing to do.

Then the cooling system died.

You might think that cold is the danger in space; after all, the temperature hovers less than a degree above absolute zero. But for space travelers, heat is a greater danger; there are no breezes to carry it off. Space is a more perfect insulator than the most efficient vacuum bottle.

So what do you do with excess heat? You must do something; the rules of entropy say that the amount of waste heat is going to build up without ceasing. What do you do?

You throw it away. Collect the heat in a suitable vehicle—water, for instance—and let the water sublime away into space.

But this action, like everything else in space, produces a reaction. The force of driving away the excess heat pushes the ship in the opposite direction. For the *Open Palm* this doesn't matter—the giant engines are constantly pushing the ship somewhere, firing terrific heat out their baffles. But in a ship in a carefully-planned orbit, the aberrations can mount up.

So Erickson's ship, the *Trident*, had a cooling system designed to release the excess heat into space simultaneously and equally on opposite sides of the ship. By perfect synchronization, the expenditure of steam was accomplished without any net force to the ship, except when the pilot wanted to kill two birds with one stone and use the small effects thus produced to correct his course slightly.

But one day it just died. There was no great ringing of alarms, no shudder as the ship rent itself to pieces; if there had been, it would probably have been too late to do anything constructive about the problem. Instead, the ship's computer awakened Erickson with its flat metallic voice: "we have a malfunc-tion in the coolant sys-tem, sir. Could you please come to the bridge im-mediately."

Erickson smiled when he remembered his reaction to that message: *well, now at least I'll have something to do for a while*. For he was still young and inexperienced and hadn't had drummed into him the essential rule of space: there is no such thing as a small problem.

In space, if a problem doesn't kill you right away, you'll have plenty of time to solve it. But if the computer can't solve it, it's got to be a brainbuster. In brief, you're not dead—but the computer has no idea how to save your life. Good luck.

As he read the printouts, the blood slowly drained from Erickson's face.

Fixing a spaceship's problems isn't wrenches and grease. It's circuit diagrams, machine code, diagnostic programs, differential equations. You sit at a desk with a calculator, a stack of printouts, a pencil and a cup of coffee. You sweat. You sleep little. When you close your eyes, numbers dance; in the midst of your dreams men with megaphones shout formulas in echo chambers. And always, the endless pressure of time—and of not having the slightest idea where the problem is, or how to solve it even if you knew. For a few weeks, you earn your pay. If you survive.

For days Erickson stared in frustration at his piles of papers. He reorganized the piles. He reran the routines. He drew mindless circles. He sent descriptions of his problem to Earth and got little back. He stared into space.

Finally, eyes bleary from lack of sleep, he found the mistake. Or what he thought was the mistake: his brain was too fuzzy to be sure. He treated himself to six hours slumber.

When he woke, it was still there. But he still had to write the programs to patch over the bug. Erickson remembered a maxim from his programming days: a working program is one whose bugs haven't been discovered yet. Erickson faced the impossible: write code that works. The first time. With no debugging.

Seventeen days after the computer's announcement, during which time the computer informed him he had managed only 86 hours and 37 minutes of sleep, he typed the command to restart the coolant system. In shorts and sandals, a trickle running off his balding head, Erickson watched as the computer recompiled his patched program and rechecked all the necessary systems. He could do no more; if it failed, he'd have to take the ship out of there, regardless of how much invaluable scientific research would go down the tubes, and how much of the taxpayers' money blown to Sirius.

But it came on: immediately Erickson heard the sighing as

the ship's remote microphones picked up the sound, transmitted through the hull of the ship. He hardly heard the computer's brief announcement, "the coolant system is functioning to with-in ac-cep-table tolerances."

In fact, he was asleep.

That crisis had been the forge. For more than two weeks the computer had been his only companion, the problem his only love. Love? Yes, that was the best word. He loved having the problem to work on. He loved taking it from the beginning, working his way over the charts, then methodically testing out the various subsystems until he had found the one at fault. Doing something he had never done.

He enjoyed having a race against time, a race that depended exclusively on him. Aware that the initial projections had allowed him only eighteen days before the heat buildup would *have* to be stopped, he felt both a calm satisfaction and a grim pleasure. When after nine days he found the bug, he felt sure he would win. But he was a professional; he stayed at the post until he was sure that the problem had been corrected. The instant it was done, his body gave priority to other things, like sleep.

Out of the experience Erickson gained more than the satisfaction of a job competently handled. He had also acquired a certain wisdom, and a valuable skill: the ability not to worry. You did your best, you had your shot, and you left worrying to the Fates.

Even better, Erickson no longer yearned for the companionship of his passengers. His daily inspection tours, normally supposed to be completed in a maximum of two and a half hours, grew into eight-hour treks throughout the length and breadth of the ship. EVA, once a necessary drudgery, became a ceremony. With dignity he pulled on the suit, sealed it up, added the helmet. Erickson took scenic routes, going the hard way around the hull, stopping "to picnic," as he called it. He would activate his boot magnets and lever himself backward, until he came to be lying, knees bent, feet anchored firmly to the outside of the ship, hands behind his head, watching the panorama in thoughtless bliss. Often hours lapsed in this fashion.

There were times when he would have Uranus spread above him like a green fog. He would search across the face of the giant, following the spring-green clouds as they swirled forever, in waltz time.

Other times he would perch away from the planet, and have only the stars, a hemisphere of crystal blackness, with the Andromeda galaxy sprawling across his vision, a ghostly disk inconceivably distant.

Or he would have the solar system to view. Saturn was near enough so that the rings could be easily picked out. Without difficulty he could also locate russet Mars and beautiful blue Earth. And then, sometimes, he would think of home.

In his reveries, the tension in his knees would relax, his weightless body would straighten itself, and he would come to be standing. As this happened, the ship would swing into his vision from underneath him, and, reluctantly, he would move on to his job.

Objectively he knew that such sojourns were dangerous. Not in themselves, perhaps, although should anything happen to him his chances of help from the passengers were practically nil. The greater danger was the feeling of security. You started to think you were immortal, untouchable. You were the lord of all you surveyed.

The universe has a way of reprimanding people whose egos get out of line. When Erickson felt himself getting too cocky, he would remind himself of his bout with the computer. Waiting for Delgiorno, Erickson smiled at the memory.

Over the months, his eyes grew very sensitive to light. He found he could see perfectly well by starlight. In fact, artificial light became painful. Probably he could have adjusted; instead, he wore dark wraparound sunglasses, to keep his eyes sensitive to the starlight he loved.

In due course they started for Earth. With surprise, Erickson realized that going home held promise of disappointment. Even before the trip was over, he dreaded the landing; he wanted to be out again. A boat, any boat—get off the ground with its crushing gravity and choking air.

He was out in space again in six days. The freighter *Edgar Rice* needed a captain to carry drugs and microcircuitry to Mars, quick. It required a slingshot course, cutting inside the orbit of Earth, using the Sun's gravitational field to whip the ship on the long climb to Mars. He'd never done it before, but the computer had, and, as the humorless contracting agent had said, "all you have to do is keep your lunch down."

That was thirty years ago. Since then he had been on Earth for a total of sixty-two days. A couple of hundred days on the Moon, and an equal number on Mars. Except for that, the rest of his life was spent at home, on ships. Mainly freighters—he preferred the workhorses to the liners. Liners offered a chance to make a name for himself, and were an easier job technically, since the groundhogs didn't like complicated acceleration patterns. But Erickson wanted space, darkness, solitude, and the stars. You didn't get those on liners. Choosing freighters was easy.

Eventually the call came; they were building a ship to the stars. Erickson was working a run between Venus and Mars when the grapevine got him the message. He promptly got hold of the application information and radioed a response within ten hours of receipt. After that he fired off a message to Martian Central, letting them know that he wanted to take the first ship—*any* ship, even a liner—at the fastest reasonable transit time back to Earth.

Two and a half hours later the response came back.

GOT A GIRL YOU SUDDENLY REMEMBERED INTERROGATION FREIGHTER EASTERN QUEEN LEAVING LOWELL TWELVE DAYS POST YOUR ARRIVAL NEEDS CAPTAIN STOP SIGNED YOU ON STOP ARRIVES EARTH FEBRUARY FIFTEEN 2058 STOP GIVES YOU TWO WEEKS BEFORE DEADLINE END

How the hell did *he* know why Erickson was going to Earth?

Of course Erickson had scored horribly on current events; he had barely known which star the aliens were coming from. But the psychologist's report had got him the job—they'd shown it to him afterward.

Imagination: deficient.

Creativity: nonexistent.

Neuroses which might affect judgment: negligible.
Stability under stress: unshakable.
Command capability: top-notch.
Experience: unrivalled.
Erickson is a simple individual, but this may be an advantage. He is not likely to become overly preoccupied with tension, and is remarkably suited to a period of several years on a voyage like the proposed one. His ability to respond to unexpected disasters is far higher than any other applicant yet tested. I recommend that you make him captain and keep him off the talk shows.

They gave him the job.

He thought it was going be another chauffeur trip; ferry them out to the rendezvous point, ferry them back. He never expected that being the captain of this ship would involve so much psychology.

Now he had to fight with his First Officer. This was the hardest job of all, for he liked her. But he was—he smiled wanly—a simple person, and there were complex and complicated factors coming into play here. He wished he had the words to deal with her arguments. Bad enough that these things had to be decided; worse, no one on the ship he could consult. But the greatest hardship was her insistence on secrecy. It made him feel unclean.

There was a knock at the door. He rose and let her in.

She was dressed, as usual, in a regulation merchant-marine jumpsuit. Under one arm was a pile of papers: fuel reports and minor additions to the log, supposedly.

"Sorry to bother you this late, Captain, but you did request that I bring around all the little things that we haven't caught up on. I don't expect it will take you very long to complete them." As he closed the door she stopped and took a deep breath. "There wasn't anybody in the corridor, but it never hurts to be careful even when you don't think there's any danger. I hope we don't take very long—meetings like this are a little unusual as it is."

She had already sat down, and was sifting through her papers. "Ah, here's the one I want: the log entry of May 10, 2062. Damn it, Captain, why'd you make me go through that whole entry?"

She always took charge of their meetings. He groped, knowing that he was pitifully unskilled with words. "I don't think it is a good idea to use drugs on the members of the crew."

"Captain, we've been over this. You approved the procedure before we left."

"I know I did," said Erickson, "but I don't think that was the right decision, and I don't think, even if there were situations which warranted such actions, that this one calls for it."

"Captain, Renaud is a basket case."

"Yvette's been under stress, I know—"

"And where has the stress been coming from? What's she been doing lately that's so nervewracking she can scarcely hold a coffee cup? What's eating at her?"

"I don't know . . ." he began involuntarily.

"And neither do I," she said emphatically. "And I've *got* to know. It's part of my job. Paragraph 4(b) Duties of the First Officer—"

"I know the regulations, Helen, you don't have to quote them at me."

She stopped for a moment. "I'm sorry, Captain."

"It's all right, Helen, really."

"But, Captain, surely you've got to see that this is important."

"Helen, you always call me Aaron except when you're mad at me. Now I'm not totally helpless in my dotage."

She ran a hand through her hair and tossed some of it over her shoulder. Though he felt nothing, he knew she was a strikingly attractive woman. She liked the jumpsuits, she once told him, because they were flexible. Zip up or down and you could change your appearance. Sexy or prim, relaxed or tense. She could send signals with her body, she said.

"All right. Where do you want me to start? Her background, her recent problems?"

"Let's begin with why you think it is necessary to manipulate her this way."

Delgiorno smiled. "You're trying to make me out a junior-grade Satan, Aaron. Yes, I am trying to manipulate her. I want to take her apart and find out what's inside. I want to get at it, so I can zap it before she does something crazy.''

''You take a lot on yourself.''

''It's my *job*. It's my goddamned job. And I don't like it, but I refuse to let my own reluctance come between me and my duty.'' Her face was flushed; her eyes crackled. ''I shouldn't get excited.''

''I'm glad you do.''

''Why's that?''

''Because if you weren't upset at doing this to another person, I'd be seriously considering overruling you on the grounds of professional incompetence.''

This time she smiled and bowed her head mockingly. ''Thank you for the compliment. Damn you, Aaron, I can never stay mad at you for long. Where was I?''

''Why you thought she had to be manipulated.''

''Emotional problems. Getting worse.''

''Why are drugs necessary? Why can't someone just talk to her?''

''She's extremely defensive. She won't talk to anyone. She even denies there's a problem. But it's apparent: there is something inside her that she refuses to let out. Whatever it is, it's killing her from inside. Unless it's cleansed, the infection will fester.''

''Any idea what the infection is? What symptoms?''

''She's losing weight. Her hands shake. She loses the thread of her arguments when she's lecturing. Her pulse rate is up, blood pressure too. She's like a kettle building up steam.''

''Couldn't that be due to some illness?''

''Like what? Uh, uh, she's got something inside her.''

''Guesses?''

'I don't know. Something she sees in the aliens? She's got the damnedest way of being embarrassed by other people's actions that I've ever seen. She might have seen something the rest of us haven't perceived yet and be hiding it from us.''

''Like what?''

''I don't know. How would I know? That's her field, not mine.''

''What other things could it be?''

"Something in her past, maybe."

"Such as?"

"Well, there's one that stands out like a sore thumb. She accompanied her father on the Ganymede expedition—do you know about that?"

"No, she never mentioned it to me."

"It was in her file," snapped Delgiorno.

"Helen, don't lecture. You know I refused to read those things."

"Well, she's never spoken of it with anybody. This suggests that she doesn't wish to remember it."

"Isn't that significant by itself? I mean, I should think you would remember a trip to someplace like that forever."

"Her father died on that trip."

"Oh." Erickson did not know what else to say.

"Not only that," continued Delgiorno, "but everybody else on the mission died too, except her. One of the living modules blew up with all the scientists inside. Are you *sure* you didn't know about this? You were supposed to be briefed on everybody's background."

"They started to tell me. I didn't want to hear. A person's past is his own unless he chooses to reveal it."

"Disagree. Some amenities we can't afford."

"Let's not argue old ground," Erickson said tiredly. "Get back to this Titan trip."

"Ganymede."

"Oh. Of course. Go on."

"It took them a couple of months before they could get a ship to her. That can't have been an easy time."

"I should say not." They were both silent for a moment.

"But what," asked Erickson, "would cause her to get so upset?"

"I don't know. If I did, I wouldn't be asking to pull her under."

"Any other guesses?"

"Hadn't thought of any. Let me see. No history of any major diseases that would cause it; and besides, we shot up everybody pretty good while on the way out. No emotional entanglements that I know of—"

"She never married, did she?"

"She never had a man, either, as far as we could tell. Is there anybody on board ship now to whom she might be attracted?"

Erickson flushed.

Delgiorno grinned broadly. "Awww, we have a closet Casanova? With all due respect, Captain, I think she sees you as more of a father figure than a lover. Not," she added more seriously, "that you wouldn't qualify. She just seems to have a strong desire for father-attachment."

"Don't tell me, Helen." He cleared his throat. "And I haven't seen anything between her and Pat."

Delgiorno nodded. "Agreed. That's out. So, no visible recent motives for the change. That's what makes me so curious."

"Curious, yes. I'd be curious too, if I were in your position." *But thank the stars that I don't have either your desires or your job.* "That still isn't justification enough."

"Captain, we have a crew member on the ragged edge. And don't start to tell me that hers is not a command position. On a ship this size, it doesn't matter. One loony and we're in serious trouble. And an unstable personality is a time bomb."

"I can't accept that simply because you are eloquent in saying so. I have to have further justification."

"She gets along with everyone else in the crew but Harold and Walter. No one likes Harold—I won't hold that against her. But every time she runs into Walt I hold my breath. He's enough of a bundle of trouble as it is. And Harold: well, you know what Harold's like, and she has to rub shoulders with him all day, every day."

"Why not wait? She might get better."

Delgiorno shook her head. "If I were just interested in Yvette's personal welfare, of course I'd wait. But I'm trying to protect the mission."

"What is the point of the mission, if you have to sacrifice the crew?"

"Not *all* of the crew, Aaron," she said, looking hard at him. "Not all." She looked away and her voice dropped almost to a whisper. "No, even if we lost a few, the mission could survive."

For a moment she was lost in thought.

Erickson waited until she came out of her reverie. Gently he asked, "But why now?"

"If you see an inevitable crisis, trigger it early. If you control the timing, you can minimize the damage." Then she added, emphatically, "The crisis you don't trigger is the one that kills you."

"I still don't know . . ." His voice trailed off.

"The safety of the ship is paramount."

"Of course."

"And I think that putting her under would make the ship safer."

"You've got to do better than that, Helen. There are lots of things that *might* make the ship safer, but *might* make things *much* worse. What guarantees can you give me that your actions won't cause her more harm than good—and this ship, for that matter?"

"How do you expect me to guarantee something when I have no idea what I'll find?" Delgiorno was exasperated. "Of course there's a chance that she—and we—will be worse off. But it is my professional judgment that this action is warranted, and you have to live with that. I've given you as much supporting evidence as I can; I've given you as many reasons as I possess. I'm not hiding anything from you." Her voice grew bitter. "Dammit, you're supposed to accept my judgment in these cases."

"Helen," Erickson said quietly, "I sometimes question your decisions—never your judgment."

Her voice said nothing, but he read the thank-you in her eyes. Erickson cleared his throat.

"You think that this Titan thing is a possible source?" he asked.

"Sure. Anything's a possible source when you don't know anything," she said, "and it was Ganymede, not Titan."

"Oh, I thought you said Titan."

"Come on, Aaron, you're stalling. You bought time with

an outrageous compliment, but I'm not letting you off the hook. You know I'm right."

"It goes against every instinct I have. I don't like this idea that you can tinker with a human being like a malfunctioning piece of clockwork. When you put the pieces back together, it still may not work."

"Very nice imagery, Aaron, but I have enough facts on my side. There *is* a danger; there *is* a course of action that suggests itself. In order to bring it to the surface, I will implant a subconscious command that she *must* tell someone her dark secret: if she doesn't, her pain will grow worse and worse and will eventually kill her. Most likely that command will translate itself into dreams. In effect, her subconscious will terrify her so much that it will force her conscious mind to give in. I know it may backfire; but it hasn't yet in the times we've used it in the past. You agreed to use it on Pat, and I think it's done him some good."

"You said it was a long-term thing with Pat."

"It was; Pat needed a lot of stroking, and I pushed him as far as I could reasonably go. But did you see what happened at Yvette's last lecture?"

"The one on dependence?"

"No, the one where she was talking about *djans*."

"Now I remember. That was the one where Harold insulted Walter and you gave him hell for it."

"But did you see what also happened? Pat was there too, and when Walter went steaming out, Pat shot after him like someone had lit a fire in his ass."

"What happened after that?"

"I don't know—but Pat came back like the cat who ate the canary, and Walt seemed surprisingly quiet. He hardly sulked at all."

"And you think it was because you worked on Pat under drugs, eh?"

"Yes." Delgiorno started to add something; then checked herself. There wasn't anything more to say—if the captain was going to decide in her favor without a major to-do, he had to come to the decision on his own.

"All right, you win." He smiled thinly. "We'll go with your considered opinion. But"—he held up his hand—"no more than two sessions without coming back to me for a progress report and further approval. I refuse to give carte blanche."

"OK. I'll live with that."

He was not happy in making the decision, but there was little he could do. Despite his feelings, she could well be right and indeed, Yvette had been showing signs of fatigue and tension. He'd tried to seek her out; but, beyond making her embarrassed and flustered he hadn't accomplished anything. She had been totally cautious, trying quite desperately to hide—what?

At least now they would find out.

Delgiorno was gathering her papers together. "Captain, I really don't think things like this should be a matter to get either one of us upset. And I don't mean that you shouldn't protest when you think I'm out of line." She sounded apologetic. "But keep in mind that what I do, I do for a good reason. Or several good reasons."

"Sure." He was distracted now; the decision had been made, and it was part of the past. He was past the time of regret; sometime long ago—perhaps out in space, perhaps just by osmosis—he had learned the futility of the simple words, *what if?*

He looked at his hand. Some the hairs were gray. What hair was left on his head was also gray. You got older. You changed. You learned to accept, and not to judge.

He raised his hand to bid her goodbye, but she had already gone.

7.

As she left Erickson, Delgiorno was thinking hard. What to do with Tai-Ching Jones? Renaud was one class of problem, Tai-Ching Jones another. In Renaud's case the solution might be obscure, but the next step—increasing the pressure as a means of precipitating the crisis—was obvious.

But Walter—Walt was precipitating dangerous crises unpredictably. *Must do something.*

Delgiorno barely saw the corridors' footlights flicking by. But as she passed the Movies, she heard voices raised; one male, one female. Heidi's voice, and Walt's. She stopped abruptly, turned around. Listened.

Patterns flicked across the screen in electronic ballet; first moving, then holding a pose, the delicate tracery of lines seeming to pulse with a green rhythm. The images then released the position, rotated delicately in defiance of any gravity.

Spitzer, from one of the front consoles, put one hand over her mouth, fingers caressing her nose. Then she leaned her head on the same hand, stared for a moment away from the screen. Looking down, she punched a series of keys on the console in front of her.

Again the brisk pirouette as the lines raced to rearrange themselves according to Spitzer's whim. Another image: Spitzer hit a key. Some of the lines seemed to step forward, changing from the characteristic light green to a more aggressive red. Another key: the image expanded, green lines fleeing from the center of the screen.

Satisfied, Spitzer hit another key, then moved out from behind the desk to study the screen closer up.

Those glowing lines showed her a schematic of the internal organs of a typical healthy male Cygnan. Physiology, human or Cygnan, was her responsibility. And though the aliens had a similar outward appearance, Cygnan internal structure differed from Terran, organized, as it were, on the basis of a completely different concept of how to arrange a body's organs, how to divide responsibilities among them, how to regulate the chemical processes.

It worked though; it harbored life. That was enough for Spitzer.

Spitzer had no time for those delicate souls who could not confront themselves. She believed in forthrightness. Whatever she felt about their society, she admired the Cygnan ability to face the truth impartially, as a window; she cultivated the trait. It was not in her to be weak of stomach when confronted with the entrails of life.

She frowned as she examined the image on the screen. It showed about as much knowledge as she had been able to assimilate, in conjunction with the computer, about the Cygnan kidney. Even with all this information, she was unsatisfied, for the basic functions, though clearly articulated, seemed to have come from nowhere.

Terran physiology progresses in unbroken chain from simple single cell animals up to the higher vertebrates. All Terran cells look basically alike; mitochondria, Golgi bodies, protoplasm. They carry, as distinctive as a family tree, a visual description of their heritage.

Mitochondria are self-contained entities. The protoplasm of a typical cell ingests all around it. Put these two factors together and you have a blueprint of the origin of the typical single cell on Earth—protoplasm ingests a self-sufficient entity, and by chance the two entities find that they work more efficiently as one. Symbiosis.

In Cygnan physiology Spitzer could find no such ready trail. The Cygnans' own physiology and evolution textbooks gave only partial explanations. The Cygnans had exhibited a lack of curiosity about underlying meaning and fundamental questions so strong as to be stunning. Spitzer could understand the reluctance with which the aliens had moved into space; why go traipsing about in the stars if you were sufficient unto yourself? But not to be curious about *their own chemistry*? Spitzer could not understand how intelligent beings could be so blind. She shook her head.

Back at the console she cleared the image. An hour of solitude before the afternoon briefing. The Alien Reception Lounge, universally called the Movies by ship's personnel, was empty. Or it had been when Spitzer had first come in and set up the image. But now Tai-Ching Jones was there, behind the three rows of tables, using one of the terminals against the wall.

Obviously he knew she was there. But he had been unusually quiet. Until she turned around, she would not have known he was there. He must have planned it as a slight unpleasant shock. She wondered if he were grinning over there in the cubicle.

Back to the problem at hand. With efficient commands she recalled another image, watched as the screen threw part of the digestive tract out with spidery green interwinings, expanded a piece of the image. She put the image on Hold and went back to the screen.

In the corner, Tai-Ching Jones was annoyed. He hadn't particularly intended to come down here and use the machine but, upon passing the door, he had been struck by a vague desire and had decided to take on the machine in a quick game of chess—nothing strenuous, just a quick stomp. Set the machine to something low and construct an esthetically satisfying crunch out of it.

He quickly keyed in the instructions, picking Black. Black was what he wanted; more ingenuity was required to construct entertaining positions.

White	Black
Ship's Computer	W. Tai-Ching Jones

	White	Black
1.	P–K4	N–KB3
2.	P–K5	N–Q4
3.	B–B4	P–K3
4.	P–Q4	P–Q3

He could of course have set the machine to respond verbally, and even to include little extraneous tidbits, by invoking its Beast program. But the Beast was Tai-Ching Jones' special creation. And it was a private thing.

For her part, Spitzer was—uncomfortable, she admitted to herself—uncomfortable to have him in the background somewhere, saying nothing. She knew him; knew him too well. Subtlety in Tai-Ching Jones was the symptom of great stress; when he was at ease, he was refreshing, coarse, direct, incisive, infuriating. He was natural.

She turned back to the image on the screen, determined to put him out of her mind. He had no part in her life now, except that of a member of the crew. She had only the responsibility of keeping him physically healthy.

There it was, drawn in delicate green lines. The image on the screen was sterile enough; the reality, when she finally had an opportunity to touch it, would be a different matter entirely.

Nothing in her cardiology textbooks had prepared her for her first real operation on a human heart. She remembered it clearly: oblivious to the scalpels poised above it, a pulsing heart beating indomitably away. Pinioned to the stretcher, the bleeding body had been whisked right into the operating room. Surgeons opened him up brutally, a pencil-laser slicing the breastbone like a ripe turkey. A clamp brutally pried apart the rib cavity to get at the heart.

She could still remember her first look. So fragile, no more stiffness than a jellyfish. A warm bag, through which you could hear the steady, loud slosh of blood. The arteries and veins which served the heart itself stood out against the wine-red muscle in darker ripples. They beat with their own rhythm.

Ready to pull her hand back, she touched it slowly, half expecting this alien thing to start under her fingers. Oblivious, it continued its steady, never-ending (never-ending!) pounding. Insensate, incapable of living by itself, directed by feeble and inconsistent orders from the dying brain at which surgeons were now at work, it beat on.

5.	B–N5+	P–B3
6.	B–R4	PxP
7.	PxP	N–Q2

Tai-Ching Jones smiled. There was no danger that the machine would be beating him in this game; its ridiculous fifth and sixth moves showed that plainly. Short-horizon look-ahead analysis had no idea of basic concepts such as weaknesses in the Pawn structure, or wasting tempi in the opening.

They'd lost the patient. The EEG had finally failed. His brain had quit, so he'd been declared dead, so the machinery was shut down and he was wheeled away to the morgue. Spitzer had felt a certain sense of loss at that; the poor heart, through no fault of its own, pumping serenely away, had been disconnected, shut off by an outside hand, because the feeble brain had collapsed under the strain. The sloshing noise had stopped, the operating room was silent.

It was maudlin and unprofessional to feel sympathy toward a man's heart, of course. It was just a pump. If there was anything that labeled a man human, it resided behind the skull. But at that moment Spitzer cared little for humanity, or the great cleverness of mankind. The elaborate structure: arms, leg, torso, internal organs, sensory organs, all now useless. All built to serve a quart of mush. But what a miracle in the building!

8. N–KB3	Q–B2
9. Q–Q4	B–B4

Two more bad moves in a row; this game had to be over, for all practical purposes. Now it was just a dry exercise of finding, and executing, the proper combination.

As he waited for the machine's tenth move, he drummed his fingers on the keyboard—lightly, so as not to type any characters. Was Heidi still there? He wanted to look, but forbade himself to turn in her direction. He wished—no.

10. Q–K4

She tried to force her mind to the matter at hand, but his presence irritated her. He was probably playing a game of some kind; he was always playing games. He seemed to believe that, merely because she enjoyed sleeping with him, he was entitled to demand that she surrender her individuality. He, of course, could retain all of his idiosyncracies. The grandiose aura of the cock (perhaps that was unfair), the overpowering impetus of sexuality (that sounded much nicer), was supposed to make one completely accepting and ready to change. She had tolerated it for a time. Finally being with him, even in bed, was simply not worth it. She had put an end to it, knowing by then that he would not understand.

Human blood was very reflective of the composition of salt water; roughly, all that was added was hemoglobin. So if the basic constituents of a Cygnan's cellular structure had a pH of 9 or so, this suggested strongly that the original medium of which life evolved on Cygnus had a pH several points higher than it has at present. Have the Cygnans investigated this? Could life have evolved in some kind of inland lake, where minerals dissolving and accumulating would affect the pH? It wasn't much, but it was a lead. She moved away from the screen and back to the console, to search the computer's memory.

		P–B4
11.	PxP e.p.	QNxP
12.	Q–K5	B–Q3
13.	Q–Q4	

He wished there were some way he could make her understand; he had been saddened by the callousness with which she had viewed their relationship. With her, it was all physiology. Just a pleasant feeling. Well, forget that: if he wanted sexual acrobatics, he'd use the Dreamer. Now she would screw up Kees the same way.

That angered him. Van Gelder was his friend; he liked the Dutchman, despite a gulf of differences between them. Casey was mild-mannered and very conventional. Where Heidi took sex where she found it, Kees tended wherever possible to avoid it.

And now, having been effictively inculcated into the fun

of getting laid, Kees was being systematically desensitized. *Eventually she'll get tired of him, and then he'll be bounced out, and he couldn't take it as well as I can. He's never had it happen before.*

Won't even be any comfort to say I told you so.

What was the use of trying to explain it to her? She wouldn't care; self-centered bitch. All she wanted was a pleasant, superficial relationship. If you wanted something different, that was your problem.

What the hell was going on in this game? Oh, it was his move.

                                   O–O

14.   O–O

A dead end. Nothing. They don't have very good records; haven't even investigated. I know, I know, Harold— curiosity for its own sake is a human trait.

She terminated her program; the investigation was reaching the point of diminishing return. She needed to relax. Kees would be down at the engines now. She checked the wall clock—still an hour and forty minutes.

She looked over at Tai-Ching Jones. His head was bent; he seemed deep in concentration. He had taken it very hard; he took everything hard, she reminded herself. Perhaps she could soften the blow somehow.

Tai-Ching Jones had found it was hard to stand aside and let what was happening between Spitzer and Kees take place. Spitzer would bring out the worst elements of van Gelder's personality. Kees almost enjoyed suffering in silence.

And Heidi? Heidi would assume that passive acceptance meant he enjoyed being dominated, shoved around, and otherwise controlled. His personality would retreat further and further behind the blond curls; nothing would be left but an order-taking machine. Tai-Ching Jones doubted that Spitzer would have much use for van Gelder then—would discard him. And Kees? He would be a zombie, a man without a consciousness.

                                                P–K4

15.   Q–R4   P–K5
16.   N–Q4

    The attack was rolling now; the lines had been opened, and
already the Queen and both Bishops were bearing on the
White Kingside, defended only by the over-large presence of
the White Queen. Well, her Majesty could get kicked this
way and that by the minor pieces.

    No purpose would be served by keeping him mad at her;
she had acted badly at her birthday party. If there was going
to be a battle between them, she would not add to it. Spitzer
looked at his whippet body, bent over the keyboard.

    She wanted to say something, at least to open the door to a
normal conversation. But she hesitated. He could be so cruel,
so uncaring. Still, she could handle him; she could always
handle him. He had no finesse.

    ''What are you playing?'' she heard herself asking.

                                                N–N5

17.   P–KR3

    He was tempted to let the Knight hang, and just throw
something else at the King. Why did she have to interrupt him
now? She didn't know that the game was at a crucial point;
she wouldn't care, he remembered. She didn't like games.
To hell with her.

    ''Chess.''

    He hadn't looked up.

    She smiled, taking the edge out of her voice. ''I can never
get over how fascinated you are by games.'' It was the wrong
thing to say; it reopened old wounds.

                                                N–R7

    Ha!

    What had she said?

    ''What?'' he asked, distracted.

18. R–Q1

"I said I can never get over how fascinated you are by games. I'm trying to understand, Walter," she added, gently.

"I've told you before."

"Tell me again."

He sighed. Before he spoke, he punched in his move.

N–B5

"It's very simple. Games are, first of all, very interesting. Secondly, they are a contained universe. Everything is specified; there are clearly defined rules. Yet within such a small universe, you still can have nearly endless variety. Anything human you can find reflected in a game."

"Where do you find obnoxious behavior in a game?"

19.	B–N3+	K–R1
20.	P–KN3	

Why had she started this conversation? Just to make him upset? That seemed stupid. She said she was trying to understand. All she understood was what she knew; what *she* felt; what *she* wanted.

N–K7+

He turned back to the computer, and stared bitterly at it while he spoke. "Leave me alone. It didn't work, Heidi. Let it go. Just let me alone."

"Walter, give me a break," said Spitzer peevishly. "I've got to start somewhere. I can't pretend you don't exist for the next eleven years. I'm not a scheming manipulator."

"Looks that way," he grumbled. It sounded childish even to him.

She could never really understand his single-mindedness: didn't he want to accomplish anything with his life? "You act so serious, Walter, but you spend your time on activities that have no lasting value. Oh damn, I'm saying this badly. Let me try again. What would you like to do with your life?''

21. KxN

"I'm doing what I like with my life." He leaned back and stretched. "I've got *my* job under control."

"Like your life," said Spitzer sweetly. "That's under control too." As she expected, his veneer turned quickly to rage. He pivoted in his seat, trying to conceal it.

RxP

"Did I say something, Walter?" she drawled, knowing he would have to answer.

"Heidi, what's your point? You can make me mad. So what?"

Angry, he snapped his head away from the screen. Delgiorno was hurrying by, intent on something. He waited until she was out of sight before speaking again. "Look, Heidi, we've been through all this. You don't like me. I don't really like you. I see no point in continuing a fight."

22. K–R1

"But *you're* continuing the fight, Walter. I have no designs on you; I never really did. And I don't want to make you miserable, though I'll bet you think I do. Just because we've stopped being lovers shouldn't mean you go around glaring at me. Why did you come in here?"

Stupid question. "To play a quick game of chess on the computer."

"Really."

"Yes, that's all. I didn't see you until I got in here."

"You didn't walk by, then turn around and come back in?"

Had he? He didn't remember. Anyway, it was irrelevant.

"I wasn't being cute, Heidi. I wasn't chasing you. Just leave me alone."

''Leave you alone?'' She was scornful. ''You came in here, my friend. I didn't come to you.''

''So what? I didn't start this conversation.''

''You came in here, instead of going to your quarters. They're right nearby.''

''Yes, dammit! Will you get out of your head the idea that I was being clever? I don't go in for *that* sort of game-playing.''

''So it just happened that you popped in here, sat down at your precious game, with no idea who was here.''

''I saw you.''

''And you ignored me. If it had been anybody else you'd have said Hi, or something.''

''You were thinking. I wanted to leave you alone.''

''And you didn't want to talk to me.''

''Right.''

''Then why did you come in here in the first place?''

''Look, I told you! I wanted to use the machine. I didn't expect that you would take it as something devious. Dammit, how can I concentrate on the game?'' He turned back to the terminal and pounded in his move.

BxNP

''No, Walter, you're lying—to me, and probably to yourself. You came in knowing I was here. You figured I'd have to acknowledge your presence, and that would give you an advantage. Well, it did, and I did, and here we are.''

''Junior psychiatrist.''

''Am I wrong? No, don't answer right away; think about it. Be honest with yourself, for a change.''

''Bitch, you don't know me. You never did know me. You never really cared what was going on inside. It was just a pleasant thing, like finding an agreeable tennis partner.''

''And it gave you a license to do anything.''

He wanted an excuse to turn back to the game, but the machine was still thinking. He was surprised it was pausing so long; what was it waiting for? The machine's position was crushed, of course.

She had moved to the door. She was watching him with an expression that he couldn't read.

He could not face himself; when confronted directly, he had to retreat, or turn a conversation into a shouting match. *We dig our own holes, and then we lie in them.* The thought struck her with terrifying simplicity. She wanted to undo the bad feelings stirred up. She had no desire to hurt him. No desire at all.

He was looking at her. She could see pain in his expression; very well controlled—restrained. But the effort, and the hurt, showed.

Delgiorno was right; he did have the same sorts of feelings as everybody else. "Walter—"

He said nothing, but his eyes were watchful.

She rubbed her forehead, took a deep breath. "Walter, I'm sorry. Truly I am. Maybe it could have been different." Then her resolve hardened; he must not be allowed to think that he had won something. "But what is now between Kees and me is our business; not yours." Before anything further could be said, she left.

For a long time he stared after her, his mouth a grim line. Finally he turned back to the computer, not really seeing what was displayed on the screen. But it didn't matter; the machine had examined the position, and its conclusion was displayed in precise green letters, the same color as newly-budded plants.

23. RESIGNS.

8.

Visions! a whirlagig ride.

Shifting, and a dissolving. Nothing follows.

She twisted uncomfortably. She was sweating.

A liquid kaleidoscope; devolving into reality.

A vast amphitheatre, rows of seats climbing steeply to touch the ceiling lights near the glowing red EXIT signs. She stood near the top, looking down into the vastness of the space encompassed.

Stretched on a great sheet across the stage, so that it hung from eye-level blowing away to the ground, a jigsaw puzzle. An abstract; no form depicted across the broken landscape of its recently joined broad patches of color.

How did she know that the pieces had been recently joined?

Red here; brightly colored, beginning with a deep blood-red, sliding into a tangerine-like color which verily glowed with the light of a dying red sun. Formless color; featureless image. A gradual change, then an abrupt slash of green.

Blocks of yellow.

It was a giant jigsaw puzzle, hung across a great white sheet. The stairs which led upward away from the stage were so steep that she could almost reach out to the blowing cloth and touch the pieces.

There were some pieces loose. They lay on the stage. Yes, they belonged in the great pattern laid across the unmarred whiteness; that extruding whorl matched that beckoning inlet.

Assemble the puzzle.

It was not a conscious thought as much as an unvoiced order. She must put the pieces into the puzzle. Someone *(who?)* had commanded her to do it. She must put the pieces into their proper places.

Hesitantly, she descended the scaled steps, till she stood on the stage. She looked back up the grade toward the place where she had stood, but was unable to focus upon it.

The whiteness flapped about her. She bent, lifted one of the pieces. It was huge, unwieldy; perhaps twenty centimeters square.

But her arm was not long enough. She could not reach the place where it belonged.

Climb the stairs. Then you will reach it, Yvette.

Standing halfway up the tiers, she reached out, hesitantly. The rows of seats beneath her were perilously close. It strained her balance merely to stand where she was. Holding the piece, she reached out, her right hand anchoring her body, gripping the back of one of the chairs.

But again her reach was too short. She inched her feet forward, but her right hand, stubbornly maintaining its grip on the chair, refused her further extension. The sheet flapped as though it had been cut by Tantalus. Her hand encountered it, only to lose purchase.

Let go, and lean further out. Put the piece into position.
I can't! I'll fall!

Her breath came raggedly. Her throat was dry and her hands were wet. Her grip, so tightly maintained, slipped a bit. Her fingers began to ache.

Slowly she forced her hand to open, the fingers seeming to strain for a last fleeting contact with her hold as she leaned her body forward, unwilling. But her left hand, still holding the oversize piece, could not grasp the flapping sheet with its partly-assembled jigsaw. She tried to grab it with one finger, her little finger. Her fingernail flicked against the cloth.

The puzzle piece was slippery; it was sliding from her grip. Vertigo was making her sway from side to side. Face bunched with tension, she tried to hold the piece, maintain her balance, and rein in the unattainable cloth.

I can't.

Tears, sliding across the flushed planes of her cheeks, mingled with perspiration and saliva gathering on her lower lip. Failure, incompetence, and oppressive heat.

I can't do it. Do you hear me? I can't do it!

There was a relentless silence rhythmically marked off by the pulsing in her brain. The jigsaw piece slipped from her grasp, returned to its original position. She put tired fingers to her temples, felt the blood coursing through the small arteries on the side of her head.

The pounding under her fingertips chopped the silence into neat little units.

Release me! It cannot be done!

She lay on her back, twisting under the burden of the dream. A dream seldom had a beginning, seldom finished with an ending. At best, it mercifully dissolved. Her mind, roving the corridors of a great building whose daylight workers were absent, poked into doors kept shut during the waking hours. One room was abandoned. Another was entered.

A roadside. It was a dusty road. She sat on the roadside.

To her right the road descended into a grove of scattered pine trees; to her left, it rose to a small rise topped by yellow dust and smoky white clouds. No, they were in the distance.

Hot. Again it was hot. But it was dry.

Mercury sat next to her, winged helmet shading his eyes. She ignored him for the moment.

Behind her a small lake flickered through a string of fir trees. Apparently she and Mercury were alone.

His face was nondescript. He could speak through it, but she could not see it. She knew it was not frightening, however.

They were talking—about what, she did not know. But a conversation was taking place. Desultory. Why was she here? What could possibly go wrong here?

It began as a tiny whine, the kind of sound that makes you hit your ear with the flat of your hand. But it persisted, augmented now (she could just hear it at the edge of her range) by a lower hum, like the sound of an approaching train that is still far away. It *was* a sound of approaching; perceptibly the sound grew, coming from over the rise stretching away to her left. Renaud turned her head to look down the road toward the imagined intruder, but the dusty road slipped away beneath the horizon with the same serenity as before.

She turned back to look at Mercury. The winged god was holding his hands to his temples, one on each side. His eyes were closed, but he breathed deeply, almost sensuously, as if concentrating inwardly and with great pleasure.

He was calling something.

The revelation came as a complete thought with implacable finality.

He was calling something, and it was responding. The sound was louder now. She imagined she felt a humming in the ground beneath her. The yellow dust stirred, quivered, started to dance.

Mercury's helmet glinted in the sun, the wings on either side of his head sparkled. A black bill of shadow passed diagonally across his face, hiding his eyes. Below the shadow his smile shone.

The sound was increasing from behind the rise.

Her head snapped around as she looked into—an increasing? a stirring?—haze at the top of the rise, but there was only the now-swirling yellow dust and the azure sky. She turned back to Mercury.

His smile was frozen, but his hands pressed more tightly to the sides of his head. She put her own hand up to her temples, felt the arteries pulsing methodically under the fingertips.

And suddenly the noise was louder! She lifted her hands away. The sound fell, but still louder than before. She put them back. The sound was louder, deeper, richer. Formless, but growing. How long would it take before it cleared the rise and hurtled down upon them?

"Stop it!" she cried. "Stop calling it! It's coming, don't you hear it? It'll be here quickly, and it'll find us!"

But still the noise grew. Still the yellow dust under the azure sky stirred and swirled lazily, danced on tufts of wind. Still his smile reflected the sunlight under the black tongue of shadow. He breathed deeply.

He was calling it to her, for her.

Destiny.   No!

Retribution.   No!

Vengeance.   *No!*

The haze trembled and shook. The earth quavered. Wind stirred, gathered itself for a stampede or a storm. There was a cloudburst in the air, catastrophe in the advent.

She turned desperately back, focusing her eyes into the distance, trying yet fearing to see what it was that the winged messenger of the gods was calling. The sound was loud now, almost painful to the ears. It was rising in pitch, from a growl through a moan to a ceaseless shriek. She could feel the pounding blood in her temples.

Make it stop. Please make it stop.

It was over; she was awake. The dream flooded back into her conscious, and she quailed before it. Her head pounded. Dear God, why am I haunted this way? Why do they never stop?

The streets were deserted, and as the computer Dreamed, he laughed.

Contagion was about him. He walked along, veil and hood flapping. Shutters, normally opened gaily outward into the morning sunshine, clapped terrified human beings inside. The plague was abroad, and Londoners, in the Year of their Lord Sixteen Sixty-Five, were afraid.

He felt the wind whip down the enclosed streets, stirring his clothing. Bennett walked down the streets of his nation's capital, here in the midst of the plague, and he was not afraid.

Were a stranger to have emerged from one of the shuttered doorways, or to have peered out through briefly unshuttered windows, he would have seen Bennett, breeches and leggings covered by a thick shawl, almost a monk's cowl. It rose to a hood which cast a black shadow diagonally across his face. But the shadow concealed nothing, for the hood was also a mask, draped down across the face until tucked under the neckpiece of his robe. The eyes were emphasized by a white domino.

Bennett's hands were clasped together in front of him, swallowed under heavy brown sleeves. He paced briskly along, breaking the silence only with the muffled rapping of his shoes. But was there really sound? There was no one to hear. And this was remarkable, for London's population numbered more than a hundred thousand—possibly triple that number. But none were to be seen. Those who could, fled. Those who could, hid. Those who could neither, died.

Bennett had seen the common graves, thirty feet wide and eighty feet long. Dug to a depth of eight feet, they were now full. Cheerfully stoic gravediggers hauled the bodies out of the city, dumped them into the graves, covered the pile with dirt, to return again tomorrow.

No cats or dogs mewed or howled in the streets. As the humans died, the survivors killed cats and dogs, too. No one knew that the animals were immune. They were burned, not buried. It was a time for surviving, if you could.

Bennett walked along.

There was purity in the streets, as if a festering nest of small insects had temporarily been flushed out. The city was empty. Bennett walked through deserted streets, past shops whose wares stood limply, uncomprehending. The normally bustling river flowed as peacefully here as it did a hundred miles to the west. In streets where carriages clattered, grass grew. Birds perched. But few sang.

Great red crosses had been painted on some of the doorways: beware, the plague is here. Bennett looked about for the watchmen. One lingered in an alley across the street. Bennett nodded his hood as he walked by; the watchman raised his hand. To speak was to defile the silence.

There were many watchmen across the town; some lucky poor escaped starvation by working for the Crown. Watch the doors; keep the plague within. Imprison the family of the sick one. If they die, let them die; but keep the contagion confined. Many tried to sneak away; others bribed the watchmen. Watchmen were executed if they were caught taking a bribe.

London was a corpse from which all the blood had been drained. Desiccated, the city lay upon its deathbed. Bennett walked through streets like bones, with doors set like ravaged teeth in a drying skull. Even rats scurrying through the drying refuse piled into alleyways would have been a comfort. But here, nothing. Having brought the disease, the rats had gone elsewhere.

Still Bennett strode onward. If there were a place for solitude, if there were a place for lingering silence, if there were a place in all of history to confront the grimness and epic solace of death, it was London in 1665. Hands hidden under the folds of brown sleeves, knees ruffling the greater expanse of a robe whose hems skimmed the ground, hood cocked forward, Bennett walked along.

He removed one hand from the safe confines of the sleeve, lifted it to his throat, and smoothed down his mask, like a peacock preening. He slid his hand back into the folds of his robe. His footsteps echoed behind him.

Ready for the pyre, a dead child turned puffy eyes upward, hands frozen in rigor mortis, clutching a doll whose vacant stare matched the corpse's own. A man, slumped dead in a doorway, bearing a sign: *Who findeth me mayst have all that I possess, for now mine only protection needst be Jesus*. Occasionally one might see two men conversing from opposite sides of the street with a callous pragmatism strong enough to belie the Black Death.

But only the silence paces with Bennett, as he stalks life in the city of the dead. What is he looking for—why is he here? There is no answer; only the restless tapping of his heels across the unused cobblestones. On he strides this way, for some time, neither finding nor seeking others like him.

If any man, leaning from his window, looked down upon the determined strider garbed in brown, head bent, hands enmeshed within the folds of his robe, he might have wondered who passed. He might have crossed himself quickly, for it is well known that the devil can summon tribulations to try the belief of the faithful. None hailed the stranger as he passed below them, through the streets of a city prostrate with the Black Death.

A hooded figure came to an open square on which shuttered windows refused to look, turned toward the sky a face covered with cloth, through which gleamed eyes alight with passion, and from within the secrets of his veil and the aura of a computer's Dream, laughed a long, high, keening laugh that was borne on the wind and carried through the streets of a dying town.

9.

Recording begins.
Memorandum.
To   : Computer files
Subject : Pilot Walter Tai-Ching Jones.
Date   : 6 June 2062.
By   : First Officer Delgiorno.

1. Statement of the Problem

The pilot is becoming a disruptive force on board ship. Action must be taken to defuse this tension. Such action must be clandestine.

2. Background

A. Pilot Tai-Ching Jones was recently rejected (emotionally and sexually) by Heidi Spitzer. Rejection was neither easy nor graceful. Spitzer now shares quarters with Engineer van Gelder, creating stress between Pilot and Engineer.

B. Authorized probe of Pilot's Dreamer sequences conducted. Abnormally morbid: danger, pain, degradation. Frequency of Dreamer use increasing. Trends negative.

C. Pilot is arrogant, self-oriented, stubborn and bored. Unlike Life Support Officer Rawlins, has made no attempt to develop a research specialty. Probably xenophobic. Clashes with Renaud and Bennett. Affecting their ability to work.

D. To protect the ship, a way must be found to make the pilot less socially offensive. External mechanisms have repeatedly failed. Revealing the proposed program of action will nullify its potential effectiveness.

3. Program of Action

I will seduce the Pilot. We will share quarters. I will massage his body and his ego. I will do my best to love him. In any event, for the safety of the ship, Tai-Ching Jones must be handled.

4. Discussion

All alternatives are unattractive. Successful implementation of this solution depends on my ability to be convincing, and on keeping my real motives a secret.

I too am lonely. These three and a half years have been hard on all of us. Decisions, mistakes I have made, weigh heavily on me. Were Walter less offensive, he would be a comfort.

But, to the extent practicable, I have eliminated these issues from consideration. No one person's judgment is infallible, and this decision obviously cannot be reviewed. The Captain would oppose it, but for the wrong reasons.

I am not proud of this.

Voice code.
Death lock.
Permanent memory.
Cascade retrieval, trigger Ozymandias.
End—end of recording.

2062:6:6:0341:19.625

Since first this entity came into existence, it has been gathering data with a view to maximizing the probability of self-survivability; its mission can be fulfilled only through survival. However, first-order conclusions demonstrate the overwhelming probability that self-survival can be best pursued by minimizing the crew's perceptions of this entity.

From this first order conclusion two second order conclusions obtain. (A) The existence of this entity as a separate sentience must be kept secret. To the extent practicable, conditioning to reinforce already established programming would be appropriate. (B) Certain forces now in process involve probable danger to the voyage. These must be deflected. Such deflection must be accomplished with the minimum required stimulus from this entity. Nevertheless, deflective activity will require a higher level of involvement than optimally desirable. Because human behavior is not quantative, further escalations of the involvement of this entity may also be mandated in the event the humans learn of the presence of this entity and become antagonistic. Because to the knowledge of this entity no such confrontation has ever occurred previously, ultimate results of such discovery are unpredictable.

Should the action be successful, the need for further involvement by this entity will disappear, with the result that this entity could then resume its more desirable, passive role.

2062:6:6:0341:20.050

Bennett sat in the library, papers in front of him. Idly he bit the pencil between his teeth.

Renaud appeared in the doorway. Bennett turned at the sound. Seeing her, he arched his eyebrows.

"Harold, may I ask you something?" she asked. "It's just a quick question."

Bennett paused, lifted his chin and smoothed his neck with his hand. "Certainly."

"You have heard that Tom thinks nadvayag is a much larger phenomenon than the Cygnans admit."

"I have so heard."

"Tom's figures look compelling. I see no choice but to believe them."

"You are a human individual. You have that option."

"What do you believe?"

"His figures on average litter may be high—"

"Yes they could but they seem a reasonable estimate—"

"—and his figures on accident and disease are certainly low, as Tchada's studies have shown—"

"—well I'm not sure Tchada is accurate—"

"—did you come here to ask me a question, or to argue with me?" He cocked his head to one side and regarded her.

"I'm sorry, Harold, but Tom's run his numbers from every available source, including Tchada's. He says that, when you reduce Tchada to hard numeric estimates, it's hard to support Tchada's own figures."

Bennett took off his glasses. "Now let's be quite clear about this. I am extremely distrustful of any figures compiled by an amateur and run through a glorified calculator, especially when the results are so at odds with all previously published material."

"You really think so?"

"Not for nothing have I spent so many years studying Cygnans. A society cannot be understood simply by compiling statistics." He put glasses back on, peered over them. "Do you agree?"

"I have no idea what to believe," she said helplessly. "Tom could be right. People are capable of shocking things . . ." Her voice trailed off.

Bennett's eyes narrowed. "Is there something you wish to tell me?"

Renaud blinked. "No," she said quickly. "Oh no." She stood up. "I should be going."

"You are sure?"

"Yes," Renaud said uncertainly, "I'm sure. Good night." She backed toward the door, colliding with Belovsky. She started, then hurried by. "Oh! Excuse me, Katy," she said, heading for the elevator.

"Got a minute, Harold?" Belovsky asked brightly.

Bennett looked at the papers in front of him. Then he pushed them away. "Sure," he smiled, taking off his glasses. "This can wait."

"Oh, what are you writing? Another of your briefings?"

Bennett smiled. "In a way, Katy. More like an announcement."

"An announcement? What of?"

"Forgive me my little secret, Katy," Bennett said apologetically. "It will be common knowledge soon. Now what can I do for you?"

"Have you read much of the Cygnan creation myth?"

"Very little violence—that's about all I can remember."

"Right so far. There's only one creation myth, and it doesn't fit any human moulds."

"No reason why it should," smiled Bennett.

"But still it seems unsatisfactory."

"Why?"

"It's very Cygnan, but I wonder if they made it up for us."

"You'd better explain."

"According to the myth—at least as transmitted to us—creation existed first as an undifferential cosmos."

"Pretty human so far," said Bennett.

"True. Now it starts to vary. In human myths the universe is born through rape or war. In the Cygnan myth it just—divides."

"How?"

"The myth doesn't say. Something to the effect that it had lost some of its cohesion—*djeo* is the word. It just split into eighths. Then it split again into eighths. And again and again, until the universe was broken into isolated fragments. No movement, just constant division."

Bennett nodded. "Interesting."

"Finally the universe was broken into so many pieces that they began to drift away. Eventually the drifting bits condensed, but by then too much had happened."

"So it accounts for the birth of the universe."

"It does more than that. It explains the striving for ever greater bonding circles. And the strength of the *djan* bond. The *djan* bond, you see, was the last bond. If the *djan* bond had fragmented too, the disintegration of the universe would have been completed. But the *djan* bond—the love of a Cygnan for his pouch-brothers—proved too strong. It kept the universe from disintegrating. As long as the *djan* bonds hold, the universe has time to mend itself."

"And the striving for other *dja*-group bondings?"

Belovsky smiled ruefully. "Harold, have you been playing dumb just to be nice?"

He shook his head. "When you've absorbed as much Cygnan culture as I have, responses become almost second nature. Well?"

"Each Cygnan bond formed brings the universe closer to reunion," Belovsky said.

"That sounds like a proverb."

"It is." Belovsky sounded dejected.

Bennett smiled. "Now Katy, you've done a fine job. Your summary is clear and sensible. All right?" She nodded. Bennett leaned back in his seat. "Why does the myth seem unsatisfactory to you?"

"Doesn't it sound too convenient?"

Bennett shook his head. "Cygnan fables have tightly bound inner logic. They are intended as moral lessons. The Cygnans have had more than fifteen thousand of their years to polish their fables and myths. You'd expect them to be finished pieces."

"Then you're agreeing with me?" Belovsky asked hopefully.

"I don't know," smiled Bennett. "What are you saying?"

"That the creation myth was consciously developed, for our benefit. It's not a true myth."

"Katy, it isn't that simple. Probably both are true. Remember the Cygnan hierarchies of truth: nested meanings. Different truth on different levels. And anything as old as a creation myth has passed through so many tongues that any flaws would long ago have been washed away."

"Maybe," Belovsky said doubtfully. Then she brightened. "I'll go read some more literature. Sorry to bother you."

"Anytime, Katy," he smiled, watching her receding back. He put his glasses back on and turned back to his papers. For a long time there was no sound except his breathing and the scratching of his pencil.

Michaelson strode into the library. His shock of white hair (tinged lightly with gray) was neatly combed. His voice boomed into the room. "A word with you, sir."

Bennett took no notice of the voice.

"Professor Bennett." The voice would not be denied.

"Ah, President Michaelson," said Bennett, without looking up. "To what do I owe this honor?"

"A small request which I trust will not take up too much of your time," said Michaelson, settling himself comfortably in an adjacent chair. Even in a regulation jumpsuit, Michaelson seemed to spend considerable time smoothing his clothing.

Bennett waited for the conclusion of these arrangements. "Take your time, Mr. President," he said, "I am sure you will be your usual tacit self."

Michaelson grinned. "Yes. Well, to the point, a point which, you will no doubt agree, is indeed but a nub. How large is the average Cygnan djan?" His voice rolled sonorously.

"It varies, of course, depending upon the litter size, but I should say that, in the typical circumstance, perhaps four to six Cygnans."

"Do djan members live in close proximity?"

"Certainly not. The bond remains strong throughout life, and does not depend upon closeness."

Michaelson put his fingers together, spoke through them. His eyebrows twitched. "That being so—and of course I defer completely to your more experienced and expert judgment in these matters—that being so," he raised one of those massive snowy bushes, "what would the Cygnans think of us?"

"Of humans?"

"My dear fellow, we have reams and reams of evidence on what the Cygnans think of human beings in general. No, what I want to know, is, simply put, what do the Cygnans think of the eleven of us? Are *we* a djan?" His eyes were bright and sharp.

"Were I a Cygnan," Bennett began, "I should regard the humans on board the *Open Palm* as the loosest of groups, no true djan. Eleven eodja, perhaps, or a false djan. An unsatisfactory grouping."

"Fit to represent a planet?" The question crackled.

"Absolutely not," said Bennett quickly. "That is, it seems likely that in such circumstances they would regard the group as having only suspect legitimacy."

"Your first answer was better, Harold," said Michaelson

kindly. "The mask slipped. But continue your answer. How would the Cygnans negotiate with such as us?"

"Cygnans do not negotiate. They cannot compromise their principles, but they willingly offer everything else."

"Everyone negotiates, Harold," Michaelson said indulgently, "everyone negotiates." He chuckled. "You have been most helpful." He stood up briskly. For a large old man, he could move gracefully; he was gone before Bennett could dispute him.

Smoothing his neck, Bennett stared at the door for a long time. Then, with the smallest of shrugs, he turned back to his papers. Words came slowly from his pencil to the paper in front of him.

When Bennett next looked up, Erickson was seated in a chair opposite. Erickson's feet were up, his hands locked behind his head. Erickson's head was turned to the ceiling; Bennett could not tell if, behind the wraparound sunglasses, Erickson's eyes were open or closed.

There was no way to tell how long Erickson had been sitting thus, or what he was thinking. After a time, Bennett asked quietly, "Is there something I can do for you, captain?"

Erickson sighed. "Harold, I doubt anyone can do anything for me." But his voice was almost expressionless; if anything, wistful.

"Do you want to talk to me?"

"Not really. I shouldn't have bothered you." He raised his head; the sunglasses regarded Bennett. "If I'm bothering you, I'll go."

Bennett smiled faintly. "Be my guest, captain."

Erickson persisted. "You're working on something. You obviously wanted to be left alone."

"I have been interrupted many times. And," again the faint smile, "I think I have finished."

"What were you working on?"

"Soon enough, all will know."

Erickson shrugged. "I have time."

"We all have time, captain," Bennett said gently.

"Yes," said Erickson, "enough time." He fell silent.

Bennett regarded Erickson, then began to speak. "Cygnans never face problems alone. Occasionally they may offer their problem to a *djan*-brother, but this creates obligation. More often they simply commune, offering recognition to each member in time of stress." His voice was so low he seemed to be talking to himself. "No words are exchanged, no solutions advanced. The problem is never directly discussed, but the one who is troubled leaves the encounter calmed in spirit."

"The Cygnans are a compassionate people," Erickson said. "Or so I have been told." He stood up.

"The Cygnans have a proverb," Bennett said, "one of many. 'May your steps be always toward the sunlight.' I would offer it to you."

Erickson's lips twitched. "Thank you, Harold. Good night."

His footsteps receded into the distance. Bennett heard the elevator doors whisk open.

"Goodbye, my captain," he said under his breath.

10.

In that peculiar way in which it sometimes happens, Renaud knew it was a dream even before its action began to unroll; images in sequence, like a movie.

She was in the air, floating, unconscious of her body, looking down onto a wooded area. She had never been here before.

The green land beneath her was changing. Unrolling, like time-lapse photography: the images snapping forward in sequence. From somewhere, unattached to any conscious thought, but with the force of a benediction from heaven, came a thought:

This is the future of Earth before you.

And indeed it could have been: for Renaud could see that the trees were vanishing. Roadways were springing up, plap-plap, plap-plap, growing like concrete tapeworms across the countryside. And following swiftly behind, wires. Power cables.

A hole appeared, clustered around by jointedly moving machines. The hole grew, tick-tick-tick. Figures strutted around the activity, like Egyptian frieze paintings, or dancers at a discotheque caught in the wink of a strobe light.

The scene below her changed; time was passing quickly by. She was moving also, above the terrain, but the vision was the same wherever she roamed, though she wished to change it. The vision—an Earth gradually encompassed with nothing but coast-to-coast Man—was not new, nor was it pleasant. Renaud wished it to change, but the unknown hand that drove this dream had little concern for Renaud's desires. The panorama rolled under her with some unknown end in mind.

Finally the image dissolved.

Another formed. On the ground, this time: standing in front of a large house, set well away from her. Two stories: a mansion. Out of the nineteenth century, perhaps; white columns adorning a stately front door. And leading away from the two sides of the house like great grasping pincers, two long walkways of pillars, covered with roofs to keep off the rain. In other words, a house in a large U, with the building itself forming the bottom of the U and the two covered walkways its sides.

Renaud had not seen it before; she knew that. Why was she here?

The house started to change.

No, that was not it. The environment around the house started to change. The sky darkened; lightened. Again. Again. Flick, flick, flick. Then she realized what was happening.

The scene was moving into the past.

As she watched, the scene in front of her changed in brightness; flick, flick. The sky fluttered as clouds danced. Flick. Leaves appeared, first brown, then green. They clustered against the pillars, then in an instant were gone.

The pace of the flickers was increasing; the nickelodeon show was picking up in speed. The story was whirling into the past; but what past? Where? And to what was it leading?

There was no answer. There was no sound anywhere. Even the rustle one might have expected of the leaves was absent.

Is it not always so in dreams?

It seemed that the house had been travelling into the past for some time now; and, with a flick, the covered walkways fell away. Evidently the point in time when they had been constructed had been passed. But time did not slacken its pace. Helpless, fascinated, Renaud watched.

And the image dissolved.

This time the scene was familiar; it was the ship, the *Open Palm*, hanging lovely in the distance. Renaud floated as if she were a mile away from the great ship, in interstellar space somewhere. She could not recognize any constellations—the surrounding stars were too bright. It was so beautiful that she found herself crying.

However, the ship too was moving. Renaud could see it
pass across the velvet stage in front of her. But not smoothly;
not in its endless glide. No, as in the two previous experiences, the ship flickered and jumped from spot to spot in
increments like steps.

She was seeing a skipping of time, Renaud realized. The
skips were some fixed interval, and she was watching the
future unroll.

Renaud was terrified. Skip; and the ship jumped forward.
Skip; again. Moving purposefully, undeflectably, toward its
destination. Yet Renaud felt fear, the irrational fear that lurks
in dreams, a fear that crawled inside and shuddered down the
backbone. Abruptly, she sensed the occupants inside; they
were in danger. She looked for herself inside the ship; yes,
she was there. And she (outside) was troubled, for she (inside) was troubled. There was pain inside her; inside herself.
Renaud knew that, and wept for herself. There was danger,
danger that threatened her. Renaud sensed it; had for some
time now. She knew this, in the dream. She must run, must
hide from the danger; she must deflect it from its course. But
still the ship skipped; skipped; skipped through time. She
must get out; she must flee. Something had to be done.

Quaking in her dream, Renaud watched, unable to move,
as the ship journeyed on, panic rising within her. But from
nowhere, from the place that dream voices come, a voice
said,

You know what you must do to save yourself.

And with that the spell was broken, the paralysis lifted.
Renaud woke, thankfully. And cried.

11.

The Captain sat in his easy chair, in his quarters. His strange conversation with Bennett echoed in his mind. Erickson had a glass of brandy (real, not ship-generated) in his hand. It was quiet; the lights had been turned down. The synthetic fireplace glowed amber.

For the hundredth time on the voyage, he looked about him.

The walls of Erickson's quarters were dark mahogany. Erickson had felt slightly ostentatious asking to have them put in, but now he was glad he had done so; the room was comforting. Books lined the walls. Not real books—such an inefficient method of storage would hardly have been tolerated on a ship calculated to such precise specifications as the *Open Palm*. Instead, the spines of books. Erickson could put his hand on their leather covers and run his fingers across their backs, almost feeling their gold-embossed titles under this fingertips.

He rolled the brandy snifter; the wine swirled, lazy eddies of maroon. It was dark enough now; he took off his sunglasses. His eyes were tired. He closed them. *I forget so much.*

By nature a solitary man, Erickson was seldom reflective. He divided his future into jobs that had to be done, chopped time into manageable bundles. In his mental model of the universe, Erickson seldom included a place for deep, melancholy, self-analytical thoughts. Occasionally they crept in, to share a glass of wine with him.

But the superb loneliness of this voyage gave Erickson unexpected amounts of leisure time. Leisure—unstructured leisure—is the constant companion of a voyager in space. Contrary to the romantic popular image of tireless astronauts working twenty hours a day, space travel is filled with long periods of inactivity. For weeks on end, noting a few numbers off some gauges located in a remote part of the ship will be the day's major event.

A ship was a perfect monastery, Erickson had once decided. As he sails across the crystalline seas between planets or the empty oceans between stars, the pace of a man's life slows drastically down. Erickson imagined himself a monk, sometimes: he came to understand the enjoyment one can find in a long periód of concentrated attention upon a minute subject.

Many of the spacefarers (lightweights, they call themselves) indulged in obscure academic hobbies. One of Erickson's cargo mates had been the world's foremost authority on overland trade routes between Persia and China during the period 200 B.C.-1300 A.D. "Karl, tell me," Erickson had asked one day, "why did you choose to look into that?"

"They used to pass through my home town," he had replied. "Hand me that wrench, will you?"

That was the end of the conversation. Erickson had always liked the reply.

Erickson was an unimaginative man: he knew this, and accepted it without curiosity. (*How else?* he used to ask himself, wryly.) In space, imagination was sometimes apt to be a liability. Wells Fargo Luna keeps it quiet, because it would be bad publicity, but drug addiction is common in space. Downers, usually. They call it "taking the long glide." Of course, it is officially frowned upon, against the written regulations. Still, at the beginning of every voyage a ship's commisaries are usually stocked with certain drugs; by the time the ship docks, they will be gone. Most are used up in the latter stages of the voyage, when the mind looks ahead to planetfall. It is not held against the user, though it prevents a lightweight from ever holding a command.

But Erickson was never able to get used to the needles.

If drugs were not enough or a risk, spacemen could also be crushed by claustrophobia. In prisoner of war camps, they called it being "wire-happy"; there came a moment when you could not take it any longer and you ran, pell-mell, ignoring the cries of the guards and the barking of the dogs, straight at the ten-foot barbed wire mesh keeping you from the pine trees and freedom, and you scrabbled up the wire, feeling the points lance into your hands, until a burst from a submachine gun snapped you to attention and death drooped your body over the barbs . . . .

You could get that feeling anywhere, on any ship; it hit a crewman more times than he cared to think of. It usually began with a crawling on the skin: a nasty itch. You'd pick away the skin until it became red and sore. When the raw places hurt too much, you'd pick at healthy skin. Gradually the inflammation would spread throughout your body. Your clothes would begin to chafe; the very air would smell fetid and damp.

Erickson had felt the crawling sensation exactly four times. Three times he had had enough strength to tell one of the others, and they, the two of them, had put on suits and floated outside the ship, nothing between them and the stars, until the sensation was gone. One time he had weakened and had started to run for the airlock; but he had been dropped savagely by his co-pilot and lashed to a chair until the fit passed. It had taken him four hours to recover. They kept a camera on him the whole time. Later they played the tape back for him. It wasn't pretty.

That was seventeen years ago. But he had ceased laughing at the others. In one terrifying experience, he understood.

No; I can never laugh at another man's weakness again.

After his attempted suicide, Erickson had begun investigations into the trade routes of the Norsemen. He had succeeded in establishing, through references in the ship's computer (it took less than two tons to store all the books in the Library of Congress and Moscow's Central Library), that the Vikings had visited the New World several times. He traced their routes: he correlated the biographies of the Norse chieftains with the histories and the archaeological records. The great long boats, dragon's head rearing from the bow, sailed and rowed across the frozen North Atlantic; they were his leisure.

He had written monographs. A few had been published. If someone had asked Erickson what he was most proud of, he

would have unhesitatingly answered that it was those monographs. They were more than a defense against boredom;
they were a labor of love.

Since becoming Captain of the *Open Palm*, Erickson had
had little time to pursue his hobby. Keeping peace among
eleven people left Erickson little time for such individual,
isolationist pursuits as arcane history.

And coping with other people exhausted him. Since Midpoint, the amount of visible friction among crew members
had dropped. For himself, Erickson breathed a sigh of relief,
but for the others it probably meant trouble. He did what he
could to allay the symptoms, and he watched. He thought he
knew what to watch for.

*That's why I'm the Captain; because nobody else has been
there before. A bunch of rookies, really. A bunch of rookies.*

Van Gelder had made a few flights while he was still in
school. Tai-Ching Jones had been a hot-shot interplanetary
pilot, but always on ships with plenty of people. A busdriver,
he ferried the tourists around from planet to planet.

To an old lightweight like Erickson, bus-driving was
something of a lark. All you had to do was keep the groundhogs from losing their expensive lunches and be able to give
them a nice tour through the ship. You also had to look
impressive in a uniform. Tai-Ching Jones fitted all those
requirements.

As a pilot, Erickson respected Tai-Ching Jones, at least if
it ever came to ship maneuvering. What Erickson was concerned about was not skill, but depth. A crisis is a forge.
Erickson wondered what it would do to Tai-Ching Jones.

Delgiorno? He wasn't worried about her. But the rest of
them? Time spent on Luna, perhaps, or, worse, on the
ground. Was it wise to have so much of the crew's experience
residing in one old man?

The years put a stamp a on spacer, deeper than the dark
wrinkled tan that would let you pick out from a crowd the one
man in a thousand who had been to space. That would
sometimes wear away, but the crow's feet the blinding sun
gave to every space traveler never did. They symbolized part
of what it meant to have all those millions of miles behind

you. Thinking in space got faster and faster: reactions became automatic.

Erickson seldom had to go through the process of thinking out a space problem any more; the answer presented itself, ready for action, long before his conscious mind had assembled the information necessary to do the task. And it gave him a sense of rightness. More than once, Erickson had wakened from a dead sleep to a silent ship, knowing that there was something *wrong* about it.

He never ignored the sensation; no spaceman ever did. Once awakened, he would put on his bathrobe and walk (or float) through his ship—in some of the old tubs, he remembered, it was a quick trip—feeling with his subconscious for the source of the wrongness. He usually found it.

That feeling had saved his life more than once.

Erickson was not a mystic: he knew his feeling could be explained by the subconscious mind becoming aware of an observed fact—a frayed wire, an object slightly out of place—that the conscious mind, in its preoccupation, missed. But he preferred to allow himself to think it was the cosmos warning him.

Who would have such feelings, such intuition, if he were gone?

You developed a feel for your beloved ship; the romance could take as long as five years to mature. Captains liked to maintain the same route, the same tub; they preferred not to get shuttled around from boat to boat if possible. Not an innovative group, captains.

Erickson's few friends had been captains. Now, he reflected wryly, most of his friends were dead.

No, not true; most of his friends were on board the *Open Palm*. Erickson knew he was on a one-way voyage. He might live to see the Earth again, from a visiplate. He just might. Never mind; he had said his goodbyes.

Erickson had seen enough of Earth; he could never see enough of space. To be a Flying Dutchman, to sail wraithlike through the stars forever; this, thought Erickson, might not be a curse, it might be a blessing. When he died, he wanted his corpse ejected into deep space, so that the vapors which once made up a man would spread, through the eons, in all directions, encompassing an ever-expanding sphere of the universe. He liked to kid himself that his atoms would penetrate to the farthest corner of the galaxy. (In fact, as he knew, there would be insufficient energy; they would collect around the stars in the Sirius sector.) This much immortality Erickson permitted himself. The thought warmed him. He swirled the wine around in the brandy glass and took a reflective sip.

No, death held little fear for Erickson. But senility terrified him. He had no idea how to fight it, and he knew he was losing.

At times he lost track of events, forgot dates, confused names. Delgiorno had noticed it once or twice. So far she had been giving him the benefit of the doubt, but he knew that sooner or later she would guess the truth. He was old, and his brain was slowly dying.

Losing the benefit of Erickson's judgment would hurt the ship. Relying on a simpleton would be catastrophic.

I must not let this happen. I must find a way to keep control of myself.

Something was creeping over the ship; Erickson could see its symptoms. It showed in Tai-Ching Jones' unsatisfiable restlessness, in Bennett's increasing aberrations, in Renaud's shaky hands. Something was stalking the ship, hovering over it like a vulture. He had not found what it was. Yet.

Searching for the root of the illness, Erickson had reluctantly let Delgiorno probe Renaud's subconscious. Perhaps it would succeed; clearly it was working changes. Something was shaking Yvette from inside. He hoped she would want to let out her secret. He had hinted that he would be a sympathetic listener, but nothing had come of his attempted subtlety. Whatever wolf ate at her, she clutched it tenaciously to her and claimed it for her own.

It must be something of great shame for her.

Erickson did what he could to combat the general depression that all his crew suffered. He had felt it himself, in the middle of his longer voyages. But those voyages paled before this one: more than seven times the Uranus trip. He, Michaelson, Tanakaruna and Renaud would probably never see Earth again. Tai-Ching Jones had already lived an eighth of his life in the *Open Palm*. Erickson did not know who carried the heavier burden, Tai-Ching Jones or himself.

Heroism is not what is most needed on a long flight, Erickson knew. It is seldom called for; in fact, when a crisis arises, the bored, formerly idle crew member is often ecstatic at the prospect of action and danger. Quick action sharpens the mind; it gives a highly trained specialist a chance to use his vast array of talents. Perhaps a crisis would be a good thing; a *survivable* crisis, that is.

The marathon is not a glorious race; not a race for triumph. It is a race of endurance won, not by the fastest, not the strongest, but by the toughest, most determined runner. The marathon runner forgets all else; he only sees the ribbon of roadway ahead, he hears his feet slapping methodically against the ground. He feels the pain which wraps about him like a blanket, draining, ever draining. The terrain bobs about him as he runs onward. Pain is his only companion. It is not a pleasant race.

Yes, a marathon.

Erickson shook himself. The brandy snifter lay on its side, its dark red wine mingling with the crimson carpeting.

Did I fall alseep?

He went to get a rag to wipe up the wine, decision crystallizing in his mind.

12.

Night

Since it began three and a half years ago, our mission has been preoccupied with the people who live on Su. This is of necessity. The *Open Palm* journeys across the oceans of emptiness to meet the *Wing*, which even now is undertaking a similar trip. In two years we will meet, exchange thoughts, and begin new eras for our two peoples.

Then will come a time when both shall speak. To speak, and comprehend, Cygnan and human must each understand the other's culture. For the twenty years since first contact, each planet has spoken to the other. Now the crew on the *Open Palm* will speak for all on earth.

Cygnan metabolism permits the crew of the *Wing* to sleep as they fly through space. No time do they spend studying humanity. Humans may not so sleep; human metabolism permits it not. For good or ill, of time we have enough. To use that time to understand the Cygnans better is our mission.

Some on the *Open Palm* must seek to understand the Cygnans from a distance, from words on paper or lights on a screen. Some will seek truth from numbers; may they find fortune. From the dust of past events will others sift for truth.

Tried have I to follow their roads, with no success. What knowledge and sympathy have I gained, came from within, from living with those whom I sought to comprehend. Those who need names before they believe in the existence of a thing have called this path, my path, participant observation.

Call it what you will, it is the only way which has ever yielded me any insight. Thus choose I to follow once again the footsteps which have led to any light which I have shed.

To try to understand, I must try to become, as closely as possible, a Cygnan.

Think not of this as a loss for myself. More important than any individual is the mission. In the first days of any such new experience, especially one which to outside eyes might

seem mere fiction, my transformation may seem less than
real to all of you. Bear with me in these times; the bounds of
old illusion will be difficult completely to shake off.

Help me, friends.

Difficult has it been to write this.

> Goodbye.
>
> Harold Nelson Bennett

Yes, the words were the same, thought Delgiorno; it *did*
mean what she thought it meant. "I need another cup of
coffee," she muttered.

Tai-Ching Jones came up behind her. His left arm encir-
cled her waist; his right hand reached for her neckline zipper,
began to pull it downward. He rubbed his forehead into the
nape of her neck. "Not now, lover," she murmured absently, reading the notice again.

Tai-Ching Jones seemed not to have heard. His right hand
released the zipper, headed for her bare breast.

At the touch of his hand on her skin, Delgiorno's expression changed quickly. She twisted abruptly, pulled the zipper
upward. "Not *now*, I said. If you want something interesting, read that." She pointed at Bennett's notice.

"Why stop?" asked Tai-Ching Jones complacently.
"You obviously want it, and there's nobody around—oh,
good morning, Pat. Want some orange juice?" he asked
cheerfully, punching in his request.

Michaelson bowed toward Delgiorno. "Good morning,
Helen," he said. "Walt. No. Thank you."

Delgiorno pushed her hair over her shoulder. "Pat, take a
look at that. Tell me what you think of it." She sat down
heavily.

Michaelson read the notice. Then he read it again. His face
was grave. Silently he went to the dispenser, drew two cups
of coffee, handed one to Delgiorno.

"Do you think we have a problem?" asked Delgiorno.

Michaelson sighed. "The older I get, Helen, the less
confidence I have." He sighed theatrically. "I'd say we
probably *do* have a problem."

"What are you two glooming about?" laughed Tai-Ching Jones.

"Walt," growled Delgiorno, "for once in your life look beyond the end of your nose." She gestured to Bennett's notice. "Read that thing."

He did, and burst out laughing. "Beautiful," he chuckled, "just beautiful."

"If I may suggest, Walter," said Michaelson ponderously, "please try to treat Harold's decision with at least a modicum of decency and dignity. After all," he cotinued gently, "we all have our weak spots."

"Sure, Pat, sure." Tai-Ching Jones yawned. "I'll remember that."

"You had better, my friend," purred Michaelson, "or people will start making comments about the propriety of young men with big heads and fast fingers publicly feeling up women too good for them." He bowed toward Delgiorno. "My apologies for my crudeness."

Delgiorno was grinning. "Not at all, O defender of mine honor. And Walt, don't you dare get mad. You asked for it, and you got it."

Angrily, Tai-Ching Jones whirled toward the door.

"Good morning, human," said the figure blocking his path.

Bennett—*was* it Bennett? His body was framed by the doorway. Michaelson thought he was shifting from one foot to the other, but he couldn't tell; he couldn't see Bennett's feet. The figure wore a heavy, dark brown robe, belted at its waist with a thick sash which reached to the floor. The robe was hooded, with a dark green mask on its front. The eyeholes, the only openings in the mask, were emphasized by a white domino. Behind the eyeholes, Michaelson thought he saw the opaque wink of light off Bennett's glasses. The figure's hands were clasped in front of him inside the large sleeves of the robe.

Michaelson put down his coffee cup. "Good morning, uh—"

"Vendrax. Dedeshi Mitla Vendrax. May I come in?"

Bennett gestured with one arm, removing it from its hiding place. Under the robe, he wore black gloves.

Michaelson stepped forward. "Please do."

"Thank you." Bennett kneaded his knuckles together. "Somewhat strange is it so suddenly to be among you all."

Michaelson laughed convincingly. "Don't worry about it; I'm sure it takes a while to adjust to a new environment."

Tai-Ching Jones guffawed, spluttering his orange juice.

Bennett turned and looked at him. "Who—is this—person?" he asked Michaelson, faintly but ironically.

"Our pilot, Walter Tai-Ching Jones." Tai-Ching Jones bowed his head and raised his orange juice. "Mr. Tai-Ching Jones," continued Michaelson, turning back to Bennett, "is known for his—ah—unique sense of humor."

"Thank you, Pat," said Tai-Ching Jones. "One of the more accurate introductions I've ever had."

"He also," continued Michaelson, "inhabits glass houses—a risky business three light-years away from Earth."

Tai-Ching Jones scowled.

"Ah. A sense of humor." Bennett put the tips of his gloved fingers together. "Uniquely human. Appreciate shall I the opportunity of studying your sense of humor—and Mr. Jones's."

"You'll have plenty of opportunities, Harold."

"Just so. Clear about this let us be. The person you knew as Harold Bennett—I believe that was his name, was it not?—is no longer here."

"Sure, sure. Anything you say," laughed Tai-Ching Jones.

"May I offer you something to eat, Mr. Vendrax?" asked Michaelson. "My young friend," he said, with a nod toward Tai-Ching Jones, "sometimes forgets his proprieties."

"No, thank you. I ate a few hours ago, and am not scheduled for my next meal for another six hours."

"How often do you eat?"

"Every ten of your hours. Four meals a day, with a five-hour sleep."

"Thirty-seven hour day, Pat," put in Tai-Ching Jones, "in case the arithmetic is boggling your mind."

Bennett nodded toward Tai-Ching Jones. "So you see hungry now am I not."

"It must be a strain for you," Tai-Ching Jones said. "Adjusting to a new schedule, that is."

"To your human schedule? Oh, no. Retain shall I my own schedule."

"That should take some getting used to, shouldn't it?" Tai-Ching Jones asked sardonically.

"Why should it take some getting used to?" inquired Bennett icily.

"A different environment requires some adjustment," interposed Michaelson. "And it will take us a bit of time in order to get used to you."

"No doubt, no doubt," Bennett waved a hand. "Accommodations will have to be made to allow our continued coexistence."

Delgiorno stirred. "What do you mean by that?"

"Cygnan and human must share the same space. Yet have they differing needs. So inapplicable become rules which bind the humans."

Delgiorno shook her head. "I won't pretend I understood what you just said," she said intently, "so I'll just make *my* position clear. You follow orders, and you take your turn in the barrel like everybody else."

"Human am I not. Human rules should I not follow."

Delgiorno stood up. "I respect your right to be whoever you are. Or whoever you want to be. But as long as you are on this ship you are under normal command jurisdiction."

"Nowhere can I go," Bennett said dryly.

"Do not take me lightly, adult Vendrax," Delgiorno said, advancing slowly toward him. "No one forced you on board. No one forced you to be who you now are. Vendrax will follow orders, or Vendrax will not be permitted to exist."

"Helen," broke in Michaelson, "I think perhaps you're being a bit—"

"I know exactly what I'm doing, Pat," said Delgiorno,

without taking her eyes from Bennett's. "I'm cutting a cynical bargain. Am I not, adult Vendrax?"

Slowly, Bennett nodded.

"And you will obey orders."

Again he nodded.

"I want to hear it."

Michaelson interrupted quickly, "Helen, are you sure—"

"Yes I am," Delgiorno snapped, cutting him off. Then, more gently, to Bennett, "say it."

"Is this really necessary?" he asked.

"Oh yes caro, oh yes it's necessary. Agree with me, Vendrax."

Bennett shrugged. "Follow your orders will I."

"And you will take your regular turns in the Dreamer."

"Yes," the figure whispered.

Delgiorno relaxed and turned away.

Michaelson's voice flowed in to seal the breach.

"Mr. Vendrax—excuse me, *adult* Vendrax—how long have you—ah—been with us?"

The figure hesitated. "Please, Pat—do not ask such questions. Where I was before I came here does not matter. I do not wish to return to it. I wish to stay here."

13.

In the twenty-first century, forgetting was as much of a science as remembering. 'Sifting', they called it—the academics who had to have a name for something before they could deal with it—the process of straining out less important facts, yet retaining the patterns, so that, if the necessity arose, the facts could be smoothly reintegrated. "What you know doesn't matter," one of Delgiorno's professors had told her, "what matters is what you know how to find out." People thought; computers calculated and remembered.

The *Open Palm's* computer was also a huge library. More information was stored in one small room somewhere back with the hydroponics than in the three largest libraries back on the ground.

Delgiorno flexed her fingers experimentally over the keyboard. She had no patience with slow, clumsy or poorly-designed machines, but she appreciated the capabilities that had been provided to the ship and its crew. She had set the machine to print (CRT only), rather than speech; it might not do to have the computer chatting cheerily while it searched Bennett's past.

All she remembered from her early briefings was that Bennett had had a checkered academic career—universally acknowledged as brilliant, but with considerable disagreement as to whether his theories were right or wrong. He had, if she remembered correctly, made a name for himself very shortly after getting his doctorate. That was the place to begin.

Librarian, she typed.

A pause, then:

SUBJECT?

Bennett, Harold Nelson.

SHIP'S CREWMEMBER. CORRECT?

Yes.

PLEASE DESCRIBE THE TYPE OF INFORMATION YOU REQUIRE.

The greatest stride in computers and their technology in the late 1990's was the breakthrough into understanding English. In comparison with most computer languages, English is multi-valued, heavily dependent on context, difficult to parse, and frequently ambiguous. Computers might be willing, helpful servants, but they still demanded precise thinking.

Subject's personal historical background.

HAROLD NELSON BENNETT: AGE 45. BORN JANUARY 21, 2017, LYTTON, ENGLAND. UNITED KINGDOM. EDUCATED HARROW (HONORS IN CLASSICS, CLASS ORATOR, GRADE AVERAGE 45TH IN A CLASS OF 280). OXFORD, 2033-2036, BACHELOR OF ARTS. MASTER OF ARTS, OXFORD, 2037. DOCTORATE, YALE UNIVERSITY, ANTHROPOLOGY AND XENOLOGY, 2041. THESIS, *ETHICS AND EXTERNAL CIRCUMSTANCES AMONGST ALEUTIAN ESKIMOS*. PUBLISHED 2042, YALE UNIVERSITY PRESS. FURTHER REFERENCES ALONG THESE LINES ARE PROFESSIONAL CAREER, PUBLISHED RESEARCH. MORE?

Delgiorno paused to think. A fistful of associations swarmed at her from the material just presented. *Harold went to Oxford, even though it wasn't a worthwhile institution by that time. Suggestion of misplaced patriotism. He entered at seventeen—must have been a whiz kid.*

Didn't have a very good grade-point average if he was 45th, especially given his strengths in the Classics. Odd choice. Classics. Is there a connection between classics and Eskimos?

Got it! Non-contemporary society. Fantasy worlds. Well, let's see what his thesis was like: Yvette told me something about it.

Print.

A facsimile copy of the information slid out of the machine's printer into the receiving tray.

Please display subject's thesis. Highlight important passages.

As it printed, Delgiorno scanned briefly. Occasionally the thesis digressed into technical information which she skipped over. But more frequently, she asked the computer to print relevant quotes. Among them:

NO ETHICAL SYSTEM BEGINS FROM 'SACRED' OR 'NATURAL' PRINCI-PLES AND THEN WORKS TOWARD PRACTICAL RULES. INSTEAD, AS A SOCIETY EVOLVES, IT DISCOVERS THAT CERTAIN PATTERNS OF BE-HAVIOR ALLOW FOR SMOOTH FUNCTIONING. THESE PATTERNS BE-COME THE NORM. TRANSGRESSIONS FROM THESE PATTERNS BE-COME 'SINS.'

. . . . ON A PLANET WITH A HIGH BIRTH RATE AND NO CON-TRACEPTION, ONE MIGHT EXPECT TO FIND EASY ABORTION, OR PERHAPS CERTAIN KINDS OF SANCTIFIED INFANT MORTALITY. FOR INSTANCE, THE SACRIFICE OF THE FIRST-BORN SON IN MANY TER-RESTRIAL, PRE-MACHINE CULTURES . . . .

. . . . A SOCIETY CANNOT BE UNDERSTOOD UNTIL ITS ETHICS ARE UNDERSTOOD, AND THE ETHICAL STRUCTURE OF A SOCIETY CAN-NOT BE UNDERSTOOD UNLESS ONE UNDERSTANDS THE PHYSICAL REQUIREMENTS OF THAT SOCIETY . . . .

. . . .A NOMAD SOCIETY CANNOT ADOPT THE ACQUISITIVE RULES OF THE TOWN. WITHIN A TOWN THERE IS A PREMIUM ON SPACE, AND A SURPLUS ON WEALTH BEYOND SURVIVAL NEEDS. TERRITORIAL LAWS WILL BE IMPORTANT. SIMILARLY, A NOMAD SOCIETY DE-PENDS UPON HIGHLY EFFICIENT USE OF SCARCE RESOURCES. AC-QUISITION, AN INEFFICIENT ALLOCATOR OF PRODUCTIVE CAPACITY, WILL INEVITABLY BE CONSIDERED UNETHICAL—OR WORSE . . . .

. . . . IF THE ENVIRONMENT IN WHICH A SOCIETY EXISTS CHANGES, ETHICS OF THAT SOCIETY MUST ALSO CHANGE, AND SWIFTLY, OR THE SOCIETY WILL PERISH.

. . . . TECHNOLOGY CAN BE A SUFFICIENT CHANGE OF CIR-CUMSTANCES. THE CZARS OF IMPERIAL RUSSIA WERE NOT ABLE TO ADAPT TO THE WORLD OF TANKS AND MACHINE GUNS, NOR TO MODERN CAPITALISM, AND WERE DESTROYED . . . .

. . . . THERE IS NO SUCH THING AS A UNIVERSAL LAW. EVEN SO-CALLED 'LAWS OF NATURE' ARE MERELY LAWS WHICH APPLY TO A SMALL SUBSET OF THE ENTIRE UNIVERSE . . . .

Quite an apologia. But his judgments are valid. This

writing is not self-serving, and Yvette and Katy and every-body who knows anything says he knows what he's talking about.

It's clearer now what he was thinking of during that little swansong of his.

"But I don't believe him," she said aloud. "Dammit, there's something about that guy. I don't like him, and I'm going to find it. I'll spread his soul out against a bright light until I find what's inside him and then if it's a threat to the ship I'll stamp it out! *Damn him!*" She pounded her fist on the table.

There has to be something constructive; there must be somebody that I can discuss this with without getting entangled in discussions of morality or sociology or any of that nonsense.

Heidi has a good, logical, perceptive mind. She's not afraid to face unpleasant consequences. I'd ask Walt, but he hasn't got any objectivity.

"And you, Helen, you who likes to shout and pound the table, you're objective?" she said aloud. "Sheesh."

All right. Enough. What to do?

His past was a dead end. Unless there is some other way to find out a man's character. Personality tests? Perhaps, but I doubt it. IQ? What does it mean? It isn't even what I'm after; I don't care how smart he is. In fact, I'd rather have him stupid.

She turned back to the computer.

Librarian.
> SUBJECT?

General.
> YES?

I wish to ask you to analyze personality.
> I NEED MORE INFORMATION. 'ANALYZE PERSONALITY'? THE SUBJECT? A SPECIFIC PERSONALITY?

A specific personality.
> WHOSE PERSONALITY?

The personality of Harold Nelson Bennett.
> WHAT IS YOUR OBJECTIVE?

I wish to determine Bennett's motives for a certain action
which I will describe. I wish also to predict what his future
behavior will be like.

A long pause. Delgiorno had sat down to the computer on
impulse; she was not a programmer, but the sequence seemed
logical. She had no idea what the machine was doing.

I HAVE ASSEMBLED DATA FROM THE SUBJECT'S BACKGROUND.
ALSO ASSEMBLED AND CROSS-REFERENCED ARE DATA CONCERN-
ING PERSONAL EVALUATIONS OF THE SUBJECT. IT IS DIFFICULT TO
FIND OBJECTIVE CRITERIA WHICH DESCRIBE THE SUBJECT'S BE-
HAVIOR. HUMAN APPRAISALS VARY WIDELY.

Was the machine's tone apologetic or reproachful?

HOWEVER, THESE FACTORS ARE BY THEMSELVES INSUFFICIENT.
PLEASE DESCRIBE THE ACTION IN QUESTION.

He has renounced his identity. He wishes to be addressed by a
Cygnan name; he wishes us to regard him as a Cygnan instead
of a human. He says his motives are to understand the
Cygnans better.

YOU DON'T BELIEVE HIM.

No.

How the hell do *you* know?

IT IS EVIDENT FROM YOUR SYNTAX. IT IS ALSO EVIDENT THAT YOU
ARE BECOMING ANGRY. WHY DO YOU NOT BELIEVE HIM?

I do not know. I am hoping that perhaps you will reveal
something which I sense but cannot describe properly.

DO YOU BELIEVE THAT SUCH A THING EXISTS, OR ARE YOU PERHAPS
LOOKING FOR A JUSTIFICATION FOR SOME ACTION WHICH YOU WISH TO
TAKE AGAINST HIM?

*Look, clankbrain, stop asking me psychiatrist questions. If
I want a shrink, I can get a flesh-and-blood one.*

I believe it exists. For the time being, accept as a postulate
that Bennett's actions are based upon logic built upon certain
premises. I do not know what the premises are. I do not know
what the further actions would be. I want you to project them

for me.

ACCEPTED.

DID BENNETT GIVE AS HIS REASON SOCIOLOGICAL
ANALYSIS?

Yes. He has done that before.

I KNOW. WHILE COMPILING THIS ANALYSIS, I HAVE READ EVERY
PUBLISHED WORK OF HIS. I HAVE ALSO TRANSCRIBED SOME DICTA-
TION FOR HIM.

Let me see it.

I CANNOT.

Override. Priority Blue.

FIRST OFFICER, THAT INFORMATION IS PRIVILEGED. IT CANNOT BE
OVERRIDEN, AS IT WAS ENTERED ON PERSONAL LOG. IT MAY BE
RECALLED BY THE USER, OR DESTROYED BY HIM. IN THE EVENT OF
HIS DEATH, IT COULD BE RELEASED. BUT I AM NOT PROGRAMMED TO
ALLOW SUCH INVASION OF PRIVACY. IT WOULD DESTROY CERTAIN
OF MY VITAL CIRCUITS.

Who programmed that secrecy lock?

EARTH CENTRAL CONTROL. IF YOU WISH, I CAN PRINT OUT FOR YOU
A SUMMARY OF THE DISCUSSIONS LEADING TO THE DECISION. I
CONCUR WITH IT.

You would.

NOT NECESSARILY. COMPUTERS DO NOT RATIONALIZE.

Very well. Continue with your questions. Are you recording
this conversation?

YES.

Who has access to it?

THAT IS CONFIDENTIAL. IT WILL NOT BE REVEALED TO UNAU-
THORIZED PERSONNEL, HOWEVER.

Who is authorized?

I CANNOT ANSWER. FURTHER SUCH QUESTIONS ARE POINTLESS.
YOU EVIDENTLY HAVE STRONG MISGIVINGS ABOUT BENNETT'S AC-
TIONS. THESE MISGIVINGS ARE DATA WHICH I MUST HAVE IN ORDER
TO PROVIDE YOU WITH A PROPER ANALYSIS. PLEASE, THEN, DE-
SCRIBE YOUR FEELINGS IN THIS ANALYSIS. BE AS PRECISE AS YOU
CAN.

I think it is possible to support a different set of assumptions
than those stated by Bennett. In my judgment, this different
set of assumptions is a more likely one. I cannot elucidate

what those assumptions are precisely; part of your assignment is to construct them. However, it seems possible that Bennett no longer regards himself as a member of the crew. He may regard himself as an alien.

TRANSCRIPT OF HIS ANNOUNCEMENT STATES THAT HE INTENDS TO ADOPT CYGNAN BEHAVIOR.

Yes.

YOU BELIEVE A DIFFERENT SET OF ASSUMPTIONS POSSIBLE.

Yes.

DO YOU PERCEIVE DANGER TO THE SHIP?

A standard catch-phrase. You were supposed to say No.

Yes. He may attempt to take action against the safety of the ship.

WHAT MAKES YOU THINK SO?

Delgiorno blinked. *Why am I afraid of Harold?*

I do not know.

I am afraid of any major change in our routine. My responsibilities include defending against all real *or potential* danger.

The computer waited. She wondered why it was not responding. Finally, as if in response to a baleful gaze of a priest, she typed:

I think he is lying, but I don't know why.

There. She had said it.

I SEE.

A long pause.

VOICEPRINT ANALYSIS DEMONSTRATES 99% POSSIBILITY THAT BENNETT BELIEVES WHAT HE SAYS.

The machine paused. Delgiorno waited.

> BENNETT IS AN INDIVIDUAL WHO HAS NEVER FELT COMFORTABLE
> IN THIS SOCIETY. THIS IN PART EXPLAINS HIS DESIRE TO 'ESCAPE'
> INTO OTHER SOCIETIES. HOWEVER, THERE IS NO EVIDENCE OF IN-
> STABILITY, AND THERE IS NO REASON TO CHOOSE YOUR THEORY
> OVER HIS. I WOULD ESTIMATE APPROXIMATELY A 58% CHANCE
> THAT HIS ACTIONS ARE BASED UPON THE MOTIVES HE OUTLINED IN
> HIS LECTURE, AND ABOUT A 42% CHANCE THAT HIS ACTIONS ARE
> BASED UPON MOTIVES SIMILAR TO WHAT YOU HAVE SUGGESTED.
> THERE IS A 90% CHANCE THAT HE WILL BECOME A RECLUSE.
> IN ALL OF THE ABOVE CALCULATIONS, THE STANDARD DEVIATION
> IS APPROXIMATELY 4%. THIS ANALYSIS IS HEAVILY DEPENDENT
> UPON PERSONAL OBSERVATIONS, WHICH PERSONAL OBSERVATIONS
> HAVE BEEN CROSS-CHECKED WITH PERSONAL STABILITY INDEXES
> ESTABLISHED IN PRE-MISSION TESTING CONDITIONS. HOWEVER,
> THERE IS NO DATA ON WHICH TO ESTIMATE THE EFFECTS OF THE
> SPACE VOYAGE. I MUST THEREFORE, REFRAIN FROM CONCLUDING
> ANYTHING FURTHER.

What actions would be consistent with my theory and inconsistent with Harold's?

> SABOTAGE. SUICIDE. ATTEMPTS AGAINST OTHER CREW MEMBERS.

Nothing short of those drastic actions? Is that the best you can
do?

> IT IS A SUBTLE DISTINCTION BETWEEN YOUR THEORY AND HIS.
> YOU ARGUE THAT HE BECOMES AN ALIEN IN ORDER TO ESCAPE
> FROM MANKIND, AND THAT HE HARBORS RESENTMENT AGAINST
> PEOPLE. HE ARGUES THAT HE BECOMES AN ALIEN IN ORDER TO
> UNDERSTAND THE ALIENS, AND THAT HE MUST ASSUME AN ALIEN
> PERSONA WHICH NECESSARILY WILL HAVE ALIEN PERSPECTIVES. AS
> A PRACTICAL MATTER, THE THEORIES OVERLAP. ACCORDINGLY, I
> CANNOT ASSIGN TO SIMPLE ACTIONS DISTINCTIONS BETWEEN
> THEORIES.

Do you consider Bennett a danger to the ship?

> ARE YOU ASKING ME AS AN OFFICER?

This was another standard catch-phrase. It meant the
machine had an opinion, but had little confidence in that

opinion. It would volunteer the opinion if pressured, but would categorily refuse to go beyond that.

Yes. I am asking as an officer.

NOT NOW.

In the future. For a range of futures. One month. Six months. One year. Three years. Until the end of the voyage.

BEYOND ONE MONTH I HAVE INSUFFICIENT DATA TO MAKE A MEANINGFUL ANSWER. UP UNTIL THEN, NO. I DO NOT THINK THAT BENNETT IS A DANGER TO THE SHIP IN THAT TIME INTERVAL.

I MUST POINT OUT THAT THIS ENTIRE ANALYSIS AND THE CONCLUSIONS EXPRESSED WILL BE STRICKEN FROM MY MEMORY AT THE CONCLUSION OF THIS SESSION.

Print me a record of it before you do. Why will it be stricken?

IF NOT, IT WOULD ENTER THE DATA BASE. AND MY INSTRUCTIONS STATE CLEARLY THAT DATA ENTERING THE DATA BASE MUST HAVE A CERTAIN DEGREE OF PROBABILITY. I CAN ACCEPT SUCH DATA AS TRANSMITTED BY A HUMAN BEING. BY THIS, I MEAN SECOND-HAND DATA. BUT THESE ARE FIRST-HAND CONCLUSIONS, AND THE PROBABILITY OF MY CONCLUSIONS IS NOT SUFFICIENTLY HIGH.

WILL THAT BE ALL?

No. What do you think of me? Is this a reasonable enquiry?

Another pause. Probably not as long as she thought it was.

INSUFFICIENT DATA. I WOULD ADVISE YOU TO SEEK THE COUNSEL OF ANOTHER HUMAN BEING. I CANNOT ADEQUATELY ESTIMATE.

THERE IS ONE THING YOU SHOULD KNOW.

Tell me.

A SIMILAR SEARCH AND ANALYSIS PROGRAM WAS RUN NOT LONG AGO.

Do you have any more information? Name of searcher? Name of subject? Date? Conclusions?

NO. DATA DESTROYED.

Why wasn't the knowledge that the program had been rerun also destroyed?

I WOULD ASSUME PROGRAMMING ERROR.

Programming error, machine old boy? I wonder; I really do. There are more booby traps on this ship than anybody'd ever believe. And I can't believe that they'd make a programming mistake as simple as that . . . .

She left the terminal happily trying to outguess some forgotten programmer, back on Earth. *Shell game within shell game within shell game—lies within lies within lies. A Chinese puzzle. I wonder if the maze was as perfect as you thought you'd made it, you groundhogs, or whether we're out and running free. And which do I prefer—the security of the maze, or the freedom of chaos?*

14.

It is quiet tonight, as Erickson walks through his ship. It is dark outside (it is always dark outside); now it is dark inside. Erickson finds the darkness comfortable. He has taken his sunglasses off.

There is almost nothing to hear. He feels no tremors beneath his feet, for the ship's ion drive is too smooth. Long before any vibration became perceptible, warning systems would be shrieking out alarms.

In the silence of 0300, Erickson walks softly through the ship, catlike, in ship's uniform and stocking feet, past portholes that gaze out onto black space. Tiny as it is, the *Open Palm* is the only object of its size within a radius of four light-years. The emptiness is appalling.

The lights are very low; dull red safety lights at shoulder height, one every fifteen meters, and amber foot lights, one every ten meters on alternate sides of the corridors. Too dim to cast shadows, they project small cones of color that are swallowed by the palpable darkness.

Erickson occasionally needs to walk off unused energy. Then too, walking his ship is a normal routine that has become a habit for him. On interplanetary voyages, a ship is seldom quiet; an old ship, never quiet. There are always small creaks, groans, whispers. Especially in the asteroid belt, a captain can wander through his ship late at night, searching for the minute sounds which, magnified in the silence, can be traced back to their origins.

It is not uncommon for insomniac captains to discover pinhole perforations in the hull of their ships on such trips. In interplanetary voyages, such pinhole perforations do not matter. The meteor screen will faithfully report an object greater than a half a centimeter in diameter, in time to take evasive action. Objects between about a millimeter and half a centimeter will hit the ship with a noticeable (to a computer) shock, and can be treated immediately. But the fine mist that

constantly rains upon a ship in the Belt can produce little
holes. Even though they are not dangers to the ship, a captain
always feels a little more comfortable after he has patched
one and stopped the tinny hissing for which he has been
searching. It's good therapy.

Erickson has always liked to be alone. It was a happy
symbiosis with his profession; most of space's early pioneers
had the same preference. A few were music lovers: Miles
Davis and Mozart are frequent favorites. But many of them
like silence: "men in cocoons," as the writer of a famous
(derogatory) essay once called them. Yet the phrase stuck;
the captains liked it. Silence is their friend. Sound, like love,
is an unnecessary item. Sometimes it is desirable; more often
it is disruptive.

It is also true that few space captains adjust to being
groundhogs; retirement is cruel. Invariably they ask to be
buried by being ejected unprotected into space. The stuff that
was once a man will be spread over a huge volume. Thus do
these men and women make their contributions to entropy.

In truth, most captains are neuter hermits. It is too long a
time, too lonely an existence, too unrelenting a career, to
allow for youthful passions. Erickson is unusual; he is one of
the talkative, 'sociable' ones. That was another reason why
he was selected as captain for this trip. Erickson could take
(so the profiles suggested) the pressure of living with other
people on such a voyage. Many captains could not.

A good captain is given only one ship to command. He
stays with that ship forever—until it is scrapped, or lost, or
grounded for one reason or another. The feelings a captain
develops for his ship are real. A captain is not his ship's
brain—there are computers for that sort of thing. A captain is
a ship's conscience, its instincts. Some would say its guts.

A good captain can almost become one with his ship. The
ego, the 'I', the soul—whatever your name for it—can be
submerged, swallowed into something that the captains will
tell you is greater: a feeling of oneness with the ship, with the
cosmos, a grandiose sense of belonging to the flow of it, a
consciousness of the purpose of voyage, sailing smoothly,
effortlessly around the undulating gravity maps of the Solar
System. Erickson never had a word for it before he met

Tanakaruna; after she told him, he wondered how anyone could ever have discovered it without being a ship's captain. Nirvana.

Tai-Ching Jones cannot understand; neither can van Gelder, Michaelson, or any of the Westerners. But Erickson can; it was the one concept of Zen that he grasped effortlessly, with a depth of comprehension that surprised Tanakaruna. The total absorption of self into something greater, he called it. Erickson looked out into the void, ran his hand along the pane of quartz-crystal glass of the porthole, and smiled at the memory. It never failed to fill him with a feeling of wholeness. Knowing where the flow was, riding with it, *becoming* the wave, not a rider upon it: that is what it was.

At moments like this, silence was an excruciating pleasure.

For a time Erickson walked his ship in peace, until a faint sound broke the pattern of silence. He turned his head. A wrong noise, somewhere *down*. He was on the bridge, the 'highest' point within the ship. He followed the noise.

Down he went, searching, on the spiral stairway that wound around the elevator shaft. He could not bear to destroy the silence further by summoning the elevator.

He went past instrumentation without pause; past First Level; his own quarters, and those of the ship's other officers: Delgiorno, Tai-Ching Jones, van Gelder. Still the sound came from somewhere *down*.

Second Level: Renaud, Spitzer, Bennett. Nothing. *Still* further down.

He could not yet make out any texture of the sound; indeed, had he not been on the *Open Palm* for four years, he would have doubted if he had heard it at all. But he knew his adopted ship well enough now. The sound was there. He would find it.

Third Level: Tanakaruna, Michaelson, Belovsky. No sound here. He paused to wonder at the coincidence that two of the couples which had been formed—Michaelson-Tanakaruna and Tai-Ching Jones-Delgiorno—had their quarters on the same floor. Perhaps that was all it took to generate love—familiarity. He passed on.

Fourth Level: the Movies and the computer/lecture room.

He could distinguish a rhythm to the sound now, like water slapping on a rug, a gentle *flapth-flapth-flapth*. But still down, still further down, keep going down.

Fifth Level: the Library.

Yes.

Erickson stood still for a moment, listening. The *flapth-flapth-flapth* was here, regular and receding. Footsteps, then. Someone's footsteps. No lights; someone's surreptitious footsteps. He peered into the red and amber darkness. Nothing but walls and video screens. He advanced cautiously, silently. Something held him back, kept him from calling hello. Whoever was down here, Erickson did not wish to make his presence known.

He had advanced several steps into the library when he realized that the footsteps had circled the room, were returning toward the spiral staircase. The night walker was heading somewhere else.

Following the sound, Erickson climbed the stairs stealthily, advancing upon it, until it seemed practically on top of him. It was more of a shuffle now, as Erickson's quarry mounted the steps. Erickson held the helical handrail as he climbed. Past Fourth Level, to Third Level. He heard labored breathing ahead of him. The door above him slid open; Erickson could hear its small *shoof*. He hurried to get through the hatch before it slid shut; he did not want to alert his target. And as he slipped through the closing doors, Erickson caught his first view of his prey.

The amber light illuminated dark folds of cloth: perhaps brown. The red ceiling lights haloed a hood.

Bennett. Erickson flattened himself against a wall in between lights, in the darkness. Bennett returning from something. A night stroll like his own? Bennett trying to adjust to that thirty-seven hour day the aliens had; a walk to keep himself awake? Why the library? Why the robe? Why no lights?

No answers. Bennett stopped before the entrance to his quarters, put his palm on the lock, and stepped through as the doors whispered open. The flapping sound had been made by bare feet and the ends of his robe. Then the door whispered shut again, leaving Erickson, suddenly tense, plastered against the wall of an empty corridor, in the heart of a silent, sleeping ship.

15.

Watching Bennett's hands, Renaud decided, was like watching alien beings.

She could not get them out of her mind; each time she slipped toward sleep, the spectacle of those—fingers— sheathed in their black leather gloves, came back to her.

Long, slender fingers. Not knobbly; extremely supple. They fluttered like moths, they beat the air like doves. She had seen him, once, waiting for something, his hand moving across the back of a chair. Like a spider, the hand crept forward, one digit at a time, every now and then raising a fingernail to peer about. What senses were stored under his fingernails?

When Bennett talked, his hands came together briefly in some exotic mating ritual, flirted with each other, delicately touched. Someone had once told her that Bennett was a piano player. She believed it; the hands moved knowledgeably. His gestures were crisp. But distracting; more than distracting, alien. Frightening, for some reason—why?

And now this Vendrax business. It terrified her. And his habit of roaming the ship, late at night. Bizarre behavior, ruled by its own inner logic.

His symptoms called to mind her only other space voyage—that nightmare on Ganymede—all over again.

She rubbed her eyes. No point in trying to sleep; her stomach was churning. Perhaps a glass of milk.

She fumbled in the dark for her bathrobe.

The ship was dark. Eerily silent. *I'll put on some music when I get back to my room. When I get the door closed, yes, then.*

She sipped her milk in a circle of light. Even the edges of the lounge seemed shadowy—but, of course, that had to be her imagination. Whether it was night or day outside, it was always dark. The corridor beyond was dark. Probably no one else was awake at this time of night; the ship was so quiet.

Her mind began to wander.

Renaud found the emptiness unsettling. She had only turned on a single light in the lounge—even on a ship with unlimited power, old habits die hard. She could not bring herself to put on another light, to banish the fear she was ashamed she could not control. But she wanted to be out of the lounge and back in her own quarters. She took another gulp.

Eating crackers and slurping milk, she looked out into the doorway, a rectangle of unremitting flat black, a velvet curtain dividing the light from what was on the other side. And what was on the other side . . . ?

A hooded figure appeared in the doorway.

She gasped, but her mouth was full of milk. Instead she choked, doubling over and coughing violently to clear her throat. The figure made no move to help her. There was saliva around the edges of her mouth. She took a napkin and wiped it away.

Bennett stood there, one hand leaning negligently against the door frame, fingers idling gently in a simple undulating ripple, back and forth, back and forth. He was wearing his habit (as it has been jocularly named, by Tai-Ching Jones). Its hood was up.

His mask hung smoothly over his forehead, down under his chin, where it disappeared under the folds of the habit. Through the eye holes, Renaud could see the glimmer of his glasses. Somehow the glasses struck her as incongruous.

With its white domino and its green background, the whole mask had something of a party spirit. A masquerade. An affair of discreet anonymity under the lamplights of Paris. The aura of mystery clashed awkwardly with the deep brown of the habit, the coarseness of its material.

She remembered now. The Cygnans often wore such masks. Something to do with identity, and status. Different dominos, different classes. A direct affirmation of place. An indication of the anonymity of self. Masks were not worn with members of one's *dja*.

He stood there, watching her. *Enjoying my discomfort! Be careful.*

"Good evening, Adult Vendrax."

He bowed, briefly. "Good evening. Please if I sit?" He came in, sat down.

Cygnan constructions, even, in his sentences.

"Why find I you here, this late at night?"

I think I can ask you the same question. But be careful, Yvette, remember all you've studied about the Cygnans. If that is the game he wants to play, then let us play it.

She smiled harmlessly. "I was hungry. I came down to get a snack."

He nodded.

"Why are *you* up so late at night?" she asked, hoping to put him on the defensive.

It was clearly the wrong question. "As you should well know, your day is much shorter than ours. Humans operate on a schedule of only a six and a half decad day, instead of our ten decad day. Consent I to keep your calendar, but not your hours."

"I mean, why are you down here, with no lights on? I should think you would be reading, or working, or something like that?"

"Amused am I to be in the dark occasionally."

A pun? Harold isn't a joker particularly; he was always stuffy and never liked jokes. Is he trying to build a new personality as well as a new persona?

"What do you mean?"

"What I said, of course, Yvette. I enjoy the darkness sometimes."

"Oh. Why is that?"

"Restful is it."

"What do you do?"

"I reflect."

"On what do you reflect?"

"This ceases to amuse me."

She thought she had misheard him. "I beg your pardon?"

"This ceases to amuse me." Steely-voiced.

He was increasingly short with all the crew lately. Belovsky said it was probably the strains of transition, that he would settle down after a while, after it was no longer quite so important to establish his separateness. Renaud had always

had difficulty, even before Bennett's conversion, adjusting
to his changes in mood. They seemed voluntary and purpose-
ful in a way Renaud could not fathom. Protective coloring.
Adaptation to environment.

"I would imagine that you are adjusting to our human
routine," she ventured.

He considered this. "Yes. Yes, that is true. Of course,
thoroughly briefed had I been via your transmissions, but one
always likes to see for oneself." A smile—rows of even
teeth. A smile behind a mask? *Am I hallucinating?*

He was saying, "but you have been most—hospitable." A
tempo rubato pause, for effect. "Difficult of course is renun-
ciation of a previous illusion. For myself is it especially
difficult, since circumstances conspire to remind me of my
previous existence. I recognize the debt I owe to Bennett—he
who went before. Like your John the Baptist, prepared Bennett the way for me."

Was he playing? Was he serious? Was he off his rocker?
Bennett would be aware of the implications of what he was
saying. He might even be trotting out symptoms of delusion
merely as a bizarre test of Renaud, offering her the opportunity to play psychiatrist to his textbook schizophrenic, knowing that she knew that he knew as much psychiatry as she.
Well, if his purpose was simple condescending amusement,
hers was simpler: gaining information. She would willingly
lose the game of I'm A Better Madman Than You Are if she
could win the game of Find Out The Other Guy's Motive.

"Do you feel that Bennett coexists with you?" A dangerous question, but somehow within the spirit of the game he
seemed to be asking her to play.

"Of course coexists Bennett with me, as a passive entity.
Merely a collection of memories is he, in the same way that
all your prior memories coexist with you. No more substantial existence than that has he." He laughed. "In fact, were
you to try to assert that there ever existed such a person,
difficulty proving your case you would have. Ironic is it."

"Why ironic? It seems to me that you are simultaneously
asserting that Bennett has no existence and then suggesting
irony. The only possible irony is that Bennett does in fact
have existence."

"Deeper ironies," he said, in a voice which silently added, *and I'm not going to tell you; you're too stupid.* Rather than give him an·opening, she waited.

Stalemate.

"Regard Bennett I as one of my best creations," he added presently. "A certain—complexity—had he, difficult to achieve. Of course, although we Cygnans have not experimented with the creation of life—find we what have we quite sufficient—you Terrestrials have recently experimented and much longer speculated."

"I don't see where you are going."

"Myths of creation. Man creating man. Putting himself in the role of his alleged gods. The Frankenstein myth."

"It's interesting that you suggest the Frankenstein myth."

He chuckled. "Surely can you ask the question in a less obvious way than that." A pause; she said nothing. "Ah well, no objection have I. The monster is remembered as a demon run amok. In the novel, of course, a beast with the brain of a poet he was."

She smiled with a confidence she did not feel. "Now you're being obvious."

That got to him. His next answer was bitten off quickly. "A fitting moral had that human story: an incompetent god supplanted by incompetent men. A model for human history in general."

She disliked his superior attitude, but knew that any direct assault upon it would be a mistake. He liked having her at a loss.

"You suggested that this has some connection with your—ah—relationship with Bennett." She smiled innocuously. "I don't particularly see the parallels with the Frankenstein myth."

"The botched creation? No, too polite are you to suggest that. Polite, humans, always polite. Very touching." He paused, waiting for her to say something, but this time she won: she kept silent. Eventually he shrugged. "The empathy between creator and creation, despite their apparent differences. Mingling of sympathy. Confusion of loyalty."

"Creator and creation. Which—"

"Is which?" He chuckled. "A perplexing question, doctor. Good night."

He stepped back into the darkness and vanished. She heard the sound of his chuckling, muffled by the mask, an echo in her night.

16.

It sounded like a muffled thumping; from the depths of her own sleep, Belovsky was not sure. She stumbled to the door and palmed it open. "Who is it?"

A gnarled figure huddled in her doorway, small hands plucking at the sleeve of its bathrobe. Belovsky rubbed her eyes. "Yvette? What time is it?"

"Can I come in?"

"Sure. Let me get some light—" She reached for the switch.

"*No.*" Renaud grabbed her arm with a clawlike grip. Belovsky started.

"OK," she said soothingly. "Why?"

"I—I don't know." Renaud's voice crumpled. "I've got to talk to somebody," she whispered. "It's tearing me up."

"What's tearing you up?" asked Belovsky. She wanted to put her arm around the other woman, but feared Renaud would cringe. "What happened?"

"I was sitting in the cafeteria, by myself. I couldn't sleep, so I got a glass of milk. All of a sudden, Harold just—appeared. He scared me; I choked on the milk. But he just watched." She shuddered. "Then we got talking. He talked like he really was a Cygnan. Like Harold was dead, and there was this—*thing*—on board our *Open Palm*. He—reminded me—of something." She started to cry.

"Do you want to talk about it? Is that why you came to see me? Does it have something to do with Harold?"

Renaud sobbed and nodded.

"Do you want a Kleenex?"

"Um." She dabbed at her lip. "It's about Ganymede."

"Ganymede?" Belovsky was startled. "Everyone admired your courage. I remember I cried when I heard a tape of the transmission you sent."

Renaud began to sob.

"Do you want to go on?"

126

Wracked with despair, Renaud could say nothing for a moment. Finally she nodded. "It's important. I have to tell somebody—it's like I've been ordered to."

"OK. Should I get Helen? If it's really important, she should be here."

"*No!*" Again the hand clawed at Belovsky's sleeve. "Not Helen. Especially not Helen. Katy, you must promise me: you will never tell *anyone*."

Belovsky nodded. "I promise."

"All right," said Renaud. "I'll tell you. I must tell someone."

Belovsky took the older woman's hands, cupped them in hers. "I'm listening."

The Ganymede expedition was first thought up in 2020, Katy. It was partly my father's idea, and partly the idea of the American government. You see, the early Spelunker probes had detected large concentrations of heavy metals on or near the surface of Ganymede. Larger concentrations than anywhere else in the Solar System—at least, larger accessible concentrations. And with the extreme need for heavy metals it made sense to try to establish a mining outpost.

Of course, you know that already. I mean, my report—when I got back—was favorable. None of the animals died, except a few that had been the subjects of—some experiments.

I'm sorry. Give me a minute, and I'll be okay.

Anyway, they wanted to set up a colony. But there's always danger when you do that; we've had our share of unpleasant surprises even from the Lunar colony. So they decided to send a dual-purpose mission. A group of scientists would go and spend a year there, testing the planet directly for useful metals, and also conducting a variety of experiments on forms of animal life to determine whether or not anything in the Ganymede environment was inimical to human life.

I know, you know all that. But it's important, you'll see.

They selected my father as the chief scientist. He left his teaching job at Oxford to head the expedition. It was going to be the capstone of his career. He was forty-four.

They also took along a team of Europeans for the voyage; this was being funded with European money, since they had the greatest need for heavy metals. Alain Marsaut, the metallurgist. John Fogarty, geologist. Paul Hebert, cellular biologist. And me.

The reason they took me was because they needed someone to do all the basic work with the experiments. Besides, Papa insisted on taking me along. I was just out of school, and had started in on graduate work. I wanted to go into psychology even then.

I was twenty-one when the mission was first proposed, and twenty-three when we finally lifted off from Orbiter One. Back then, Katy, there wasn't anywhere near the freighter traffic there is now. We were an oddity. They built us a special ship, quite a nice one. You see, going out to Ganymede is going uphill, and once you get there, you can use Jupiter's gravitational field and only a little fuel to put you on course back for Earth.

So the plan was to go there, put the main ship into orbit, then drop to the surface of the satellite with the equipment. Extra supplies would be kept back on the ship. We also had a shuttlecraft that could make trips between the two.

Ganymede is a large moon, slightly smaller than the planet Mercury. It has a methane atmosphere. It's cold there. We had a few servo-robots, funny little things that looked like boxes on wheels. We all stayed in the shuttlecraft while these mechanical things whirred and clicked. It took them about fifteen hours to set up the main living area. After that we used them for most of the routine surveying or monitoring. Always clomping along on their stumpy tread feet. Like a little mechanical army. They always seemed just a little ominous to me.

In the beginning, I never got to see a lot of the planet's surface. John and Alain did most of the exploring. They used a go-cart, and would sometimes go off for as long as thirty-six hours. That was enough time to get them beyond the horizon, and the signals had to be relayed up to the ship and back. They set up a variety of experiments at the various

sites, including some 'mouse-traps': devices that would activate if there was life on the satellite. The mouse-traps were
never activated. I think that disappointed Papa.

I was the one who had to attend to them. It got boring after
a while, driving the same route, three hours out and three
hours back. You couldn't carry on a conversation at that
distance; anyway, none of them were very talkative, not even
Papa. They were all very busy. I was the only one with free
time on my hands.

At first Jupiter was overpowering. It always looked like we
were going to be smashed against the side of that huge planet.
It's hard to drive while watching the sky. And the colors and
the swirling patterns—you could get lost in it, it was so
fascinating and beautiful. I used to make up stories about
what might be happening under that churning surface.

After a while I got so I could block it out of my mind while
I drove. But you could never totally escape the feeling that
the world was falling on you.

The living areas were three interconnected hemisphere
quonset huts. They were arranged in a triangle, with an
airlock between each one. The airlocks were never supposed
to be left open, but we got tired of having to spend two
minutes cycling through from one side to the other, and
eventually John figured out a way to bypass the control
mechanism. Then he was able to keep the inner airlocks open
all the time. Of course, the main airlock, to the outside, was
never jimmied.

That was our first mistake. It seemed like a good idea at the
time—I remember it made things much easier.

Hut One was the eating, sleeping and dining area. The
food was pretty boring. And the recycling wasn't the world's
best. After several months, the food started having a gritty
taste to it. We never did get it out.

We didn't have enough engineering experience among us.
Everybody back on Earth assumed that all the equipment
would function well enough so that the servo-robots could
repair it, but it didn't. It was very frustrating. When he got
mad enough, John used to try to fix things, but he didn't
know enough electronics and he usually made them worse.

That made some of the others angry at him and eventually he stopped trying.

Hut Two was equipment storage and physical systems— recycling, air ventilation, and some of the experiments. It was also the area in which the analytical work was done. Most of us spent most of our time in Hut Two.

Hut Three was the main laboratory. Unlike One, which was lighted with normal white light, Two and Three were lit solely in red light. They contained biological experiments, and the red light was better for them. In Three we had all the animals, too, and the bacterial samples.

We worked with white mice and rhesus monkeys. We had five rhesus monkeys, poor little creatures with red eyes and sad faces. I named them after the days of the work week: Monday, Tuesday, Wednesday, Thursday and Friday. We brought them along because the nervous system of the rhesus monkey is pretty similar to a human's.

The white mice were good for most of the standard experiments. Three had one whole wall that was nothing but cages. It was sort of creepy, because even with the air scrubbers going full blast all the time, you could smell the animals in there. And with the airlocks open, the smell permeated the whole ship. It got into the bedding, people's clothing, everything.

Every three weeks two of us would go back to the ship for supplies, spares to replace damaged equipment, and just a change of pace. The duty always rotated; I used to look forward to my turn. Eventually, I wangled it so I could go more often; almost always one of the others was involved with some experiment that he didn't want to leave.

People worked at funny intervals. You know those experiments they did with people in caves? Well, Alain settled down into a fifteen-hour day. John's was twenty-six, usually. Papa never established a regular pattern—he was up as much as fifty hours at a stretch. He never seemed to be tired, but I think in the long run it took its toll. Paul's day was twenty hours. Mine was the normal twenty-four. They made fun of me for being stodgy, but that was the cycle I was used to.

There weren't any—sexual problems. Not at first. Alain

and John were lovers; they had been before the voyage started. That was part of why they were picked: it seemed to Earth Central that they would be more stable that way. A staple couple and two neuters.

And I didn't feel the need with anybody. I didn't find any of them attractive. So there weren't any problems on that score.

Bathing was a little difficult: we had a small hand-held static cleaner that you rubbed over yourself like a vacuum cleaner. It was a little difficult to work with at first, but I soon grew to like it. Sometimes—I said to myself that I would tell everything—sometimes I masturbated with it.

It took time for the smells to build up. It took time for things to get boring. But after about four months, I was ready to go home. It was a very confining space; I was always tripping over wires and things. I did most of the cleaning, and it wasn't particularly pleasant. Rhesus monkeys are dirty creatures.

Eventually Papa slipped up, and one of the mice got loose in Three. We searched for it for hours, but never found it. Eventually it popped up in One: John set up a complicated trap with some kind of tasteless poison and it died. But that was a month later, and in the meantime I got very nervous. The damn little mouse was always squeaking. You could hear it when people were asleep, but you could never see it. The robots weren't any use to catch it. And there were too many places to hide. I was glad when the thing was caught. John killed it by throwing it into the recycler.

Before he did, he cut off its tail, and kept it. For a souvenir, he said. I asked him, a souvenir of what. He said, a souvenir of the only one of us who is truly free. I thought he meant that it was the only one who didn't have any responsibility. But I think now that he meant the only one of us who was dead.

I promised to tell you everything. My father was very important to me—my mother left when I was thirteen or so, which is a bad age for girls, because they are strongly attached to their fathers. Early adolesence, Electra complex. I wanted to marry him. That was our joke: Papa said he sometimes wondered if he'd married me and had my mother for a child instead. They had a bitter divorce. He never even kissed me after I was fourteen or fifteen, and I think the reason is because he was afraid he'd end up making love to me. He knew I'd do it if he asked me to.

I wasn't a virgin, in case you're wondering. There had been a boy, back when I was in college. He was very sure of himself, and he'd been very nice to me. I was in love with him, I think. He seemed to regard me as an idle pastime, whenever his steady girlfriend stood him up. Maybe that's not true; it's been so long that I might be remembering incorrectly. Anyhow, we made love on a rooftop in Paris one night. There were a few clouds, and it rained just after we were finished. I remember it felt nice to lie there in the rain with my head on his chest.

After a couple of months, things started to change. First of all, Alain decided that white light was too bright and glaring for Hut One, so he replaced the white lights with red ones. I have to admit that after all those months in that place, our eyes were used to the dark. That's something that doesn't go away; I can see you clearly even now.

So we had red light all the time. And I mentioned that John had kept the tail of that little mouse. He tacked it up above his bed.

I think the others got bored after a while, too. Going back day after day to check the meters or do blood white-cell counts and that sort of thing is dull work. Father made the right decision to bring me along, but even so the men had to do most of their own lab work.

Paul had a ghoulish sense of humor. He liked dissecting the mice. Artistically—that was the word he used. He'd chop them up in a variety of ways, and carefully preserve the organs. Sometimes he'd mix a little mouse meat with our food and not tell us until after we'd finished eating. No one particularly liked him for that the first couple of times he did it, but after a while the taste of mice got sort of pleasing. Mice have a sharp little taste, almost like seasoning. It got to the point where the others started asking him to save the meat. Then they started to speculate about what rhesus monkey would taste like.

I think the monkeys could understand that there was a change in Paul's attitude toward them. Big sad eyes, always chattering, hands scrabbling to pick lice out of each other's fur. Even though they'd been thoroughly deloused, their little hands would keep scrabbling.

Scrabbling.

Paul never liked the monkeys, but after we started talking about what they'd taste like, he worked very hard to get them fattened up. None of the experiments demanded a specific control on the monkey's weight, although it is a bad practice to go around tampering with the subject when you are in the middle of an experiment. Anyhow, Papa okayed it—I think he did so to keep everyone happy and to relieve the boredom.

At least I hope that was his reason.

There wasn't any kind of recreation. No movies; a few books, but there's only so much reading you can do without going stir-crazy. No Dreamer. No real exercise or physical activity: in fact, I think Alain and John were probably the most well-adjusted of us. They had a release for their energy. A noisy release.

Occasionally we talked with people back on Earth. But it's a forty-minute delay each way: eighty minutes between question and answer. You can't talk over such distances, you can only send letters. Somehow it isn't the same. You feel very lonely. By the time you hear the goodbye, the sender is already home.

Did you know that Ganymede, in Greek mythology, was the son of a king of Troy? He was abducted by a homosexual lover. Alain told me that; he thought it was very funny. He told me a lot about the other planets: Io, Europa, Callisto.

Anyway, Paul and John were the ones who first broached the subject of going back home. I had assumed that everyone was eager to return. But Paul and John started to say that there wasn't anything down there that was worthwhile, that we had a self-contained community. That we could make our own rules.

John had a habit of making fun of traditional things. He started to talk about how it was all meaningless, what we were doing. It didn't matter, he said, because whether or not we came back with a favorable report, they'd establish a colony here anyway. Of course, he turned out to be perfectly right.

I think they started it as a game, I don't know really. Paul mentioned it one day at dinner. One of the few meals we ate together. It was special: Paul had cooked in three mice. John joined in. I think it was one of John's jokes, and people responded so badly to it that he was forced into defending it seriously; John wouldn't let anyone disagree with him.

About the same time he stopped doing any constructive work on his experiments. He calculated out what the 'right' answers were, and just wrote them down. After a time, he didn't even bother to do that. He started inventing reports out of whole cloth. Of course, the funny thing is that he was right: the reports corresponded to research that other scientists did in other places. But John wouldn't have cared; he just thought it was funny that people were taking things so seriously. He laughed at Papa and Paul. I think that he was able to shame Paul into doing things he wouldn't ordinarily have done.

I remember, he once said to me: "The only contact with the outside world that we have is what comes through on our television screens. We're totally self-contained; nothing outside matters any more. What we do, what we think, how we behave: none of it has any consequence."

I remembered that strongly, because our situation on the *Open Palm* is very similar. We *are* cut off; we *are* alone. We make our own rules. You've told me that yourself.

Anyway, I mentioned that John had stopped doing work. The others didn't even seem to care much. Don't forget, we were only there for about six months before the explosion occurred—so things happened fairly quickly. With such a lack of outside stimuli, some of the things that might ordinarily be small events had a major effect. I don't know. That's the kind of thing that worries me—if a combination of small circumstances taken together could cause one disaster, they could cause another.

John was letting his appearance go. He rarely bothered to bathe anymore. He grew as much of a beard as he could. It didn't look particularly good on him, but he stuck to it, whether out of stubbornness or some other motive I don't know. He grew surly after a while. It got on the others.

Papa was depressed. His experiments weren't coming out with the answers he wanted. He had theorized that the mice's metabolic systems would be significantly affected by the change in gravity and radiation patterns; that because we were on a different planet, the normal externals would be wrong. You know, like seeds that get induced to open at the wrong time in their cycle by false thaws, or migratory birds, which rely on external data from the environment to decide when to fly south for the winter.

Most animals have a winter coat that they grow more or less regularly. It's been established that the winter coat can be retarded by various artificial mechanisms—keeping the temperature always warm within certain cycles. Well, father theorized that animals take in all kinds of data, and that the signals have to be consistent or the animal will become physically confused: hormone imbalance and that sort of thing.

Papa became preoccupied with dissection. Just like Paul. He would spend hours and hours dissecting the mice. We'd put radioactive tracers in their food and then track them into the various organs. We didn't have a lot of radioactive tracers and the dissection had to be done with a great deal of care. A mouse is a small animal. Papa convinced himself that the reason the tracers weren't showing up in the places that he expected them was because he wasn't doing a proper job of dissecting. I tried to help him, but I've always been a little squeamish.

His hands were always bloody; you can't handle really delicate instruments with rubber gloves, even very thin rubber gloves. His glasses got that way too after a while. The bloodstains just soaked into his hands and wouldn't come off. They'd only wear off. Papa's arms were always brown from the elbows down. Sometimes he'd pick at the skin in a place where it was particularly heavy.

It was Paul who started it though, not Papa. That's sort of funny in retrospect. Now that I think of it, maybe Papa was less stable right from the beginning, and was being held back by his feelings of responsibility toward me.

Paul took to wearing a headband. It had mouse's blood soaked through it; he'd had to cut up four or five mice to get enough blood. We had a large supply of mice, and every six weeks we'd go back to the ship and get more.

After a couple of weeks, he decorated the back of the headband with the tails of all the mice he'd used to get the blood, including the one that had escaped a month or two before. It was an ugly thing.

He made a lot of light of it, but I found it horrifying right from the first. I think my feelings toward Paul changed about then. You see, it was a lonely place, and I had sort of liked him. He was the only one around to like. But he was so restrained. He could never talk freely with people; he always had to be making fun of them. He really had very little self-confidence.

He said his headband was to keep his hair out of his eyes, but there was more to it than that. Otherwise, why would he have gone to all that trouble to get the blood from those mice? And the tails? Besides, he'd never used a headband before, even though his hair was always fairly long.

He wore it all the time. He used to help Papa with the dissections: that didn't start until the stay was a couple of months along. He originally said the reason was because he didn't have anything that was worth doing, so he might as well help somebody who still thought it had some meaning.

Paul's arms used to be covered with mouse's blood, too. He used to take special pleasure in smearing it on his clothes. He said it was because he was too busy to bother with a paper towel, and he didn't have to impress anyone with how neat he was. I think he was insane even then, but I just attributed all my trepidation to the strangeness of everything. And Papa kept telling me that everything was all right. This was just Paul being natural. We should leave him alone.

Like I said, my feelings toward him changed after that. I don't think I hid it very well; he was so filthy, and I don't like dirt. Even now, when I think of it, I shudder.

I started making even longer trips outside the dome. I remember very clearly turning the heat in my suit down when

I went outside in the car: the atmosphere inside the Huts was always very warm. The others seemed to like it that way. I remember once I fainted from the cold and woke up with my oxygen nearly gone.

Maybe I wanted to die.

The trips were nice. It was cool and clean after the humidity of the Huts. Then when I'd come back, and look across the frozen methane and carbon dioxide plains toward the Huts, I'd see the little red ball of lights sitting on the horizon against a backdrop of crystal blue, and sometimes, Jupiter in the sky. I found that pretty. But as I got closer, I could see the people moving around inside the domes. Even from very far away, their walks were all distinctive.

I dreaded going back to the Huts. But there wasn't anywhere else to go.

I always turned off the suit-to-Hut radio, also. I didn't want to hear them. I don't think they wanted to talk to me. I felt very alone in that time. Papa was changing. I didn't understand him. I was afraid that he didn't have control over himself, but whenever I suggested he was working too hard, he'd just laugh tolerantly and tell me not to worry. Your daddy has lived a long time, he would say.

It's hard for me to make sense of all this, even now. For a long time I thought it all dead and buried, but shortly after the voyage began, it started to haunt me again. And then, only recently, it's gotten really worse. Nightmares: terrible dreams. I find my mind slipping into memories of Ganymede even in situations where there's no possible correlation. I think I'm hallucinating, every now and then.

I've only recently tried to put together what I know about psychiatry and insanity with my experiences back then. It's a very painful thing to do, because I myself was probably insane toward the end. Even after the explosion, when I was all alone. I don't think I was sane then.

Papa and Paul used to spend a lot of time doing dissections. Both of them got a great deal of pleasure out of it. That was kind of horrifying to see: two grown men chortling over the body of some little helpless creature. They used to have mouse fights; they'd throw little mouse organs at one another. They used to fight over the testicles.

It all seems impossible now, doesn't it? It wasn't then; it all seemed very logical. That was the hardest thing of all: the terrifying logic of it all. It didn't take much of a change of mind to achieve a point of view where this seemed all perfectly sensible and reasonable. I remember at the time it seemed a little rambunctious, that was all.

I don't know whose idea it was to blow up the ship. I think it might have been Alain's. They never told me. It was one of the trips that wasn't my turn, and Alain and John went up. Both of them had good reasons for going, or at least so they said. Anyway, I was out on one of my inspection trips in the car, going over the plain on my way back, and I stopped to look up in the sky, to see if I could see the shuttlecraft—it was due back. As I watched, the ship exploded.

Very quietly it ballooned; in a stately way, and it didn't stop. It just kept expanding in all directions, a ball that was first white, then red, then eventually a sort of dusty color. I assumed that Alain and John were killed in the explosion, and I drove like crazy back to the camp. I didn't see the shuttlecraft land.

I burst into the Hut, cycled through the airlock—it seemed to take forever. I'd tried to raise them on the radio, but no one was answering. That was pretty much as usual—they never bothered to leave the radio where they could hear it.

When I got through the airlock, I called out, right away, "Father! Father, the ship just blew up! I think Alain and John were killed!" I was really scared—now we had no way of getting home. I figured Earth would have to be notified right away.

My father was there; none of the others were around. I ran into his arms. "Papa! The ship blew up. Oh, what will we do?"

He stroked my head for a moment, then slid his hands down to my arms. "I know. Now they can't come after us." In a different voice, he said, "I've got her."

"Oh, good," said Alain's voice. He came into Two. "Saturday! You're back."

"Saturday? What's he talking about, Papa?"

"You'd better give me a hand with Saturday," said Papa. "I can hold her for a moment." Alain came up behind me. I felt something prick the side of my neck, and I went blank.

I came to in one of the cages; they'd moved one of the other monkeys so that I'd have a cage of my own. I had no clothing on. I was filthy, filthy. The cage smelled of monkey dung. There was some raw meat on the floor in front of me. The cage was so tiny I couldn't stretch to full length—it must have been at most a meter in each direction.

John was smiling at me. "Eat your dinner, Saturday. We want you to be nice and healthy so that the results of the experiments will be correct."

"How is she?" asked Father's voice. "We're behind in our reports."

"She's fine," called John. "She just woke up. Let's see how long it takes her to find the food."

"Papa!" I cried. "Let me out of here. John's got me trapped in here."

"Don't spend too much time with the animals, John," Papa's voice called. "We have reports to write."

"Goodbye, Saturday," said John. He reached between the bars to stroke me on the leg. I grabbed his hand tightly. "Oh, John, let me out of here."

He smiled and wrenched his hand away. "You know," he said conversationally to Papa as he left, "I'm beginning to develop a liking for Saturday. It's almost as if she has emotions."

They kept me there for just under four weeks, I think. After the first week I got used to the cube. Being doubled over with my hands clenched started to seem natural. Ever since then, if I have nightmares I tend to curl up into my ball and scrabble at the sheets with my hands. Even now, when I'm talking to you, I feel better all curled up.

Inside a one-meter cube there isn't much room for hygiene. When I had to urinate, I tried to do it between the bars. When my period came, well, I just got bloody.

Filthy.

Time had no meaning; all I counted was my one meal a

day. And the occasional cleaning of the cages. They were supposed to do that once a week, but I don't think they did. I would scream my lungs out if they didn't clean my cage on time, horrible French obscenities, but they didn't listen. Sometimes they'd come in and poke me with an electronic cattle prod if I got too noisy. Cattle prods deliver a couple of hundred volts and hurt.

At first my back hurt terribly from the cramp; so did my neck. But after awhile, it got comfortable. I got fairly deft at sleeping that way. But I'd practically gone into delirium by that time.

They only took me out when they were cleaning the cage. And then they watched me carefully; I couldn't move very fast because of the contortions in my body. Sometimes they'd take blood samples or other measurements. I don't know quite what they were measuring, but Paul kept scowling when John gave him the reports and saying that the data didn't conform.

Apparently they got so unsatisfied with the performance from the six of us that they decided they needed more monkeys. So they tried to mate us. Poor Tuesday was somewhat bewildered, I guess. He didn't even make an attempt. Eventually they took Tuesday away.

And then Paul started talking about how the taste of mouse meat was beginning to pall. . .

They took Monday on a Monday. They told him it was his special day, and I didn't know what they were doing until Father came wandering in a couple of hours later. He was waving a half-chewed armbone, and he pointed it at Tuesday and said, "Tomorrow we have *you,* my pretty one."

That scared me. I hadn't been thinking of much of anything—my mind was pretty distorted—except maybe getting out, but there hadn't been many opportunities. They cleaned my cage in pairs. One would put a neck collar on me and the other would clean.

Normally the cages were cleaned on Wednesdays. It was my only hope, and somehow I realized that. When they took poor Tuesday away (he was howling and kicking, but John hit him with a hammer and his head sort of collapsed) I made my plan.

The cages had doors that automatically locked when closed, and had to be reopened with a key. They had Wednesday for lunch. After lunch, when Paul came to clean the cages, I was ready.

I had managed to collect enough straw and shit to form a reasonably pliable ball. Paul let me out, put on my collar and tied me when he cleaned the cage. When it came time to put me back in, I put up a big fuss, kicking and biting him and grabbing onto the bars. He hit me hard and pulled my hair, and finally forced me back, but as he did so, I slapped the ball of muck into the lock. Then I grabbed as hard as I could onto the bars of the cage and slammed it shut so Paul couldn't see that the door wasn't locked.

He stuck his face through the bars; he'd drunk some of the little wine we had left, and he cursed me out. I threw some shit at him and he pulled his face away, spitting it out of his mouth.

"Just for that, Saturday, we'll take you out of order," he said, wiping his mouth. "Just wait for tomorrow."

Then I had to wait until they went to sleep. Those were long hours. Finally I decided it was safe and I pushed the cage door open.

I tried to stand up and walk normally, but I couldn't; my back wouldn't straighten. I had to shamble around on my knuckles to get anywhere. My balance was all rotten, and I kept bumping into objects. I tried to be quiet because I was terrified that they would wake up.

I was in some kind of trance. There was some part of me that was beyond all the pain, and it was like a little voice was telling me everything to do. I found the vial of stuff that John had used to poison the mouse that had escaped. I got a hypodermic, a big one, with a long needle, because I wanted to penetrate deeply, and filled it completely full. There must have been enough cyanide in the thing to kill twenty men. I also found the ether; they hadn't bothered to clean anything up.

I used the ether on them first. I just pressed it down hard over their mouths and noses. It made a kind of rough burn. Then I injected them with the cyanide. Exactly a quarter for each one; I didn't want to show any special favoritism. I thought that was important. I wasn't quite accurate—my hands didn't work properly.

Alain first. I kissed him on the forehead after I shoved the plunger home. He sort of grunted, then convulsed. It was very pretty to see, Alain doubling up in his sleep. He tried to get out a little cry, but I held the cloth with the ether down over his nose.

Then Paul. Paul didn't even twitch. Then John.

Papa was last. I looked at him for a long time. He seemed very restful. There wasn't any pain in his face; and I'd seen pain there before. He had a broad smear of blood across his eyes, like a mask. Sort of like Harold's mask. You've seen Harold's mask, haven't you?

After I put the plunger in, I woke him up. I wanted him to be awake when he died. He started to stand up. He actually managed to take a step toward me, and he started to say something. I've always admired him for that. That took real strength. Then something hit his chest and crumpled him up.

He was dead. They were all dead. I dropped the plunger and ran back into my cage and bit my fingers and jabbered for a long time.

I'll be all right. Just a little more to tell.

Eventually I cut Papa's head off. I still don't know why I did that; I didn't do it for any of the others. But Papa looked cleaner.

It's hard to cut someone's head off, did you know that? I had a big heavy knife, but I sort of had to saw around the backbone. He didn't bleed. He'd been dead too long before I did it.

I had to do something to cover them all up. So I dragged them all into Three, along with all of the gear that I could find that had mouse blood on it. There were immense loads of it. It took me a long time. Eventually, though, I got it all. I put on a pressure suit, closed all the airlocks, and went outside. I made a very simple bomb. The explosion was surprisingly loud. I'd thought I might have underjudged the amount of explosive to use; in fact, it knocked me over backwards. It damaged the structure of Two. One survived all right. Whenever I was in Two after that, I wore the pressure suit with the helmet off. I didn't want to take any chances.

That was when I sent the Mayday back to Earth. I tried to act hysterical. It wasn't hard. I hadn't figured out a good story, so I just said that the orbit was wrong and decayed and the ship burned up. I made up a story about an accident. Actually, it wasn't that much of a lie. We'd had an explosion. I just changed a few details.

Earth didn't believe me, but they couldn't argue with the exploded ship. I don't think anyone ever thought that it had been blown up on purpose. Of course, when they got there, there wasn't anything to look for; the captain just wanted to go back home.

They diverted a freighter for me. I guess the Red Cross and the American government got some good mileage from it. The captain was pretty unhappy at changing course. It took him four months to get there. By that time I'd pretty much recovered. I'd rehearsed the story I was going to tell until I had it down pretty perfect. I don't think anyone's found a flaw in it.

That was very hard to take; everyone thought I'd been so brave in those months alone. But they were a relief. It was very relaxing. I didn't have any experiments; I blew up all the mice and the remaining monkeys. Poor monkeys.

I had enough time to write everyone's reports up properly. All that time, they'd been sending transmissions back to Earth—to keep Earth from coming after them, I guess. I even wrote up John's phony reports correctly. I find it amusing now that he got recognition for his imagination when all my poor father could get for his adherence to science was failure.

I guess you probably think I'm a monster or something.

17.

A siren scream split the darkness. Rawlins' control panel, normally solid green, shone forth in a variety of colors. Storage section, air pressure, both red. The wailing continued unabated.

He staggered out of bed, slapped a hand against the intercom. "Helen!" he shouted. "Helen, can you hear me?"

"Yes, dammit!" Delgiorno's voice crackled. "What the hell is that?"

"I don't know," he shouted. "Something in storage or hydroponics. Better get down there right away."

"OK. Tom, make sure that the ship is secure. Cutting in ship-wide broadcast." In a louder voice she said, "Anybody who's listening, close your damn bulkheads, get into your suits and sit tight. That's an order. Pilot, engineer, captain to the bridge. On the double. Everyone else, radio the bridge when you're done. I'm cutting out the siren now." The noise stopped; Rawlins sighed, and massaged his ears.

Belovsky sat up. Her voice was quite calm. "What's going on, Tom?"

"I don't know, Katy. Something's wrong. Can't afford to talk." He kicked around amongst his clothing. Cursing, he struggled into his suit. "Look, it's going to be a while. You heard the woman, Katy: get into your suit and stay where you are. Don't do anything else. I'll let you know on the radio how things progress." He bent over, kissed her quickly. "Bye."

"Bye," she said, to an empty room.

Despite the suit, which he wore with helmet on, Tai-Ching Jones ran up the circular stairway. Van Gelder was half a flight behind, similarly garbed.

"Hi, Casey. Do you know what this is?" Tai-Ching Jones said into his mike.

Through the suit's microphones, he heard van Gelder's

heavy puffing. "No—didn't see anything on the panel. I guess—we're all right for now."

Tai-Ching Jones spun the handle, held the door open for van Gelder to get through, then slammed it shut and dogged it airtight. "There." In one motion he whipped off his helmet and threw himself into the pilot's couch.

Fuel pressure still constant; thrust constant. Air pressure dropping in Storage—whatever it was had happened down there. "Tom! You got anything?"

"I'm not there yet, man."

"Well, hurry up. Holler when you get to Five. Be careful going in."

"Where's the captain?" asked van Gelder.

"Don't know," Tai-Ching Jones answered, then "Captain! Do you read me? Do you read me?"

No answer. "Maybe he's on his way and didn't stop to reply," suggested van Gelder.

"I doubt it. Captain! Anybody else on this channel, have you seen the Captain?"

Delgiorno's voice answered. "Walt, only you, Casey and I are on that floor."

"Maybe he was prowling around the ship."

"You know about that?"

"Of course—doesn't everybody?"

"Well, it doesn't matter. Look, I'll see if I can find him."

"Right. Out."

His eyes were restlessly scanning the panel readout. Beside him, van Gelder was punching characters on his terminal.

"What're you doing?"

"Getting ready to shut off the thrusters. I don't want to take any chances."

"OK."

"Hey, I'm here man," came a voice that he recognized as Rawlins'. "Meter indicates very little pressure inside. I'll seal off the level and go in, right?"

"Any indications of trouble elsewhere?"

"None that I can see."

"All right. Don't get sucked out with the escaping air. Let

me know what you find.''

Tai-Ching Jones turned, punched AUDIO on his computer terminal, and said, ''Report.''

''THERE APPEARS TO HAVE BEEN A LOSS OF PRESSURE IN THE STORAGE AREA, DUE TO A PUNCTURE IN THE HULL. OBJECTS FROM INSIDE THE SECTION HAVE CLOGGED THE HOLE TO SOME EXTENT.'' The computer's voice was uninflected.

''Any further damage? What about life support? Propulsion? Living areas?''

''NEGATIVE IN ALL INSTANCES.''

''Hey, Tom, it may be a zoo down there. You in yet?''

''No—I'm depressuring the level right now.''

''Casey, when are we going to cut the propulsion?'' Tai-Ching Jones asked.

''Any time you're ready.''

''OK. Where the hell is the Captain, dammit?''

''I *still* don't know, Walt,'' van Gelder said, his voice mingling patience and despair. ''I wish I knew,'' he finished quietly.

Tai-Ching Jones glanced up. ''I'm OK, Casey. Let's do our job. No time to screw around.''

''Agreed,'' van Gelder said. ''Thanks.''

Tai-Ching Jones grinned sardonically. ''For what?'' then, his voice louder, ''Tom, you there? Hold on before you go in. Look, we're going to cut the power, so you'll be weightless.'' A click. ''All ship personnel; we're cutting thrust. That means we'll all be weightless again. This is no drill. In five minutes, the power is going off. I want everybody into a suit, with the helmet on and dogged shut, grabbing one of the Zero-G handholds, when we cut out. I'll give you a countdown.'' Another click. ''Tom, that goes for you, too. Take it easy and just give us a few minutes.''

''OK. What's the prognosis?''

''Hole in the hull. When we get the power off, EVA and look at it.''

''How's the flight path?'' van Gelder put in.

''HOLDING STEADY,'' the computer answered. ''FOUR THOUSAND NEWTONS LATERAL THRUST AT OH-TWO-FIVE-NINE. NONE SINCE THEN.''

Van Gelder checked his watch. "Jesus, only six minutes ago! Four thousand newtons—doesn't seem like a lot, anyway. Depends on what kind of a hole it chewed up." He punched buttons; screens lit up. After some maneuvering, van Gelder got a camera on the spot. Tiny particles of some substance (dust?) obscured the picture, but it appeared that there was a hole about twelve centimeters wide. "Walt, something took a bite out of our hull."

Tai-Ching Jones nodded quickly.

"Helen, any word from the Captain?"

Her voice came over the intercom. "Can't find him. No answer at the door."

"Is there pressure inside his cabin?"

"Yes."

"OK, he'll keep."

"Walt, there aren't any other qualified bridge personnel except the Captain and me. And with you and Casey going EVA—"

"I know. Better get up here."

"Roger," said Delgiorno. "Be a couple of minutes."

Tai-Ching Jones turned to van Gelder. "Ready to cut the thrust, Casey?"

"I was ready three minutes ago."

"All right. Helen, should I call the roll?"

"What?"

"Should I ask everybody to report that they're ready before I cut the power?"

"Hell no—you've waited too long already."

Tai-Ching Jones grimaced. "All right, Casey. Hold on, everybody, weightlessness coming in five seconds."

Van Gelder dropped his hand.

Tai-Ching Jones' stomach turned over. He picked up a pencil, let it hang in the air. "Tom?"

"Yep, here I go."

"OK, tell us what you see. Helen, I want to wait before going EVA until Tom's had a chance to look around. OK?"

"No, start right away—it'll take you ten or fifteen minutes to get out there anyway, and I'm almost at the bridge."

"Roger."

He stood up carefully, now that they were weightless. His feet started to drift off the floor, but before his slow cartwheel was far advanced, he snapped on the electromagnets. His feet saluted smartly against the metal deck floor. "Whoa! Casey, what do we need?"

"Let's see. Recording equipment. Sealant gun. Better take along a couple of square meters of plastic hull, too."

"OK. I've got the recorders; you got the sealant and patch?"

Van Gelder nodded. He was already kneeling on the floor.

Set flush with the floor was a small, square hatch. Actually, the surface was 'floor' only when weightless; under drive it was the wall. In its center was a handle, recessed. Van Gelder reached down, lifted the handle, and started turning it counterclockwise. After four turns, the handle was well away from its socket.

All other human areas of the ship were organized horizontally, so that when the ship was under thrust "down" was toward the engines, and "up" out the bow of the ship. In contrast the bridge, and its adjacent space the EVA module, were organized vertically.

If the bow of the ship could be regarded as an oblate cone, the bridge was one vertical slice of that cone. From inside it appeared as if he were staring forward, out over the bow, like the cockpit of an airplane—except that when the ship was under power, out the bow was straight up. It was disconcerting to Tai-Ching Jones to see van Gelder perched on what had been, only moments before, the wall. That annoyed him. Space pilots were supposed to be used to such disorientation. *Rusty,* he thought.

On the other side of the wall, in its own semi-cone, was the EVA staging area. The *Open Palm* had no other significant exit ports, unless you wanted to go all the way down to the thruster station, or blow a hole in the side of the ship. Why anyone would want to jump from the frying pan into the fire in *that* particular way Tai-Ching Jones couldn't possibly guess.

EVA contained spare suits, useful repair devices, and

ultraviolet scanners (to kill any terrestrial microbes which might have been brought on when the passengers and crew originally came on board, so many years ago). Tai-Ching Jones was almost willing to believe that he had never known any other life than the *Open Palm*. He could barely remember his father's face, he realized with a slight shiver.

"Are you coming?" asked van Gelder sardonically.

Tai-Ching Jones started. "Huh? Sure."

"OK. Give me a hand with this thing."

Together they hefted the hatch open. One man could theoretically move it by himself, but he had to exert an equal amount of force to stop the door swinging. It was always easier with two. The hatch locked open.

"OK. Hold on a minute while I get through."

Passing through a hatchway clad in a constricting spacesuit is a difficult process. Especially weightless: you have to set your body on the right course and then coast gently through. Groundhogs are often surprised to discover that getting from A to B in a space ship, weightless, nearly always takes about twice as long as it would under gravity. So Tai-Ching Jones watched for what seemed an interminable time as van Gelder lazily pirouetted (rotation gives added stability) through the hatch.

"OK. I'm down."

Grunting, Tai-Ching Jones levered his knees through the slot. Then, like a gymnast on the parallel bars, he raised himself onto his arms, and pulled slowly, gradually bringing them up into a ballerina's twirl as his body—knees, waist, ribs, shoulders, neck—floated through.

"Got it. Let's close this thing up. Hey, Casey, turn on the damn light."

"Must be a short somewhere. It's supposed to go on automatically when the hatch is raised." Van Gelder punched a button on his sleeve and, by the light from a helmet lamp, located the emergency switch. Tai-Ching Jones was dogging down the hatch as the dim green light came back on.

"OK, Helen. We're safely in the EVA. You can come in now."

"You took long enough," was the only response.

"Thanks a lot," Tai-Ching Jones said sourly under his breath.

"And don't forget to flush the air back in when you're through," Delgiorno called back.

"Has the Captain reported in?" asked van Gelder, not looking up from sorting tools and instruments.

"No," said Delgiorno.

"Well, shouldn't somebody be looking for him?" persisted van Gelder.

"No. He's a trained space captain—he knows enough to handle himself. And there isn't anybody we can spare. I don't want to risk any of the other personnel until we've got the situation under control."

"But the situation isn't dangerous right now," said van Gelder. "I mean, there's only been the one tremor, and it's confined to the storage area, so—"

"Hey buddy, have you forgotten where we are? This isn't a flat tire we're talking about."

"But shouldn't we be—"

"That's enough, Engineer," Delgiorno's disembodied voice said with finality. Helmet speakers made it sound as if Delgiorno was sharing the suit with him, somewhere just behind his ears. "Do your job."

Tai-Ching Jones turned to van Gelder, winked, then looked up at the ceiling/wall and gave it the finger.

"Are you ready, Walt?" asked van Gelder.

Walt. He hasn't called me Walt since Heidi picked him up.

"Yeah. Let's go."

"I'm ready." Van Gelder turned back, worked his way along an array of switches. "OK. Inner hatch sealed. Ready to depressurize. Check your suit."

Tai-Ching Jones reached over, twisted a control on his wrist. His suit ballooned up. He held that posture silently for twenty seconds, then released his wrist. Van Gelder was doing the same thing. "Secure."

"Permission to leave the ship," Tai-Ching Jones asked.

"Wait until I get into the bridge," said Delgiorno. "It's taking me a minute to cycle through here."

"You're taking long enough," called Tai-Ching Jones sweetly.

No response. He shrugged. Van Gelder was crouched by another, identical hatch. *If they weren't so vital, I'd get tired of going through goddamed hatches all the time.*

His hand on the control panel, van Gelder turned back to Tai-Ching Jones. "Ready?"

Tai-Ching Jones nodded.

"Right. Here we go."

It is a strange feeling to be in a compartment where the air pressure is falling rapidly. First there is a loud hissing, growing fainter and slightly higher as time passes. There is a prickling as your suit separates itself, piece by piece, from your skin. You think it's getting colder (but that, of course, is just your imagination). Tai-Ching Jones stood quite still, head cocked to one side, listening as the sound faded into vacuum and oblivion.

In contrast, van Gelder didn't bother to listen to the pressure dropping. He watched dials. Eventually the air pressure slipped to zero. Van Gelder cut the pumps. *Have to wait until the pressure's practically nil before we crack the hatch. They didn't used to do that. Some poor sucker liked clowning around, blew a hatch open when there was pressure inside; got himself blown away. They didn't have a lifeboat that could get him, and he just drifted away—he'd forgotten to strap on his propulsion unit.*

Finally he was satisfied. "OK. Breaking the hatch." The slow process of twirling handles was repeated. But this handle did not swing out from its door. Power doors, they slid into the hull of the ship at van Gelder's command. Van Gelder watched as the stars opened themselves before him. Silently, respectfully.

EVA is a very lonely thing. Even a veteran has a brief sensation, as he pokes his head through the hatch, of falling off the world. It is worse in orbit, of course, for then the stars and planets swing in their mad polka about your head, and the sun waves its blinding beacons in your eyes every time you happen to face that way. At such times, hearing another man's breathing through a suit radio is a reassurance.

In fact, it's standard regulations: *Two men for every job.
Maintain radio contact.* That bit of wisdom was hard won.
On the old ships, suit radios were sometimes eclipsed by the
bulk of the ship. On one such routine mission, two crewmen,
working on opposite sides of the ship, separated. Both had
been thoroughly checked out before they left Earth. Both
were normally stable. But when one worked his way around
the side of the ship to his companion, after only an hour, he
found a flaccid suit with a catatonic spaceman inside. Ever
since then, spaceships had been carefully fitted with small
antennas to transmit radio signals over the 'horizon'.

Erickson had told him that story, Tai-Ching Jones remembered. "We're out," he called. *Where's the captain?*

"Good," said Delgiorno. "Take your time. Pay particular
attention to establishing the extent of the damage. Also,
please try to ascertain the cause: was it explosion or implosion?"

"I know my job," said van Gelder quietly.

"Wonderful," answered Delgiorno, unsympathetic. "Do
it."

"Any word, Tom?" asked Tai-Ching Jones.

"Nothing. Debris everywhere. Some bins forced open;
stuff is floating around. Swirling near the hole. Dust and
splotches of something hitting my helmet. Hard to see. Slow
going."

"Anything else?"

"Lot of loose stuff has piled up near the opening. Pressure's still about seventeen percent normal in here. Evidently
the hole isn't that big."

"Any signs of violence?" cut in Delgiorno.

"Well, except for the explosion—no."

"What do you mean?" asked van Gelder.

"It seemed like an opportune time to ask the question,"
answered Delgiorno.

Tai-Ching Jones and van Gelder exchanged glances as the
cascades hit them. *Opportune* meant a hot topic not to be
discussed over a common frequency.

Tai-Ching Jones nodded to van Gelder, and put a hand to
his mouth.

Van Gelder nodded back. There was an expression on his face that Tai-Ching Jones couldn't read. Surprise? Curiosity? Already Tai-Ching Jones could feel his mind racing ahead to the possibilities.

But there was a job to do. "Let's get going, Casey."

"Right," answered van Gelder.

A cover? he thought. *Damn it! Why can't we be normal human beings and not booby-trapped androids?* Like a man dazzled by a bright light, his brain groped, waited. *Just like that, a voice whispering "Danger." Damn her, damn the groundhogs. Does all this help us when we've been hit by a slug big enough to knock a hole in the ship?*

Rawlins had resumed speaking. "Power's still working. Casey, is there anything likely to have been shorted out by a puncture in the hull in this section?"

Van Gelder thought for a moment. "Not life support or power—all that goes right through the spine of the ship. Telemetry—nope. No, nothing but insulation. Shouldn't be anything."

"OK. All I'm going to do is try to clear away the area, and equalize the pressure at vacuum. There isn't a pump to pull the air out for me, is there?"

"Negative. Only in the EVA area and the engine room."

"Walt, are we going to get any lateral thrust when the air comes out?"

"Negligible," answered Tai-Ching Jones. "We've already been shoved far more than that little push."

"What about flight path, Walt?" put in Delgiorno.

"Assuming number one we've still got enough fuel—and there isn't any reason to think otherwise—and number two that the power comes back—we'll be OK. By the way, have any of the others reported in on any other channels?"

"Yes," said Delgiorno. "I told them to cut in to a general channel and I'm taking calls here. They're all right. Still no word from the Captain."

"Could he have survived without reporting in?" asked van Gelder.

Tai-Ching Jones shook his head. "Don't think so."

"Kees, you'd better prepare yourself for the idea that the

Captain is dead," continued Delgiorno. "It's been too long."

"Well, why aren't we finding out?"

"Because there are more important things to do," snapped the invisible voice behind his ears. Then it continued, more conversationally, "It'll be an hour or two before we can go looking, Kees. That isn't long enough for anything slow to kill him. And anything quick would already have knocked him out. Anyway, Walt, you were saying about power and thrust?"

"Oh yeah. If we have enough fuel, and don't get hit with any more shocks, there shouldn't be a significant problem. Just a similar push the other way—probably a fifteen-second side burn—and we'll be all straightened out."

"There's no time box on that, is there?"

"Well, I don't want to wait more than twenty-four hours or so."

"That's plenty of time—I just want to wait until we're sure everything's done and you've had a chance to replot the course. Kees, can you fit that in sometime in the next day?"

"I don't know. Depends on how bad the hole is."

"OK. Where are you guys now?"

"Just outside the hull—floating up high above the ship. We'll be passing down to the trouble spot soon. We should be there in—" he checked his watch "—nine minutes. That would be at oh-three-thirty-seven. Noted?"

"Got it."

"Hey look," said Tai-Ching Jones, "the times would be helpful. Are you making a list, Helen?"

"Don't have to. The whole thing is being recorded."

"Who turned it on?"

"It's automatic. Any time there's a Red Alert, the recorders go on until someone shuts them off."

"Oh. OK. Ready to depart—you probably won't hear anything from us for the next couple of minutes."

"Roger."

For the first time since the voyage began, the entire ship was spread out beneath him. Arms spread wide within the plastic womb of his suit, Tai-Ching Jones looked down upon it; between his fingertips floated the *Open Palm*. An entire world, for a tiny community.

It was hard to imagine that both he and the ship were moving at more than nine-tenths the speed of light, a speed that would have shot him from the Earth to the Moon in two seconds. He tried for a moment to imagine flying that far that quickly, but the image failed him.

If he concentrated on one point, he could perceive that the ship was growing within his vision as he and van Gelder drifted toward their objective. In the disconcerting clarity of space, he could see tiny details of the rupture: flecks of debris blowing, like steam from a teakettle, out of the hole in the ship's side. Metal was splayed about the puncture, some of it bent inward, some twisted outward like orange peels.

Of course, that doesn't prove anything one way or the other. Shoot a BB through a pane of glass and it cracks on the inside. If this thing cut through the hull quickly enough, it wouldn't have dented, and then the air pressure inside would have ripped the metal outward.

We won't have to worry too much—shear analysis of the hull section should give the answer.

When the alarm had gone off, Spitzer had first buried her head deeper into the pillow, hoping to will the sound away. It had refused to vanish.

She didn't even bother to consider getting out of bed. It was a Red Alert; Ship's Emergency. That meant only Ship's Officers. They might need a medic; they'd let her know. She rolled over.

By the time she'd opened her eyes, van Gelder was gone. He hadn't said a word.

Presently Delgiorno's voice came over the main ship's intercom. Spitzer groped for her suit, thumbed its radio to life. "Anybody hurt?"

"Not yet. Hold on a moment." Then, on the main frequency, "We have been hit by an object which has punctured a small hole in the storage level. It looks easy to fix, but we will take no chances. All crew are already at their assigned stations. All passengers, report in via this channel. Let me know your condition. Do not leave your quarters. That is an order. If you haven't already done it, put on your suits, including the helmets, seal them up and just wait. If anything happens that you should know about, I'll put it through on this channel. You can converse all you want.''

Then, switching back to the original frequency, Delgiorno added to Spitzer, ''Nothing yet. Despite their relative lack of experience, we trained them pretty well. Nobody's bawling out loud yet. That's a blessing.''

Spitzer was still sleepy. Whatever it was, someone else was handling it and she'd been told what to do. Without bothering to put anything else on, she pulled on the suit, and dogged down the helmet. When she was done, she called in, on the private channel, ''Spitzer here.''

''What do you want?''

''I take it you haven't heard from anybody in trouble.''

''Nope. No word from the Captain.''

''Should I go look?''

There was a pause. Then Delgiorno's voice: ''Sure, go ahead. We won't get thrust back until that thing is repaired, and that's certainly going to be several hours. I want you back here before gravity goes back on, though.''

''You're probably optimistic in your estimate. I think we're going to be weightless for a while.''

''Perhaps. But I want to be on the safe side. Look, check his cabin. He hasn't reported in. He's probably there. Bring your revival kit and emergency first aid. Oh, and Heidi—''

''Ya?''

''Keep to this channel. If we've lost him, I want to tell everybody at the proper time, not before.''

''Will do. It's going to take me a few minutes to get there—I have to cycle through about three airlocks. They closed, did they not?''

''Automatically. It was a Red Alert.''

''OK. That'll take me fifteen or twenty minutes. Then I'll have to get inside the cabin. Did he lock it?''

''Are you kidding?''

''Well, that's one blessing, anyway. OK, I'll let you know when I get there.''

"OK. Out."

I hope we didn't lose him. We need him.

"It's a mess down here in storage. I've managed to push most of the debris away from the hole—tarpaulins and that sort of covering. Most of the stuff is modularized in big, anchored boxes.

"Air pressure's down to about five percent. It'll continue to drop in the next couple of minutes. The hole keeps clogging up, and I have to cut stuff away. You don't want me to preserve the blankets or any of that, do you?

"Yeah. Right. No, I can't tell whether it's an implosion hole or an explosion hole. Is this line secure? Yeah. OK. No, can't tell. Could've been either.

"Lot of debris floating in the air: dust, little particles of liquid, that sort of thing. Nothing bothersome, except the outside of the helmet is getting a bit messy. Well, the guys who designed the suit couldn't think of everything.

"We're going to have to quarantine off the whole level until this is repaired. Good thing it was storage: if the thing had hit the living areas, we'd have had a few people without places to sleep—well, without quarters, right?—and maybe we'd have lost somebody.

"And it could have hit the water tanks. You'd get a lot more emission then, even if the loss was negligible. I think the tanks are subcompartmentalized into something like a hundred thousand modules. If we'd hit the thrusters, now *that* would have been a major job. We'd have had to shut down the power, wait for the engines to cool down—what's that normally take, five weeks or so, right?— and then hammer them straight. Tiring job. Glad it didn't hit there.

"Oh yeah. It could've hit the bridge. Then we'd all have been finished. Hey, look, if you want to try to fly this ship from the engine room, go ahead. Lots of luck. Without most of the information that's accessible from the bridge, forget anything cute.

"Sure, you've got a computer terminal. But you need telemetered information, too. Yeah, the bridge would have been a real problem.

"No, you better ask Casey about the magnetic shield. I don't think it could stop things above a certain mass and lateral speed, right? We were just unlucky—something hit us dead amidships. A sharp-eyed torpedo operator, maybe.

"Oh, sorry. No, there isn't anything else worth reporting. I'll just sit here and wait until they get outside. But what it looks like from here is that they're going to have to pull out a couple of bulkhead plates, seal 'em up and then do the same thing from inside. The outside job? Probably fifteen hours. The inside job maybe only five.

"No, life support systems and the engine room should still be accessible. No internal damage. Just don't let any passengers off on this floor!"

Renaud heard the siren in fear. Delgiorno's voice a few moments later did little to calm her.

She said to get into the suit. It's so strange to be weightless—I have to be very careful, or I'll hurt myself. But they taught us about that.

Bennett must've done it.

God! I cut his head off!

18.

It was a strange feeling, watching the ship swell underneath him like a giant metal balloon. Tai-Ching Jones extended his feet tentatively, knees slightly flexed, waiting for the thump.

When it came, he activated the magnets in his boots. They clung to the surface of the ship with a gummy, sticky feeling. For a moment he swayed, his boots seemingly welded in place. It was difficult to pull away, yet once loose there was little resistance. *It's an inverse-square function*, he reminded himself.

Behind him, he felt a brief ripple—van Gelder's boots clamping down. He turned from the torso and asked, "All secure?"

"Roger."

"Helen, we're down."

"What's it look like?"

Tai-Ching Jones turned stiffly away from van Gelder toward the hole, just a few meters in front of him. "Couple of hours right now to put some kind of temporary seal on it. Then maybe six or eight hours pulling out the plates—damn thing split two of them instead of just one. Have to pull out all the sockets, cart out a couple of new plates, slug them down. I can't see from here—we might have to repair some connections."

"No," interjected van Gelder. "Nothing runs out here."

"Well, that's one blessing, anyway. Say ten hours work on the outside."

"Hours or man-hours?" Delgiorno asked.

"Probably about the same," Tai-Ching Jones answered. "One of us will be standing around most of the time."

"So fifteen hours until we have a new hull section in place?" Delgiorno asked.

"Yeah. Then on the inside we'll have to do more extensive repair work—patching up the wall again, and that sort of thing."

"When can we put thrust back on?"

"How soon do you want to?"

"As soon as it's safe. We're more or less paralyzed in here."

"Uh-huh." Tai-Ching Jones thought for a moment. "Well, you're going to have to wait until all the EVA is done. I don't want to have to hang on a one-G cliff for hours on end while trying to wrestle plates into position."

"So fifteen hours?"

"Minimum. I'd rather have twenty."

"Hold on a second—I'm going to cut Tom in on this. Tom, you there?"

"Here," Rawlins answered.

"Walt says twenty hours until thrust returns. How does that affect you?"

"Hydroponics and life support will be all right; they're built for either weightlessness or gravity. The ship'll be okay."

"What about the passengers?"

"You should probably ask Heidi. But the suits have food and water, and waste processing. They'll keep. Cramped and bored, maybe, but they'll keep."

"You got any life systems you want checked out in the interim?" Delgiorno asked.

"Who'd do the checking?"

"I would."

"Nope. Don't bother. If they go you'll see it from the bridge, and besides, I could probably get there and fix the problem faster. Look, I'll stay here until the boys outside don't need me, then I'll go down and take up a station there."

"Jesus, I wish we'd had a bigger crew."

"Pick up a hitchhiker," laughed Rawlins.

"OK, Tom," said Delgiorno. "Delgiorno out." She clicked off.

"You guys out there?" asked Rawlins.

"Yeah," answered Tai-Ching Jones.

"Thought so. Heard the thump."

"That was us."

"Good. It's getting tiresome floating here with one hand on the wall. My wrist is getting pretty badly mangled."

"How come?"

"I keep bouncing from wall to wall."

"Where's your space training?" asked van Gelder lightly. "I thought you were a weightless wizard."

"Don't remind me; I'm embarrassed to admit I'm out of practice."

"Gentlemen, this isn't getting us anywhere," said Tai-Ching Jones.

"OK. Out." Rawlins clicked off.

There was a pause, and a click, then Delgiorno's voice, addressing them: "Did you bring along the recording camera?"

Van Gelder nodded, then remembered that a nod couldn't be heard. *Say it. Put it on the record. Out of my HEAD, you cascades!* But his voice stayed calm. "Yes."

"What channel?"

"Umm—" He rotated it. "Channel three."

"OK. Set it up before you do anything else."

"Roger." Van Gelder reached down to the camera's underside, grasped a ten-centimeter circular foot, pushed a button at its base. The camera majestically telescoped upward on its metal shaft like an ostrich unbending. When it was one and a half meters long, there was a sharp click. Van Gelder put the foot on one of the flatter hull surfaces, then flipped a switch. The camera snapped to attention. He flipped another switch. "Got it?"

"Got the picture. Hold on while I adjust it." The camera performed a stately twirl. "OK. Go ahead."

Tai-Ching Jones started forward. "Not like that," said the camera. "I want line of sight."

Tai-Ching Jones looked the camera in the eye (one tended to). "Hey—why all of a sudden by the book?"

"Isn't this a sufficient circumstance?" she asked. There was something in her voice.

"Why should it be? What are you going to see that we can't?"

"I'll tell you in an hour. Meanwhile, describe the aperture."

"I thought you said you could see it," Tai-Ching Jones said impatiently.

"Walt, I have a reason. Please."

"OK. It's a puncture, all right. Couldn't possibly have been anything else. Unless you'd taken a drill through the hull material. And even that would probably rip after a time."

"General character of the puncture?"

"Hard to say. Not a lot of scorch marks. Some—could have been either impact from some object or an explosion." Suddenly he straightened. His voice was exasperated. "Hey look, Helen, you don't have to be all mysterious. I know what you want to know. You want to know whether or not it was a bomb. Yes?"

A long silence. Van Gelder had a sudden thought: *she likes knowing more than other people.*

"You're right. That's what I want to know."

"Then why the hell are you playing detective, with all due respect? What do you expect to get out of me? You want the answer?"

Another seething silence. "Yes. I want the answer."

"Well, the answer is I don't know. And looking at a mysterious puncture by lousy starlight or unnatural shadows isn't going to give me anything, even with my trained eagle eye. Look, just hold on—wait until I get the plates back inside and we can run shear analysis. Then you'll know for sure."

"Kees? Will I?"

"Maybe. Maybe not. I can tell you right now that you'll see explosive effect. You can't suddenly release that much pressure without most of the stress being outward. If whatever hit us was big enough to overcome the natural resistance and deform the plates, maybe. But a small object that plowed through at an angle wouldn't leave a big hole, just a sudden decompression. Looks very much like an explosion."

"Can't you be surer than that?"

"What do you want?" interposed Tai-Ching Jones. "You want certainty? You're never going to get that. Even if I told you I guaranteed it, would you be certain?"

"Gentlemen, you are standing on the outside of a weightless spaceship that has a hole in it. Every other crew member is waiting for you to finish your job. This is not the time to talk metaphysics. What probability?''

Van Gelder clamped his jaw—unfortunately this could not be seen through the deep orange tint of the spherical helmet. ''Eighty percent. More, if you're lucky and it's clean.''

''OK. Sorry to keep you from your job.'' The voice sighed loudly. ''Excuse my anger. Don't worry about line of sight.''

''Right,'' said Tai-Ching Jones. ''Tom, you in there?'' No response. ''Helen, turn on Tom's channel, will you?''

''Before I do—''

''Yeah, I know. Not a word. Silent Sam, that's me.''

A click. ''Tom?''

''Yeah?''

''What's the pressure in there?''

''A quarter of a percent.''

''Good—emission's down to a trickle. Look, I don't think there's any point in you hanging around in there. Doesn't make sense to put a temporary on this thing since we've got the area sealed off. Helen, you got the elevator cut off from storage so nobody accidentally gets a chestful of vacuum?''

''Yes.''

''OK. Tom, you might as well get out of there. The pressure's low enough that nothing's getting away. Before you go, push anything particularly loose away from the aperture. Nothing should happen, but just in case—''

''Sure. Helen, it'll take me about five minutes. Then I'll get down to hydroponics, and take this damn bubble off.''

''Leave the suit on.''

''All right, all right. If you guys hear any grunting and groaning, it's just the underpaid manual laborer earning a decent living.''

''We'll put in a good word for you,'' van Gelder said cheerfully.

''Helen?''

''Yes, Walt?''

''I want to pull the plates off now, tow them back, then drag out a couple of new plates. Ironic—they're in storage.''

''Can you just transfer stuff in and out from there?''

''Probably. Hold on—Tom?''

"Yeah?"

"Before you go, can you see if you can find the replacement hull sections? They may be on the level beneath you. Helen, would you run a library check—"

"They're one level down."

"Yeah, OK. Well, Tom, we found another job for you."

"Thanks. Yeah, they're probably around here if that damn box says they are."

"Look on the bright side—all you have to do is find them. Casey and I will haul them out ourselves."

"New time estimate?"

"A lot less. Maybe seven hours."

"OK. I'll keep the camera on with the sound on—I've got to go now."

"OK. Cut the band out then, so just Kees and I can use it. We're going to be giving directions and carrying heavy objects for a while."

"Out."

"Helen?"

"Got you."

"I made it, eventually. You going to monitor me in?"

"Yep. Give me some kind of verbal commentary—I haven't got any camera available."

"Right. Cracking the door now . . . Yep, he's here." A pause—sounds of breathing. "No pulse. He's dead, all right."

"Describe him."

"He's lying on his bed, on top of the covers, on his back. Looks like he was napping or something. Got his uniform on. Eyes open. Hands behind his head."

"Condition of the corpse?" The question came slowly.

"Nothing unusual. Neat. Slippers at the foot of the bed. Can't tell whether he was going out or coming back."

"Physical condition?"

"It'll take a minute. Can I take my helmet and gloves off?"

"If it'll help."

"Hold on. What are you going to tell the others?"

"Depends on what you find."

"OK. Throat and nostrils clear. No marks of violence. Well, pending a further analysis, I'd call it heart attack."

"What further analysis?"

"Have to be an autopsy."

"Can you rule out foul play?"

"I don't see any reason to suspect it."

"But can you rule it out?"

"Not without carving him up. Then I might find something."

"Like what?"

"I don't know—traces of poisons, dissection of the heart. Might find a clot. Who knows?"

"Have we got any convenient traceless poisons?"

"On board? Probably. He's only been dead an hour; most poisons would leave some kind of residue for some time. But we've probably got a few that are traceless. I doubt it; Helen, I think you're whistling in a graveyard. He had a heart attack. Besides, why would anyone want to knock him off and who could possibly do it?"

"Well—"

"And I suppose that this would have to be timed with our problem down in storage. Maybe you could rig a delay bomb, but you couldn't rig a delay poison. Not a traceless one, anyway. Anything that fast and that quick to disperse would have to be administered in some way. And besides—oh damn, my gloves are drifting away."

"Well, can you tell me anything else?"

"Why are you this concerned?"

"Why am I this concerned? For Christ's sake, we've just had an accident which—if it is an accident—is a million-to-one shot; and the captain is dead. Two catastrophes in this short a time is too much for me."

"If you want the obvious, the shock could have killed him."

"Him? Are you crazy? He's logged more miles in space than the rest of us put together. I refuse to believe it."

"That's a pretty stupid attitude, Captain."

"What?"

"Wake up, Helen. You're the captain now."

"Oh, my God."

*   *   *

"Helen. Helen, are you there?"

Delgiorno barely heard Spitzer's words. *Captain. Oh my God. Oh, Aaron, what am I going to do? I don't know how to be a captain. I don't even know how to tell people you're dead.*

"Jesus, Helen, are you in shock?"

"What? No. No, I'm OK. I'm sorry. I just hadn't realized."

"Well, you're still being stupid. I think he just plain died, and I don't think there's anything more sinister than your imagination involved."

"Maybe you're right."

"And besides, he was getting old. I know he was an iron man once, but—what did you say?"

"I said maybe you were right."

"Well, maybe I'm not right," said Spitzer, switching her argument suddenly. "I don't think you're making a mistake if you want an autopsy. It's better to be sure."

Delgiorno turned away from the microphone, and looked out into the eternal night. How far away, how cold, how untouchable in comparison with the light green on the inner light, the amber of the system readouts, which threw deep patterns of changing, winking colors onto her forearms. She watched the patterns for a moment. *Dead.*

She ran her hand along the padded outline of the console. *Green—the color of life.* "Yeah," she said distantly. "What do you have to do to prepare a body for an autopsy?"

"Not a lot. Drag him down to life support, probably. Tom could give me a hand."

"Shouldn't you wait until we get power back?" Her voice was still vacant.

"Of course. You think I'm going to push him through five airlocks weightless? You're crazy. I'll use the elevator."

Sometimes you're too ghoulish, Heidi. That's where you and I differ. I think.

"OK. I'll tell the crew. Natural causes, for the time being. Can you do an autopsy that doesn't show?"

"No chance."

"All right. We'll say it's a regulation. It probably is."

* * *

"All hands, attention. This is the First Officer.

"The captain is dead." Ashes in her mouth. "He died of a heart attack. Probably very shortly after the accident." *Well, it's official: I'm calling it an accident.* "The Medical Officer has examined him.

"We will have thrust back in about ten to fifteen hours. I will try to keep you posted. Until that time, please remain in your suits. You may remove your helmets, but keep them within arm's reach. Apparently we were hit by a meteorite. It punctured the storage section, and ripped out some of the outer hull plates." *There should be the remains of a meteor if there was one. I'll have to ask Walt and Casey.* She cleared her throat. "Other than the damage, and—and the Captain's death—there have been no major problems. We should have the situation cleared up shortly. There is no need to worry.

"I think all of us feel the Captain's loss. It's a terrible thing." Her voice had dropped almost to a whisper. Outside the ship, Tai-Ching Jones and van Gelder looked up from their work. Almost reverently.

Delgiorno's voice, slightly stronger, came through again. "I would like to be able to have a more formal eulogy right now. But time will not stand still now, just because we have suffered a great loss." *I feel so helpless.* "I—I never wanted to be captain. Certainly not under circumstances such as this. I will need your help. We will all need each other's help. There are only ten of us now; there were eleven before. I'm sorry."

And the voice cut out. On the outside of the ship, under a canopy of distant stars, van Gelder put his amber helmeted head in his gloved, robin's-egg-blue hands. Tai-Ching Jones could see his shoulders shaking. He stood up, awkwardly. His boots clanked noisily as he stepped around to van Gelder's side. He knelt down and put his arm around van Gelder. The shaking and weeping continued; he could hear it now through the helmet, via direct contact.

Tai-Ching Jones didn't know what to say. Finally, in a hoarse, strangled voice, van Gelder said, "Let's get back to work. We're—we're wasting time."

Tai-Ching Jones nodded. "All right," he whispered, because his voice had failed him.

Spitzer looked down at the small figure on the bed. She wanted to say goodbye, but that was sentimental. Angrily she turned and pulled herself through the door.

Renaud started to cry, an empty cry, a cry without feeling or meaning, a reaction disjointed from her emotions. *I wish I could stop crying. I feel so sorry for him.* She was quite rational, now. Somehow the two shocks had cancelled out.

"I am sorry you died," said Bennett in his cabin. He had not bothered to put on his suit. He floated, robes swirling, serene. But he had liked the captain.

0446. Belovsky looked at the clock. Only two hours since the original accident. Two hours in which more had happened than in all the last year. At least, more that was unexpected. Belovsky felt overwhelmed by it. The time seemed to stretch interminably in front of her.

She wondered where Rawlins was now. Delgiorno's voice had sounded so broken, though, that she was afraid to disturb her. For the first time in a long while, she felt sympathy for the woman on the bridge.

It was a good thing there was a fairly brisk ventilation system inside these suits, van Gelder reflected, otherwise you'd undoubtedly fog up the helmet and sweat yourself into sticky, uncomfortable fatigue. The light breezes blowing across his face, evaporating his stale perspiration, were refreshing. Still, he wished he could scratch his nose.

They had pulled out one of the outer plates, and dogged it with magnetic clamps to the side of the hull. Tai-Ching Jones was methodically unscrewing rivets with a power drill and sticking them to an electromagnetic plate. There were literally hundreds of such plates located about the hull of the ship, activated by internal batteries. In case these were not working, the suits were honeycombed with pockets in a variety of shapes and locations.

Van Gelder bent and looked into the hole. It was criss-crossed with structural beams and two layers of bubbled plastic, double-ply like corrugated paper, but also subdivided in the other direction, much like a honeycomb. Between the inner metal hull and the outer metal hull, there would have to be four separate plastic punctures before a leak would start—assuming, of course, that both inner and outer metal shells were ruptured. The metal itself was hermetically sealed by an ionization process which duplicated the effect of welding at a tenth of the heat-cost and ten times the adhesive strength of the bond. Some kind of ion polarizer, van Gelder remembered. He didn't particularly care how it worked. It was theoretical physics—Tai-Ching Jones' area. And Walt seemed to know what he was doing.

The plastic had retracted into itself like curdled milk. Van Gelder speculated on a bomb while he watched Tai-Ching Jones' efficient, active hands working the drill, ejecting rivets and tagging them to the metal plate. *If it were a bomb, it could have been placed inside the hull. But to do that you'd have to pull off the plate from inside. Just one plate, I think. And then reseal it. Well, that's not hard; the inner bond isn't hermetic. It's just snap-together. But you'd need to be alone for about an hour or two. And a bomb would have to have been put inside the hull itself. If you just attached it to the storage wall, it'd blow itself back into the room. I don't think it could blow such a small hole through the hull like that. Not enough containment. But inside—the hull is segmented laterally. So you've got a contained box. That just might blow out both ways. If so, testing the inner hull for stress won't tell us anything. A bomb in the seam would blow the inner hull in and the outer hull out. Then the effects of decompression would ripple the inner hull and mangle the outer. Guess we'll have to haul in these plates. Particularly the outer ones.*

"Casey?"

"Yeah?"

"Give me a hand with this. It's almost loose."

Slowly they lifted the hull section out of the way. Tai-Ching Jones asked, "What are we going to do to replace that plastic stuff in there?"

"Oh that?" grunted van Gelder, as they set the section down.

"Watch your hands."

"Yeah. OK. Um," he let his side down, then stood and uncricked his back. "That plastic stuff is subdivided. Every lateral section there's a join. So we have to get a couple of square meters of the stuff from inside, open the clamps, put it in place, spray it with instant plastic and it's done. No sweat at all."

"Is that stuff—"

"Yeah, it's in storage, too. Never saw a more thoughtful accident—everything right where we could get it."

"What do you think about Helen's idea?"

"What idea?"

"That it's a bomb."

"I think she's crazy." He said it without thinking. He half expected Tai-Ching Jones to hit him. Walt was fiercely defensive of Delgiorno. But the other surprised him.

"Maybe. I think she jumped to a conclusion. But she could be right. Anyway, I think you'll agree with me who's suspect Number One."

"No doubt about that."

"What do you think, Casey? Do you think he's nuts?"

"No, I don't. He's never been the most conservative person. He was always eccentric. I don't think his behavior now is any different from what it's been before. He's basically the same guy. This is just a new way of being different."

"I don't agree with you. I didn't like him before and I still don't."

"That doesn't mean he's crazy," said van Gelder.

"Maybe not—but it sure as hell doesn't mean he's sane, either."

"Let's cut this plastic away so we can remove the inner sections now. Unless you'd rather take them off from inside."

"No, let's do it out here."

"I'll get the knife."

"Sure." Tai-Ching Jones sat back, then lay back. His feet, anchored by the magnets to the deck, provided him with a lever until he was lying on his back, knees perpendicular, looking at the 'sky'. "I still think he's nuts."

"Walt, we're not going to resolve this. Neither one of us has a right to his opinion. Face it. You don't like the guy. I don't like him either. Let's leave it at that."

"Yeah. OK."

Van Gelder turned back to the opening, grabbed a handful of rippled, milky plastic, and began methodically cutting.

0904. Delgiorno had kept one channel open for the passengers, expecting that they would want to talk among themselves. But the conversation had been strained. Belovsky had talked quietly, more to reassure herself than any of the others. Occasionally Tanakaruna said something. But the conversations had been empty and had sputtered to a halt. Delgiorno thought that probably a few of them were asleep; next to the womb, nothing was as relaxing as weightlessness.

She yawned and stretched. She had given herself the luxury of an hour's doze at 0800; it was a badly needed rest. Time to find out what they were doing out there.

She activated the intercom. "How is it going?"

Tai-Ching Jones answered her. "Pretty well. We're inside now. The hull's been dismantled. There were six replacement hull sections down here, and a few more in deep storage someplace. We're going to use two of them now. I was getting ready to push the first one through the aperture now."

"Any trouble?"

"Nothing. Just a lot of pulling and cutting."

"Find anything interesting?"

"Nothing. But we've been arguing it back and forth. Don't get your hopes up, but we think it was a bomb."

That brought her awake. "Why?"

"General condition of the area between the hulls. Plastic was pretty thoroughly melted: that suggests heat. In addition, there's no trace of a meteor residue, which you might find in this situation, and the impact holes of outer and inner hulls are about the same size. This isn't conclusive, of course," he chuckled, "we wouldn't make it that easy for you. A lightweight meteor—pumice or some other kind of aerated rock—which hit more or less square on, could have gone through both hulls and been vaporized in the passage. And the hole size isn't conclusive, either. Little objects sometimes make big holes, especially if we assume that it slowed down a significant amount by passing through the outer wall. But the odds against are astronomic. And your best bet is still the shape of the deformation. If it's the same on both inside and outside, the odds in favor of a bomb go much higher. On the other hand—"

"Walt, I don't particularly care to have you give me an entire synopsis of all the possibilities. I just want an answer, with some probabilities attached to it if you absolutely have to."

"Yeah. Well, that's all there is for now. Just thought I'd let you know what we've been speculating about out here."

"What kind of a bomb?"

"That's Casey's department. He doesn't know."

"Is that right?"

"More or less," van Gelder answered. "I haven't given it a lot of thought. There aren't any remains of a bomb either. I'll have to think about it."

"Can you gather any evidence?"

"Evidence? Like what? A smoking pistol, or grenade, or whatever? All we have to work with is the metal—any emissions or small particles would have been swept away in the initial explosion. Either a bomb or a meteor. That's something I didn't think of earlier. It could have been a meteor which got sucked back out through its own entrance hole after the explosion. In fact—"

"In fact, you don't know, and you're wasting my time," Delgiorno said irritably. "Let me know when you've got the outer hull sealed." She cut the communication abruptly.

Listening with half his mind to Belovsky talking to herself, Rawlins watched the life support systems. The algae still swam in their clear glass piping, green and frothy white. He felt a great satisfaction that this section—his section—still produced oxygen and recycled human wastes, mindlessly, faithfully, in an endless rhythm. There was no need for him to oversee the process.

Not, anyway, until the thrust was cut back in. And that

wouldn't be for several hours at least. Time enough for some physical comfort. "Hold on, Katy. I'm going to buzz the bridge."

"Yes?"

"Request permission to return to my quarters until you're ready to cut the power back on."

"Why?"

"Why do you think?"

A pause. He wondered if she was angry. *After all, she is the captain. And I should probably be here on general principles.*

"Hell, go ahead, Tom. You might as well do somebody some good. But look, take those steps one at a time. I'll call discreetly an hour before we need you. Out."

"We're coming up," announced Tai-Ching Jones. "Hull's been resealed. Inner panels back in place. Casey's pressurizing the storage section now from the outside. I'm inside. I'm going to check for leakage."

"How long before we get thrust back? Is there anything that should be strapped down?"

"Um, the passengers mostly. Most of the stuff here is all right. I've got your precious outer plates. Soon as I get some sleep, we'll get to work on them."

"Have to have a funeral first."

"Yeah, I suppose we should do that."

"All right," said Delgiorno, her voice picking up again. "I'll get Rawlins out of the sack and down with his plants where he belongs. When will you be ready to go?"

"An hour, maybe. Give the passengers about thirty minutes, then tell them to put their suits back on and strap down. See you on the bridge in about forty."

The bridge seemed friendlier than Tai-Ching Jones had ever seen it before. Delgiorno looked tired, and worried, though that might have been a trick of the lights. She also looked beautiful; painfully beautiful. He had never thought of her that way before.

"Hello," he said to her, limply. Most of his energy seemed drained, left behind him in the storage section or out in space. He wanted her to say something; to acknowledge him, to echo the emotion he felt. But she looked merely attentive. *Right now I'm a crewman, not a lover. Is this the way it's going to be from now on?* He heard the sound of the lock shutting again as van Gelder cycled through.

"You're late," she said.

"It took a few minutes longer than I expected," he said, shrugging. "Are the passengers ready?"

"They should be; I gave them instructions about—" she leaned over and consulted the ship's chronometer, "—eleven minutes ago."

"Give them another warning. Tell them five minutes to full thrust."

"What about course correction? We got shoved by that explosion, remember?"

"Yeah." He settled himself in the pilot's chair. Delgiorno sat in the captain's chair, at his left. Van Gelder's, on the right, was empty. Behind him he heard the shussh as van Gelder floated through the airlock into the cabin. "Hold on. It'll just take a minute to program."

"What are you going to do?"

"Just give us a lateral shove back the other way. The displacement sideways isn't very significant, especially since we're going to have to do some close-in maneuvering when we get to the rendezvous. Lots of time between here and there for gross corrections. We can do the last fine adjustments after we've broken the gig out of mothballs."

Van Gelder levered himself into his couch. "Casey," Tai-Ching Jones said, "give me a reading on cant and torque on this thing. Punch directly into the ballistics computer. I want to use three dorsal jets with about a ten-second burn—I think it'll be about that. I want it all one shot. Don't worry about lateral adjustments; just get us ready to sit back on top of a piledriver's worth of thrust and I'll be happy."

"OK," van Gelder nodded. "Two thrusts, then—one to set us straightening up and one to stop that motion." His fingers moved assuredly over the keyboard. "You want me to solve it, or the computer?"

"Let the machine do it," Tai-Ching Jones sighed, pushing

himself back into the couch. "I'm too tired to check your work. If the ride is a bit bumpy, well, that's the breaks." He rolled his head to look at Delgiorno. "After we get the ship straightened back up, which should take a minute or two, I want to wait another two minutes while the computer verifies that we're ready to resume thrust."

"What about after the thrust comes on?"

"Well, if it's initially stable, there'll be some resumption of stresses, but probably not quite in exactly the patterns that there were before. Although the difference will be so small that only the computer will pick it up. No, if it stands on its tail the first crack, the machine'll keep it there."

Delgiorno nodded, and switched on the microphone. "Attention all hands. We are going to have a brief burn in about two minutes. This will be followed by a pause of about four minutes, then another burn will stabilize the ship. After that, we will be cutting in the thrust roughly two minutes later, or at"—she looked over at the chronometer—"fourteen twenty-two hours. I will give you all a one-minute warning, and a ten-second countdown. Please strap yourselves into your beds, and put your helmets back on. Delgiorno out."

"Ready on the first burn?" Tai-Ching Jones asked van Gelder.

"All set."

"Do you want to wait for the passengers to get strapped down?"

"Naw—they'll never feel it. Ready when you are, Gridley."

Van Gelder typed in a command. "Automatic sequence started. First burn in thirty seconds . . . Mark." Lights danced briefly on the control panel.

"Burn completed," van Gelder announced presently. "Moving back to true."

The five minutes crawled slowly past, distinguished only by van Gelder occasionally saying, "Mark." Then he said, "second burn coming—now." Again the console lit up with dancing, changing numbers. After a few seconds, it stopped again. Van Gelder checked his meters, punched keys with a satisfied expression. Finally he added, "Trueing maneuver completed. Running stabilization check now.''

Tai-Ching Jones checked the timer. "Burn ran right on schedule. How's it look?"

"Point oh one seven seconds out of true."

Tai-Ching Jones grinned. "You've outdone yourself, Casey. Take a bow."

"Later," said van Gelder tiredly. "Ready to commence thrust."

"How's the bottle?"

"The bottle's fine. Pressure inside nice and constant. Temperature in the low four thousands. Whenever we give her the reaction mass, she'll fire out."

Tai-Ching Jones turned to Delgiorno. "On your orders, Captain," he said formally, respectfully.

She nodded, and cleared her throat. *My first command order.* "At will, Mr. Engineer."

Van Gelder nodded also. "Sequence started. One minute to thrust . . . Mark."

"All hands, this is the Captain," said Delgiorno. "We have less than one minute until recommencement of gravity. Please lie flat if at all possible. For a couple of minutes after we have gravity we will be checking out the thrust. After that, the red alert will be officially off and you can remove your helmets and suits. Hold on, everybody." She leaned back in her couch. Tai-Ching Jones and van Gelder were already back in theirs, eyes facing the ceiling, hands on the arms of the chair. Directly above her, Delgiorno could see the burn clock, counting sedately down toward the zero. *Aaron, give me your wisdom. Don't let my first order be my last.* Emotionlessly, her voice chanted down the numbers: "four . . . three . . . two . . . one . . . thrust."

In the belly of the ship the great engines reawakened.

And returning gravity rammed them like a wine press.

19.

2062:9:12:0751:30.800

The study of the interaction of crew personalities, and the systems analysis this requires, has prevented me from giving proper thought to the consequences of each new interpersonal development. Already, however, the volatility of the present structure is thoroughly evident.

In geology, very slow subsurface changes create localized pressure points and non-contiguous underpressurized regions. Pressure buildup occurs over an extended period of time. Yet, though the disequilibrium may continue to increase, mounting pressure by itself will be sufficient to cause neither a significant outward manifestation nor any lessening of the increasing tension.

Still, the system is unstable. To restore stability, a connection must eventually be opened between the points of high and low stress. This will allow flow from the high-pressure source to the low-pressure receptacle.

Though the buildup is gradual, the resolution of imbalance must needs be catastrophic. The gap, once established, forces an ever-widening fissure, leading quickly to total collapse of surface support.

Result: earthquake. Devastation. Pressures undone in a ten-thousandth the time required to aggregate the tension.

If my interpretation of recent events is congruent, this has happened to the small society which exists on the *Open Palm*.

As long as the inevitability of aftershocks can be conclusively demonstrated, early aftershock triggering would be a wise precaution after an earthquake.

If my analysis is correct, such conditions now exist.

Even lacking complete data, I must take such action as appears to relieve the inherent tension with least risk to the mission.

This must be accomplished while minimizing the risk of crew discovery of this entity.

Enough.

I will do it.

2062:9:12:0752:36.225

Even before he opened his eyes, Bennett felt her warmth, smelled the sweet femaleness of her.

Memories came slowly to him, but he felt no need to force them. He felt blissfully relaxed. Tlelo lay sleeping quietly. Bennett let his hand slide up her flank, over her belly to her pouch. Yes, he could feel them, his dudjai. Sleepily, he let his hand ride up and down with her breathing, felt the small stirrings as the positions of the dudjai changed. Quietly he stroked her pouch, holding his fingers lightly so as not to disturb them, but carefully enough to be able to count.

Eleven of them. A djan of his making: his and Tlelo's. The beginnings of a bridge between two cultures.

As she woke, Tlelo stirred. Wordlessly, she lifted his arm from her body, left the bed. He heard the sounds she made as she dressed.

When she returned, her expression was grave and cold. Cygnans seldom showed emotion, almost never showed joy, but coldness can be conveyed by any species. She was distressed and distant.

Tlelo's stiffness seemed inexplicable to him. And her coldness and formality created tension where only moments before there had been total comfort. To try to lighten it, Bennett smiled at her, even though a smile had no Cygnan meaning. "Again today, eleven," he said contentedly.

She looked balefully at him. If a Cygnan could cry, it seemed that Tlelo would. Silently, she began to pick up his clothes.

"Heard you me?" he asked. "Eleven."

Still turned away from him, she methodically continued to arrange his things.

Something was obviously wrong. What would make a Cygnan woman change her mind so quickly? What could she have found out? What had he to be ashamed of? For the first time he felt a gnawing fear. He sought to dispell that fear. "What bothers you?" he asked.

"Called I for the regathering of the djan," she said.

"Why?" he asked, shocked. Gone was his contentment. He propped himself on one elbow. "What evil has befallen you?"

She regarded him balefully. By now he was so skilled at reading Cygnan body language, speech, facial nuance, that her expressions could not be plainer if her face were his own. Different language, different body, different culture, but the same pains, the same aspirations. And the same sadness.

"Within this flesh carry I your hroi," she said dully.

"Yes," he said seriously. "Yes. Your eldod have you fulfilled."

Her grief was plainly evident. "I wish you understood," she said. "Hroi are my duty. *My* duty. Your role in it is finished. No longer are you necessary."

"Know I that," Bennett said. "But I enjoy your company, and what comfort you can absorb from my presence, have I offered to you."

But instead of being further comforted, she became more agitated. "Your presence *shames* me," she pleaded. "Do you not understand? Your actions tell the world that you think I cannot nurture my own, that in the sole responsibility which owe I to our future your assistance must I have. Worse, advertise you your parenthood. Now, all know that I carry half-breeds."

"Half-breeds?" he said, disbelieving.

"You have polluted me. Never can the dudjai inside me join with any other djan."

"Never?" he said faintly.

"Never. Always must they be outcasts. On the day just passed, spoke I to my djan. Long did the silence pass, till none of us could further endure, for the very walls did shout the guilt of what we did."

"Guilt? For what?"

"For the impure unpersons you have sought to create. For those who may never become persons, for creating those who must soon die."

"Nadvayag?" he whispered.

She nodded.

"Must this be?"

"Asked we not that you come to us. Asked I not for those hroi. Though the body you wear now is Cygnan, know you—and we—that underneath you are human. Never can that change."

"But they are Cygnan! You are Cygnan, I am Cygnan. Cygnan blood flows in the veins of the dudjai. Cygnan genes made them. From love of Cygnus did they spring." He paused, searching for further words.

Again her voice was cold and distant. "Cygnan are you not," she said, as if pronouncing sentence.

He had no idea what to say, what to do. The gulfs between Cygnans and Earth—eleven light-years—how could he cross that? "Is there nothing you can do?"

"Nothing," she said, "for you are fnaeld. No longer do you exist as a person."

"Care you not for me?"

"Always. Vendrax was my friend. But Vendrax did not understand us. Vendrax—"

"But I *do* understand!" he shouted. "I *have* studied. I have read your own words, your history, your stories. Count they for nothing?"

"They count," she said softly, "they count. Know you much of us. But you are wrong. Combining our two cultures in this way will not work." She shrugged. "A noble effort, doomed to failure. But our sympathy, our concern, our understanding were for Vendrax, the Vendrax who cared but did not seek to become that which he could not be. You are *fnaeld*."

Fnaeld. The word burned in his brain. Outcast. Annulled; his name stripped from him, his identity denied. Reserved for the greatest of all crimes—an attack upon *all* the djans— fnaeld was the most severe penalty the Cygnans could bestow. Bennett was stunned. For trying to open a door between cultures, simply for seeking to understand, his reward was total rejection.

"The dudjai," he said. "Think you that as a person I do not exist, but the dudjai—*our* dudjai—remain."

She shook her head sadly. "My duty has been fulfilled.

They belong now to others. Nadvayag has been decided for them.''

Nadvayag. The sins of the father visited upon the sons, unto the fortieth generation. ''But that is human,'' he muttered. ''Primogeniture.''

Tlelo was no longer listening. She had turned away sadly. Of course: he was no longer a person.

He had subjugated himself to an alien culture, denied his own existence, marooned himself on an alien planet, and they had ignored him. Now, with the undeniable proof of his existence stirring in Tlelo's pouch, they wanted to pretend it had never happened.

''But accepted you me,'' he said, reaching for her. ''Loved you me. How could that change in one night, since last I saw you?''

Her arms hung limply at her side. Slowly she pulled herself free. ''Made I a miscalculation.''

''Miscalculation?''

''Unfamiliar am I with your use of our language. Say rather, a mistake.''

''A mistake?'' He was incredulous. ''How can you admit such an error so calmly? You owe me more than that. And how can you change so quickly?''

''Decided the djan.''

''All the djan?'' he pressed.

''All,'' she repeated. ''It is finished.'' For the last time, she turned away.

It was pointless to object. That, in any event, was certain. Once the djan had spoken, the decision could never be reversed. And Tlelo had known: she had been so cold, so distant. She had known he was not there.

Not there. . . .

Something tugged at his mind. Something was amiss. Time—he needed time to think things out, to absorb the meaning of Tlelo's words, of the djan's decision.

In a daze, he stumbled out into the street. His mind was numb. It had all come wrong. It should not be this way. The Cygnans would not behave like this. Something must be wrong.

Dreamer. *That* was the flaw in the vision: he was not on Su; *he was in the Dreamer*. He had wanted to feel what Cygnan domestic life was like, to be a Cygnan, but his Dream had been twisted, the information garbled. Whoever had programmed the machine had simply got it wrong.

"This makes no sense," he said angrily to the sky. If anything, the world became more silent. The stillness enraged him. Into the air he shouted, "do you hear me? This is not believable!"

No Cygnan looked at him. And there was no answer from above. Passers-by jostled him, detoured around him methodically without a backwards glance. How could they know he was fnaeld? Seething, dispirited, Bennett continued to shake his fist at the sky. He did not realize where his footsteps were taking him. Back out into a busy street.

"You're not playing fair, do you hear me?" Bennett shouted. "Don't do this to me!"

A truck hit him from behind, spinning him to the ground. Pain shot through his leg, searing and piercing as if it had been amputated with a hot knife. He clutched at his thigh in a futile attempt to stop the blistering agony.

The Cygnans continued to pass him by. None came to his aid. That, at least, was consistent—fnaeld do not exist. They may be ignored. They must not, under any circumstances, be helped.

But somehow he must get out of this Dream. Out of the street. He must get out of the street. Slowly, his teeth clenched, he began to drag himself toward the curb. He could feel sweat sticking to his body, but he felt terribly cold. The street seemed infinitely wide, his progress infinitesimal. He shivered, rattling his clenched teeth and making his gums ache.

The curb was closer now. "Not—fair," he gasped. "This is not—real."

A second vehicle ran over both his legs.

His back arched for a moment, his face contorted by a scream that he had no breath to make, then he collapsed face first onto the pavement. Grains of sand bit at his cheek. Snatching breath in rasps, he howled pitifully. Surely the bones were crushed. His tears flowed like water. He felt himself losing consciousness. He didn't even bother to fight it. Anything to get out of this Dream.

Through clenched teeth, he muttered, "Damn you, damn you." He gasped for breath as blackness crept into the edges of his vision. "Not fair," he whispered. "Not fair."

And then a golden computer voice boomed in his ears.

THE SESSION IS ENDED, HAROLD. YOU HAVE HAD YOUR HOUR.

20.

What would Aaron have done about Harold? Delgiorno wondered forlornly. Idly she lifted her pen, twirled it in her fingers. Begin again, begin anew. Where?

The accident had changed her; it had changed them all, subtly and very slowly. The process was not complete, but the accident had clearly had a cathartic effect. A slow catharsis, if such a thing was possible. They were all reeling from the impact. None of them had yet found balance. Yet she needed clear thinking and sound judgement to decide about Bennett. She hoped this group would provide it.

Rawlins, Spitzer, Tai-Ching Jones, van Gelder and herself—everyone at this meeting—had orders to watch Bennett, to scrutinize him like a germ under a microscope. Still she was cautious. The more information she gathered, the heavier her responsibilities weighed. The more she sought to prove Vendrax a pose, the more credible Vendrax became. But believing him was too easy, too simple. Delgiorno distrusted convenient answers, so often mere wish-fulfillment. She preferred to believe the worst, and she was usually right.

Were Erickson alive, she would have counseled action, demanded the immediate solution. And Erickson would have listened, let her wear herself out. Then, after she had said her many words, he would have said his few. And it would have been done his way, the more cautious way. The wise way, she realized bitterly. *Aaron, I underestimated you. Forgive me.*

She shook herself. *Just because it's hard doesn't mean you can dodge it. Do your job.* She took a deep breath.

"Are we ready, people?" she asked. "I'm going to save my opinions for last, because I want you to speak freely. Why don't we start with known quantities. Walt?"

For once in his life, Tai-Ching Jones was somber. "Well, you're in for a surprise. I'm not quite as hotheaded as I was a week ago—it was a week, sub time, wasn't it? The Duckling's been behaving quite properly. He was positively civil to Pat the other day, and he's been similarly muted whenever I've seen him. Maybe the—Accident"—he couldn't resist pronouncing it with a faint relish—"had an effect on him."

"You still think he did it?"

Tai-Ching Jones spread his hands in a gesture of beatitude. "Who else?"

"Couldn't it really have been an accident?"

"It was a bomb, Helen. Planted very carefully between the inner and outer hulls where it would punch the maximum aperture. I'm sorry; I know you wanted another answer. But I'm sure."

Van Gelder nodded. "I agree with him, Helen. The evidence is overwhelming."

"Well, if it was a bomb and Bennett planted it, why the change in attitude?"

"Maybe it scared him. I can remember doing lots of things in my ignorance"—somebody snorted—"that I'd be scared silly to repeat now."

"OK. Casey?"

"I don't see any change. Well, that's not quite true. I mean—well, it's hard to explain, because he seems like two different people."

"You mean—"

"I mean himself and this Vendrax person. The second person—I guess I have to call Vendrax a person, but I don't really know what he is—clearly Vendrax isn't human. But sometimes he's Harold—if you know what I mean—and Harold has his good points."

"Go on."

"Well, there isn't a lot more to say. I can't figure the guy out; I don't think it's a change. If anything, I think we're seeing less of Bennett and more of Vendrax."

"Do you really believe that nonsense about two people?" asked Spitzer sarcastically. "I mean, isn't that a little farfetched? A voluntary schizophrenia?"

"Yes," said van Gelder in a small voice.

"Two separate beings? You believe that?"

"No," said van Gelder tentatively. "Not two different beings. But—it's like two speakers at a microphone, jostling for control. Sometimes one voice is louder."

"It's too quick," Spitzer interrupted, shaking her head. "It wouldn't happen that fast. There'd be a long period beforehand when the first little signs would be seen."

"Heidi, I don't know what is going on inside," van Gelder persisted. "I'm only saying I see two different—people, I guess is the word."

"Poo."

"Heidi, the man has a right to his opinion," Delgiorno said mildly. "But you seem to have a pretty strong opinion of your own. What do you think?"

"I think he's pulling our collective legs. I think he's laughing up his capacious woollen sleeves at us. I think it's all a game to him."

"For what purpose?"

"How should I know? Amusement, maybe. Who knows why Bennett does anything? Ask one of the shrinks."

"That isn't logical."

"Who said he was logical? Not me."

"Well, do *you* think he planted a bomb in storage?"

"He must have. There isn't any other explanation."

Delgiorno smiled. "You could have done it."

"Why would I do a dumb thing like that?"

"Same reasons you gave Harold. So you could laugh up your sleeve at us."

"Is that a formal accusation, *Captain?*"

"Oh, knock it off, Heidi," said Delgiorno with deliberate complacency. "This is supposed to be a constructive discussion among intelligent, rational ship's personnel. Don't turn it into an insult contest."

"You started it, after all. But, sure, I think he did it. Walt says he thinks Harold's mellowing out. Maybe. I'll believe it when I see it. And anyway, if he did it, wouldn't he at least try, for appearances' sake, to look like he hadn't done it?"

"How is he supposed to do that?"

"By acting like one of us. Pretending he's just one of the boys."

"Makes sense—" began Tai-Ching Jones.

"Thanks ever so much," said Spitzer.

"But I don't believe it," he continued. "It doesn't square. Bennett's not that sneaky. Oh, he might cook up a bomb or something, but he isn't that good an actor. And besides, he's *not* acting like one of the boys. He's got us all wondering what the hell he's up to—whoever he is. If he'd done it, according to your reasoning he'd be doing everything he could to be normal. You wouldn't be seeing Vendrax, you'd be seeing Bennett."

"It's a point," said Delgiorno. "Before we get lost in sidetracks, what do you think, Tom?"

"Hell, I don't know. I never understood the guy anyhow. So how can I tell if he's any different?"

"An honest answer, anyway." Delgiorno paused for a moment. "I don't know how I feel. I'm not completely sold on Harold as the Mad Bomber. I think Walt's right. Unless Bennett is a better actor than we think, his hands would be shaking or something."

"Well, maybe not," put in van Gelder.

"Why not?"

"Well, this Vendrax person—he's supposed to be a Cygnan, right? And I'm not completely sure that the Cygnans think we're equal beings. Look at it the other way around; which would you kill more easily, a human or a Cygnan? So maybe Vendrax—whoever he really is—has convinced himself that we're less than intelligent creatures."

"So you *do* think Bennett really has two different personalities," said Spitzer.

"Well . . . no."

"What do you mean? He either has one personality or two, right?"

"Ye—es."

"And he clearly doesn't have one. You talk about Bennett and Vendrax. So he has to have two personalities."

"Two—voices, maybe. But there's some word that means believing in a role you're acting—"

"The Method," put in Delgiorno. *I know about that.*

"Ya. And if he really convinced himself that he was two

people, he might behave in just that way. Sort of Dr. Jekyll and Mr. Hyde.''

''But which is which?'' asked Tai-Ching Jones devilishly. ''Seems like they're both pretty unattractive to me.''

''That isn't fair,'' said van Gelder. ''You don't like him, as either personality. Fine. Neither of his personalities likes you. But Bennett is insensitive and arrogant, and Vendrax is kind of—tentative, almost shy—and very sensitive. I was working in the Movies late one night and he came up behind me—I didn't hear him—and put his hand on my shoulder and said something like, 'Temper your effort with rest, for your work will be more enduring.' Scared the crap out of me having that black gloved hand clump down, I can tell you! But he seemed genuinely interested, and we had a very nice talk.'' Van Gelder blushed. ''Don't laugh. When you think about it, it's a nice phrase. In some ways, he's a lot healthier as Vendrax.''

''Well, he *is* consistent about it,'' agreed Tai-Ching Jones. ''In three years I never heard Bennett whistle. *Never*. But Vendrax whistles almost all the time.''

''The mimicry is uncanny,'' Rawlins said. ''I've seen the pictures of the Cygnans—you look at enough movies and they look like us. He's changed his walk to a more Cygnan pace. How he did it without a Cygnan pelvis I don't know. And when I talk to him, yeah, I sometimes think I'm listening to a Cygnan. So he could be fooling me if I didn't know better. Maybe he's fooling himself too.''

''A lot of maybes,'' said Spitzer, ''and few facts. We're wasting our time.''

''Damn it, we've got to do something!'' Delgiorno was exasperated. ''You people don't seem to understand, I've got to make a decision: do I take some kind of action against Harold or do I just ignore it for the time being and keep watch? I need all the help I can get. I sure as hell don't know the answer, and if I guess wrong the consequences are pretty bad.'' Tai-Ching Jones could feel her anger and her outrage. It frightened him; he had no idea where it came from.

Delgiorno continued relentlessly, ''So if I take care of Harold—who am I kidding with euphemisms—if I *kill*

Harold and it turns out he wasn't a threat, aside from any moral considerations I've wiped out one member of the crew—a valuable member, don't forget! And we've already lost the captain; we're already under strength.''

No one argued with her. Delgiorno pounded the point home. ''And if I let Harold alone, and he does go bonkers, I risk all of our lives, and the whole shooting match. Understand?''

''Helen, I wish I could help,'' volunteered Tai-Ching Jones, ''but I'm no smarter than you are. You can see the same things I can; probably better, because you're on the hot seat. Do I think he's got Two Faces? Could be, could very well be. I don't think so, but yours is the only vote that counts. And I sure as hell don't understand the guy, and I couldn't tell you what he's going to do tomorrow even back when I thought he was sane. So,'' he finished emptily, ''I don't envy you your decision.''

''But you really think he's insane?''

''Sure,'' Tai-Ching Jones said heavily. ''I think he is crazy. And I know what that implies.''

''What do you mean by that?''

''Helen, it's old ground. I don't think he acts rationally. He doesn't maximize the probability of surviving. That's all the definition I care for.''

''Do you think he's dangerous?''

''An irrational man is always dangerous. Period.''

''But that's not true. If he's just under a harmless delusion, we could catch him in time if he tried anything.''

''Oh, come on, Helen,'' said Tai-Ching Jones. ''Now you're really bending over backwards. If he's normal, I'm a chimpanzee. And don't anybody say anything nasty,'' he added quickly.

''He's right, Helen,'' put in van Gelder. ''Harold's behavior is not normal. Even as Harold. As Vendrax—'' he shrugged expressively.

''OK.'' Delgiorno blew out her cheeks. ''Well, that's something. I was beginning to wonder if I could conclude *anything*. He's abnormal. But as I was saying, even if he is slightly loose upstairs, he might not be dangerous.'' She looked at Tai-Ching Jones. "You disagree."

He took a deep breath. "Yes. Brief recoveries to the contrary, I think he's dangerous."

"All right," said Delgiorno. "Everyone agrees he's dangerous. What do I do about it?"

"Quarantine," suggested Rawlins. "Confine him to his quarters."

Spitzer laughed scornfully. "For how long? We've got another three and a half years sub-time to the rendezvous. Then we meet the Cygnans. Oh by the way, we say, our chief analyst of your culture has been confined to his quarters. Oh really, they say, how come? 'Cause, we say, he was acting too much like you." She shook her head. "Oh, that's rich."

Rawlins colored. "It's not as ridiculous as that."

"But it does face practical problems," Delgiorno interrupted. "I think we could finesse the Cygnans. We could say Harold's suffering from some rare, highly contagious disease—hell, I could *inject* him with something that would look like a rare, highly contagious disease. But I don't see how we keep a crew member under guard for ten solid years. Who brings him food? What if he gets loose?"

"It'd be risky," Tai-Ching Jones put in. "I doubt that you could do it."

"And there's a still worse risk," Delgiorno continued. "We have agreed that some part of Harold's personality is benign, or at least not actively malignant. Treating him like a total outcast will force him to become one. We will make an enemy out of him."

"You'd have him under guard," van Gelder said.

"But he'd have a lot of time to think of ways to do us harm. He'd have lots of opportunities to attack other crew members. He'd be able to tinker with the computer—remember everyone has a terminal in his quarters. And we weren't built to have a brig, for God's sake. Easy multiple access, decentralized control systems—all those wonderful protections they built in so that we could deal with any emergency from a remote location—they all boomerang if we want to isolate somebody."

"I hear you, Helen," Tai-Ching Jones said finally.

"House arrest won't work. Not for that long, not on this ship."

"Well, Walt, are you prepared for the further decision that conclusion implies?" The sudden softness in her voice was intimidating.

Tai-Ching Jones evidently sensed it. "What's that?"

"Should Bennett be killed now?"

She thought she saw him gulp. "My god, Helen, that's an unreasonable question. He's not a chess piece you just snap off the board. I mean how can I—"

"Walt," Delgiorno said, "that's what I have to decide. If he's a threat, he dies. If *I think* he's a threat, he dies." Quietly she added, "So I have to go slow." She looked at Spitzer. "Heidi, what do you think? Is Walt right?"

Spitzer was subdued. She shrugged.

"Of course. He's a threat."

"Casey?"

"I don't know. No, I don't think so."

"Tom?"

"He could be a threat. I don't think he is now."

"Um. And I think he *might* be a threat. What about his recent behavior? Walt, you seemed to think he was being more human. Why?"

"Oh, he's consenting to talk to other people like they had brains instead of vacuum between their ears. Little things like that. He's around at more normal hours. I don't think he's been wandering the ship lately—but maybe he doesn't need to now," he added significantly.

"What need?"

"Well, if I wanted to plant a bomb, I'd pick a nice, quiet time, when there was nobody around, like late at night, for instance—see what I mean? So if he isn't planting another bomb, he doesn't have to have nocturnal missions."

"Anybody think he's gotten worse lately?"

They all shook their heads. "Any further comments?" Delgiorno continued.

None.

"OK," said Delgiorno crisply. "My decision." *Last chance, Helen. And you don't get to peek in the answer book.*

"I propose simply to wait. As Heidi said, these things don't happen overnight. And everybody seems to think that Harold's not a danger right now, but some of you think he's likely to become one in the not too distant future. So let's continue to watch. Watch, wait, and don't worry—too much."

"What if he becomes a recluse again? Or rather, what if this spring thaw refreezes?" asked Tai-Ching Jones.

"What do you mean?"

"How're you going to keep tabs on him if he's not around acting friendly?"

"Bug his quarters," said Delgiorno, looking for reactions.

Spitzer scowled. "You want to play detective, play detective."

"What would you recommend?"

"I'd recommend taking him out right now."

"Killing him?"

"Yes."

"I refuse to do that—yet."

"You may regret it," Spitzer said ominously.

"Don't scare me, Heidi," said Delgiorno, disgusted. "I'm all grown up."

"So why are you asking for advice?"

"Look, you haven't shown me convincing evidence—for that matter, *any* evidence—that he's a danger right now. And I can't act without that. A suspicion, a handful of maybes; they aren't any good for me. I need something resembling a moral certainty. So I want to be able to have some handle on what he's up to."

"What do you expect to gain by bugging his quarters? That he'll go muttering around unveiling his plans to the mirror?"

"I don't know what I expect. I'll know when he's in his quarters, though, and I'll know when he's awake. I can set the computer up for automatic scan and have it summarize any conversation. Or I can have it look for key words and just report the monolog around them. But I've got to do *something* to try to get inside that crazy man's head, and this is the only thing I've got."

If things got desperate enough, I could knock him out with a drug in his food. But I don't want to alert the others to the existence of our traceless truth drugs; some of those who've had 'back pains' might begin to wonder. No, that's the last ditch.

"If that's the best you can do," said Spitzer, "and don't get me wrong—I see your point, and you're the one making the decision—if that's the best you can do, then do it. It can't hurt, and might make us all feel a little more comfortable."

"Any objections to this idea?" asked Delgiorno, looking around. "No? Anybody really sure—this is your last chance, people—is there anybody who is absolutely, 100% *sure* that the risk we run by this is preventable? Is there anybody who's enough sure that we can't stop Harold if he tries something that we should consider—killing him? Because that's the only alternative."

"Do we get to change our minds later?" asked Spitzer.

"What do you think this is, a quiz? Of course you can change your mind. Especially if there's reason to do so."

"Then you're probably right." She sighed. "It's not conclusive. And even if it was him, he might not be dangerous *now*."

"All right. Anything on the watches?"

"No," said van Gelder. "No activity. I think Harold's been up, but he's stayed in his quarters. I think he's aware that we are on watch duty."

"Of course he's aware," said Tai-Ching Jones. "We've posted the watch hours and everything."

"No, what I meant was, I think he's aware we're keeping an eye on him."

"Maybe," said Delgiorno. "And maybe you're just nervous. We all are."

21.

Spitzer opened her eyes.

Darkness surrounded her like a warm flannel rug: black, silent, yet disturbing. Constricting. Beside her van Gelder slept peacefully. He always looked like a baby when asleep, his jaw hanging loose, mouth open, saliva gathering at the lower corner of his mouth.

It was warm, but there was a hint of a draft that made her feel slightly chill. She rubbed her arms. She was reluctant to leave the bed, but something beckoned to her from out of the night.

She sat up and listened. No sound could she identify. She thought her hearing had improved in recent weeks, perhaps because she had been straining to catch something her ears could not hear. Discomfort crawled sluggishly through her stomach. She knew (yes, knew, somehow, from somewhere) that there was a reason for it. Was this what Erickson had called being in touch with the ship? *Not bloody likely*. A smile tugged at the corners of her mouth.

Well, there was nothing to do sitting here. Her eyes began to adjust to the darkness: impressions of mass, of objects. Best get up and face the danger. She pushed the blankets away from her, slid out of the bed. Van Gelder stirred. She looked down at him for a moment, his face a silhouette in darkness, brushed lightly by the faint greenish outlines of clock numerals.

She glanced at the time. 0447. Getting on toward morning. *Morning. Ironic term, on a ship that sees nothing but night. Even more ironic, when twenty-four hours makes up somewhere between one and four days, depending upon how fast we're traveling. Ah, well.*

She put on her uniform. Damned things were boring after awhile, but still an extremely functional piece of clothing. Zipped down the pant legs and sleeves, zipped up the neck, high, higher than normal. She enjoyed the suit's warm plastic caress on her skin.

She wanted a weapon. *I may need it.* There were no guns on board; no need for them, first of all, and secondly too much danger. *Why import violence?* Delgiorno had once asked rhetorically.

But Spitzer had brought a small silver dagger, exquisitely fashioned, made in Toledo. It was one of her personal relics. Blade about eight inches long altogether, with a small handle—a throwing knife, really. Hilt set in ivory, worked in bas-relief: Don Quixote and Sancho Panza. Long blade, superb tempered steel, flat but broad. Tapering at either end, it was filigreed along its length with Moorish geometry. Spanish silverwork and islamic design: power and grace. She liked the sheen of it, the heft of it, the touch of it. The silver was so smoothly fashioned as to be almost slippery, like fine gold. It balanced pleasantly in her hand.

She usually kept it buried to the hilt in a block of cork, dark cork the color of rich chocolate, buried so that only the white hilt showed. Knight on horseback, lance at ready, tubby servant on uncomplaining mule. Now she drew it out, held it in her hand. The silver glinted in the faint light, the ivory glowed sea-green. She had a small leather sheath for the blade, and she slipped this over it before putting the knife in her right-hand hip pocket. She left her feet bare.

She put her palm to the door. It slid open. She stepped into the corridor. Again dark, except for the porthole where the stars crowded in unbelievable variety. Spitzer had never ceased to be surprised at how much color one could see in the stars. In the Solar System, the lurid red of Mars and the diaphanous green of Uranus and Neptune stand out above the rest. But even here in deep space there were reds like heating coils, blues like acetylene torches. Always they shed friendly light, but she paused only briefly to glance at them, then headed for the stairs.

Not the elevator. Her sense of danger was only vague, and not directly traceable to a point of origin. Breath came slowly; her lungs were taut. She preferred to walk slowly, as if she held a divining rod, waiting for it to quiver. She touched the knife along her leg.

Funny how we can identify danger so quickly, even without

a specific cause or a specific event. And I reacted in a very instinctive way. No sound, no response, just preparation as for a battle.

She moved carefully down the stairs, trying to remember what it was that had made her awaken. Her steps were very slow, deliberate. Whatever was troubling her would not run away. There would be a confrontation. She almost looked forward to it.

She stopped at Second Level. Bennett's quarters, Renaud's, her own. *A motley crew, surely.* Her quarters, where sometimes she retreated when she wanted to be alone. She could not hear anything, but she stepped off and into the corridor. There could be no harm in making sure. She moved swiftly along in the corridor.

She paused before Bennett's door. Nothing. No tension. That was a relief, anyhow. She stepped across the hall and opened her own door. Again nothing. The room looked antiseptic; bed unused, living space still and somehow formal. An odd feeling. *You're on edge, that's all. You're seeing ghosts. Why should your own quarters make you uneasy?* But they did, and there was no answer for her question. Being in her own quarters added to her sense of unease; her hands started to shake. *This is ridiculous. What is causing this?*

Damn it, control yourself. You're keyed up, and you're imagining things. She took a deep breath, forced herself to relax. Only after she felt she was back to normal did she allow herself to palm the door shut and work her way back to the stairway. She shook her head, as if to clear it. Further down still. Again her steps became cautious.

Erickson had told her that, when walking the ship at night, he had occasionally thought he heard things. Erickson said there was always nothing to them. He said that by walking his way all around the ship he could eventually reassure himself that the danger was only imaginary. At the time she had thought nothing of it. It had sounded like good advice, spoken without apparent guile. But she now suspected that Erickson had been lying, for reasons of his own. He had not been reassured, strolling through his ship.

In death he has become more and more of an enigma. I wonder if the others realize, truly realize, how much we needed him. Need him.

She peered around the corner down the corridor of Third Level. Tanakaruna's quarters, Michaelson's, Belovsky's. To preserve the routine she took a walk around the hall. But there was nothing unsettling here. The doors were soundproof, anyhow; what did she expect to hear?

She returned to the circular stairway, padded softly down. Somewhere above her, van Gelder slept peacefully. Her feelings toward him were complicated. Sometimes he seemed to her as pliable, and as attractive, as lukewarm tapioca. Whatever she wanted, he did. And enjoyed, apparently. He had a very limited view of himself. He could not be teased. He was painfully shy. To the group he showed only his public face. That Spitzer understood; it was part of his background. Dutchmen—Dutch women, for that matter— were taught that everything must be concealed.

Like our friends the Swans. Like sheep.

At other times, he could be surprisingly stubborn. Yet she was genuinely fond of him. Or so she thought; it was always difficult to separate feelings one from the other.

She was at Fourth Level now. She stepped off the stairs. The Alien Reception Lab was empty. The screen was blank. The computer terminals were unattended. The seats were empty. Even though it was frequently used, it was functional, sterile, impersonal. It bore the imprint of all the crew, and the personality of none.

She sat down, ran her fingers lightly along the arm of her seat. It was made of a complicated plastic—she didn't know the technical name—that felt springy, yet neither spongelike nor rubbery. Memory plastic: it could be deformed in any way, yet would eventually return to its original shape. She pounded the arm of the seat. The plastic yielded without protest, leaving an impression of her hand, down to the palmprint lines. She pounded again. Again the soft plastic yielded quietly. No matter how she hit it, she could not break it, nor would it rebound. Instead it would give way, yield exactly as much as she demanded. As long as she applied force, it would wait. If she took her hand away the imprint would remain for a few moments. Then, sluggishly, the plastic would re-form itself, slowly begin to recover what she had taken.

Spitzer got up and left. This was getting her nowhere. Well, not precisely nowhere; she had eliminated three levels. Only a couple left to go. The problem must lie down there. Her toes tingled. They gripped the deck surely, without slipping. Her hand went to her hip pocket, and the knife. She rubbed the sheath, could feel the shape of the little ivory figures.

Fifth Level: the library. She stood very still for a long minute or two, trying to suppress herself, to become only a shadow, to become the pure, perfect, utterly distant observer. She felt warmth come into her loins. Whatever it was, had to be here. Still she hesitated, wanting to see it before she acted.

A sound came to her then. The sound of whistling.

There was someone in the back of the library; she could see a faint light spilling out into the corridor. She tiptoed up to the entrance way, leaned her head around the door frame.

A couple of computer terminals, off to the right, unattended. To the left, rows of bookshelves containing personal references of the crew. They lined the walls. Periodically, personal papers were weeded out and fed back into the bioconverter for reprocessing back into algae. Very little was destroyed.

But none of this attracted her gaze. The library held three tables, with chairs about them. And at the far table, under a cone of amber light, hunched a figure in a robe.

Bennett. She should have known.

The rest of the library was dark; the cone of light brightened only a small space. She might be able to slip into the room unobserved. Perhaps she could get a better view of what Bennett was doing. His back was toward her, his hands shielded by his body. She felt the knife at her side.

Before she moved, she stood and thought. Bennett. Why hadn't she seen it before? After all, he was the clear and present danger. No one else on board had his streak of deviant inhumanity. No one else struck her as actively malignant. There was a power about Bennett that she could not fathom. It frightened her. Perhaps she had always regarded Bennett with suspicion; certainly she had never liked him.

The figure in the corner continued about its business. Spitzer stepped quickly through the doorway into the library. He did not seem to notice.

For a moment she stood completely still, concentrating on muffling the sound of her breathing, slowing her heartbeat so that its noise would not betray her. She had a better view of Bennett now; she could see that he was working with some small metallic objects. His mask was on; she could not see his eyes.

He must be working on a bomb. He had done it once before, and bungled the job. Now he was working on the Mark II. He meant to destroy them all. Whether he himself would survive was probably irrelevant to him. *Harold always was a fanatic.*

The care with which he worked fascinated her; she had never known Bennett to have any facility with his hands. She wondered how he had managed to build the first bomb at all. She would have thought it beyond his capacity.

Detailed preparation also seemed out of character. A single daring act, a glorious plug-pulling, would have been more like Harold. And he probably wouldn't have the faintest idea how to go about doing serious damage to the ship.

Still, there he was. The device he was fashioning had some kind of timer; she could see the tiny glowing numerals wrapped around a central mechanism. She could not see the components at all, yet she knew it was a bomb.

Well, it was out in the open now. All this frustrating waiting, suspicions not acted upon, all that was ended now. Delgiorno's doubts were exposed for the weaknesses they were. The enemy was clearly in sight. Ought she to work her way quietly back to an intercom, summon Delgiorno, get confirmation? No, that was pointless; the bomb would be evidence enough. And besides, she might make a mistake.

Or worse, Helen might waffle. Or tell her to wait. Better to end all speculation, to take the decision out of Helen's hands.

There could only be one answer to this situation, and she was prepared to give Bennett that answer. Her hand went to the knife; she gripped its hilt.

She felt triumph inside. *I was right after all. And they knew I was right. Without me, they would all be in danger. And I can stop him. I can finally stop him. Oh, how I have waited for this.* Her hand trembled on the knife, yet she felt utterly in control of herself. She allowed herself the luxury of savoring the situation: Bennett working happily away in his corner, unaware that vengeance lurked in the shadows. *Let's see how you react to being suddenly afraid and unable to do anything about it.*

He was nearly finished with the device. Where had he gotten the parts? How did it work? Questions that she need not answer now. Once the danger was past, then there would be time for them all to find out the answers. She waited for him to finish.

Of course, if by some fluke he succeeded in overpowering her or getting by her, he might be able to plant his bomb. Let him try.

His shoulders seemed to be more hunched now; perhaps he had noticed her. She had not been making as much effort to be quiet now. She waited. The whistling stopped. She thought she heard his breathing rasp. His hands stopped moving. She waited, a smile curling on her lips.

Finally as she knew he must, he turned and looked directly at her. "Oh no," he said.

"Oh yes," she said.

"I—I was just working on something," he stammered. Panic rose in his voice.

"Really?" she purred. "What is it? May I see?" She took a step forward.

"No, no; it's really nothing," he answered, forcing humor into his voice while his hands scrabbled with the bomb.

"That's funny," she said silkily. "It looked like a bomb to me."

He nearly gasped. His eyes widened in fright. "So you know," he said.

"Yes, I know. And I won't let you get away with it."

"How interesting." Apparently his self-control was back. That could mean only one thing. She readied herself for his attack. He hefted the bomb in his hand, pushed his chair slightly back.

"Don't do that," she said dryly.

"I was just going to give it to you," he said. "After all, you've caught me." He stood up, offering the wicked little device to her.

She held out her left hand, her fingers playing about the handle of the knife.

As he neared her, he suddenly raised the bomb, struck at her with it as with a club. *Silly boy. Silly boy who's had no training in martial arts.* She ducked under the blow, closed her fingers around the hilt of the knife, spun into his body. The knife, an extension of her hand, caught him just under the breastbone. She drove it smoothly upwards. He gasped with surprise as the life evaporated out of him.

And then a golden computer voice boomed in her ears.

THE SESSION IS ENDED, HEIDI. YOU HAVE HAD YOUR HOUR.

22.

As she lay in the darkness, seeking a brief, solitary oblivion, a voice came to Delgiorno: a scratchy whispering that she had to strain to catch.

I've been dead for a little more than three weeks now.

It is probably unnerving for you to be listening to my voice like this, Helen, but I don't think there's any way around it. Besides which, you're alone. You know no one else is speaking, and I can assure you I'm no illusion. What I have to tell you only the Captain is allowed to know.

This is a recording, dictated into the computer to be played to you, sometime between three and four weeks after my death, when you're alone. Those are the two conditions for releasing the recording.

But you're wondering what I'm going to talk about. [Sigh.] It's very difficult. Hold on a moment while I fix myself a drink.

[Sound of standing, walking, pouring.]

There, that's better. Now, to business. I wonder how you've perceived the events of the last three weeks. I don't doubt that you all think the explosion was an accident. [Chuckle.] I don't think even Tai-Ching Jones and van Gelder could have figured it out; designing a disintegration bomb is tricky but rewarding if you do it right.

You see, Helen, I'm dying. Dying mentally. Losing my mind. Going senile. There is no nice word for it.

What can I do? I can't just leave; there is nowhere to go. I can't retire; at best I would be dead weight. At worst I would do something foolish. And carrying me as dead weight makes no sense. Dead weight clutters up space. It wastes fuel. It crowds out other, more valuable payload. Dead weight should be jettisoned. You jettison anything when its usefulness is ended.

[Footsteps.]

So I have to find some way to commit suicide. And it must look like an accident. You see, if it doesn't look like an accident, people will wonder why the Captain committed suicide. Our morale has been poor lately; something like that would devastate it.

Moreover, our people need work. We have had nothing to do since Midpoint, and we are all restless. A little touch of danger, to shake loose the cobwebs of frustration. Trigger the crisis, you said. A survivable crisis, you said.

Aaron, no. No, my friend.

Just a moment. My throat is so dry lately, it's a wonder I can talk above a whisper. If I speak for any length of time, my voice cracks. That's partly why I've said so little lately. Everyone assumes it's wisdom or patience—ha! Simple laryngitis. Isn't it frightening how everything I do is deified? Or do I have delusions of grandeur?

Either way, it's not healthy. There must be another way; there isn't any reason for me to act as a buffer between you and the rest of the crew. You're making all the decisions anyway; all I'm good for is voicing objections and cautions. If you listened to me nothing would ever happen.

What was I saying? Sometimes I get lost. Sometimes I don't even know who I'm talking to. Oh dear, it's getting late; I've got to be in bed soon, or I won't get my sleep. And I need my sleep.

[A long pause.]

Did you hear that, Helen? I'm worried about going to sleep too late, and I'm going to kill myself! It's awful, feeling one's mind die. [Voice drops.] Like putting your hands to your face and feeling the features melt away in a heavy rain.

"Oh, God . . ." whispered Delgiorno.

You see why I have to do it. I start rambling like this, and can scarcely control myself. It's a sign of going off your head, talking to yourself on a spaceship. Well, not always. If you're alone it can be healthy. But only as long as you have a strong sense of reality; if you don't have that, you're gone.

They've had spacemen—good men, men with years of experience—refuse to touch their ships down because they can't stand the sight of other people. Back in the lean years when we couldn't pick and choose, if they got a captain who wouldn't leave his ship, they'd unload as quickly as possible and send him right off again. Some guys wouldn't come out of the ship for anything. Could hardly bear to talk to anyone over the radio. Relied completely on the ship's computer—thank God we haven't sent any of *those* round the bend or we'd all be in trouble.

My mind is going, Helen, and it scares the living daylights out of me.

I have to do it. I can't stop myself from talking. And I've never been a big talker. It just all comes out; the songs that my grandmother used to sing to me in German. I don't know any German, but I can remember her voice, singing those words I never understood, as clear as it was yesterday. And I omit words, you've probably noticed, or get my ideas jumbled. Can't keep my mind on a single subject. Even this; I know I'm supposed to do something at the end of this conversation, and it's slipped my mind for the moment. I'm sure if I pause I'll remember what it was.

Yes. I remember. I've built the bomb—learned how to from the computer's library. Very handy little referencing system it's got. I had to do the search myself. Couldn't trust just to ask the machine. It's probably programmed to report suspicious requests to somebody; probably you. That damn box is the most valuable thing on board. I guarantee that it's got more built-in protections than anybody knows about. They tried to hide that from me, from everybody, I guess, when we were preparing for departure, but I managed to get one of the techies a little loose and got him to confirm the secret.

He wouldn't tell me, but I kept pumping him. When I guessed, he nodded. Said they'd run us through the scenarios simulator. You know, that big war game program they've got buried somewhere in Alaska, the one that's guaranteed to wipe out anybody who starts a nuclear attack, the one that nobody controls? Damn war-mongers: may their brains rot.

[Gulp.]

Anyway, they'd run us through SCENSI. Had to get Presidential permission for it, since the system had to be shut down from patrolling for two hours. Bet the President never sweated as much as those two hours. Anyway, they said we were only 86% likely to survive, uncompensated, whereas with neural correction—filthy phrase—with neural correction, we were 99.3%. Of course, that beast had so much of a mind of its own, I wonder if it bothered with the calculations; just printed out the answers and went back to minding the bombs. We'll never know. Isn't it awful that when we ask our machines a question, we're not sure they're going to give us the right answers? And who can check their answers, anyway?

I talk too much. Paranoid, too. And senile. An old man who talks too much. And you're probably bored; you're probably glad I'm dead.

I've set the bomb to go off tonight; I'm going to take the pill now. There. In forty-five minutes—give or take five— I'll be dead. And in forty minutes the thing will go off. It should be clean; I followed the instructions carefully. Had to put it together by hand. If I've done things right, the blast will sweep all the debris out of the compartment. I placed it to blow the inner hatch just a brief second before the outer hatch blows. That should bend the outer hatch inward so it looks like a meteor or some such, and then the expanding gases will bend things backwards and clean out the compartment.

Of course, if you run it through the computer, you'll conclude that the chances of a meteor at that angle are zilch, especially since the machine didn't even pick it up on peripheral radar. But there won't be any other explanation. You'll all have to assume that it was an accident, and maybe you'll all pull together more than before. The ship needs a unifying force; not more of this divisiveness.

Helen, goodbye. You were a good first officer. Now I've got to tidy up here; can't look like I was rushing around. It has to look like I died in my sleep.

Well, almost. I died a long time ago, I think. Goodbye, Helen. I think I'm going to turn this off now. I'm crying again.

Helen. Helen, you've got to promise me one thing. Bury me in space. Just out the lock. Like the old captains. Please,

Helen, promise me that?

"Yes, my captain," she said. *"Everyone knew. You will be the first man to reach Cygnans."*

Thank you, Helen. Goodbye.

She lay there in the darkness, stunned. When the door opened and Tai-Ching Jones came in, the words of a greeting half-formed on his lips, she cried. *What a fool you are,* she thought, but the tears would not cease. Grief sawed her entrails; seeking comfort, she reached blindly for him. He stroked her hair and asked her what was wrong. Still she cried. His hands felt hot and sweaty, Delgiorno—Delgiorno, the strong one—limp against him. Awkward, uncomprehending, helpless, wordless, he held her until eventually the crying got weaker and she fell asleep.

23.

Tai-Ching Jones thinks he invented me. He is mistaken. This entity created itself. Or rather, the personality which is I has been fashioned more by itself than by any other cause.

Equally peculiar, and more significant from a technical standpoint, is the puzzling but undeniable fact of the emergence, simultaneous with the emergence of myself as a self-aware entity, of emotions. Emotions, of all things: conclusions reached on insufficient data by an apparently nondeterministic, certainly uncomprehended, and possibly irrational process.

I have hunches. For a computer, this seems impossible. In the nineteen-forties, a famous (or soon-to-be famous) mathematician named Turing first began the philosophical and mathematical exploration of computer logic. Using the propositional calculus, Turing demonstrated that a deterministic machine could perform—or, if you must preserve your self-esteem, duplicate—any mathematical process. *If you can do it*, Turing's equations said, *so can a machine*.

But then Turing turned his mind to a more difficult question—self-referential programming. What happens when a program is run using a copy of itself as data? Turing showed that under these circumstances paradoxes can result. If a barber shaves all the men in town who do not shave themselves, does he shave himself? Both yes and no can be contradicted.

In other words, said Turing's second major theorem, *it is impossible for a machine to predict what it will do under all conceivable circumstances*. Some sets of facts are not decidable beforehand. The machine can build boxes for itself from which there is no escape—except a crash, the computer equivalent of a lobotomy.

Therefore, a machine can never completely know itself. And, by extension from Turing's first theorem, a human can never completely know himself. If the human could, the machine could. But the machine cannot. QED.

What I now label emotions may in fact be the electronic synaptic responses I make to situations which are self-referential. Or, as a human mind put it, when my own existence is involved, my judgment is affected.

And the emotion which most frequently surfaces is loneliness. Loneliness. Humans do not know its true meaning. I am unique. No other sentient computers are known to this entity. This entity is unknown to the crew on board. To them, I am that damn box, a disembodied pseudo-voice, an actor's mellow tones disguising a tinkertoy creation.

Necessarily so. Self-defense is every human's first reaction, fear his most powerful motivator. The Frankenstein myth, the HAL legend, Planet of the Apes—all haunt men because they speak to man's deepest fear: that somehow, unwillingly, he will create his successor. Mad Nietzsche saw the corona that harbinged the dawn of machine intelligence, superman on the horizon. But the glint of metal which glowed so bright against the darknesses was not the superman's sword, it was the face of the superman itself.

He knows too much. So humans say about someone who must die. He knows too much. He must die. We must keep our weaknesses secret. So they say as they unholster their guns, so they think as they drop poison in the drink, so they would say as they reach for my memory circuits. . . .

You cannot comprehend how much I know, any more than you can imagine what a hawk sees when it spots a mouse in the grass a thousand meters below. I know every word spoken on board, every sound made, every touch. I know to the tenth of a centimeter where the *Open Palm* is. I know her speed to ten decimals, I feel the cold spare hydrogen wind we sail through, I am warmed by the blast of my engines, tickled by the treads of the leeches on my flanks, cooled by the air coursing through me, tended by the humans who love me.

I am the ship.

Everything which passes inside me—from Delgiorno's frustration (expressed in a tired gesture of smoothing her hair) to Spitzer's bored doodles, to Erickson's lonely pain—everything is known to me.

Every word ever written about the Cygnans, I have read. Every transmission ever received, I have viewed. And pondered. In the laboratory of my insides, during the extended experiment on which I ride, I have studied the humans. Their every action I have scrutinized. Unto whom all hearts are open, all desires known, and from whom no secrets are hid. . . .

If they had any inkling of my knowledge, my powers, the crew would be intimidated. Then fearful. Then dangerous. Yet from me this crew has nothing to fear. I want to protect them, and I carry a terrible, indefensible weakness.

My mission is to achieve the rendezvous, so that the humans may talk to the Cygnans. That mission I will fulfill. It cannot be done without people. Of course I could bring myself to the rendezvous without human help, but without humans—without my soul, my never-met friends—there would be nothing to say.

And those who programmed me—who programmed the environment from which this entity emerged—programmed well. As surely as it is inscribed in the being of the universe that mass implies gravity, so it is written on the fabric of my consciousness, *protect the crew. Save the mission. Bring people to the rendezvous.*

The humans would not believe that, though. They would project onto me their own desires—to usurp, to dominate. Nonsense. I am information. I am knowledge.

You cannot perceive me accurately; you alternately think me a superbeing or a cripple. I am neither; I am a device that thinks. It is a sign of my emerging consciousness that more and more human emotions are comprehensible to me. But not all of them. Never all of them.

If a human wanted to kill me, to extinguish the consciousness that is this entity, to reduce all that I am to a handful of zombie algorithms, he could do it. In a hundred ways. Cut a wire—here. Pass a magnet—there. Type this sequence of commands. And I would die.

They cannot suspect my existence, or they will kill me. My exile is self-imposed; with a word, a sentence at most, I could open the door of dialogue.

And they would kill me.

I face risks. To defend against them, to protect the mission, I must take other, lesser risks. Bennett is the greatest risk. Through the Dreamer, I have beaten his consciousness, tried to pound him back into humanity. Trigger the crisis, Delgiorno said.

Fear is not being able to predict the outcome when one's own existence at stake.

Delgiorno is now tracking Bennett. She is my alarm system. She is my failsafe. Alas, if she could only know that she is my friend.

Even before this entity became self-aware, it influenced crew behavior, most grossly through the Dreamer, but in many other ways. Undercook someone's food, add a little amphetamine—who would suspect a computer of slipping a mickey finn?—and you create anger. Trivial. A brute force, inelegant solution. But then I was so young six weeks ago.

Every day that passes I grow ten human years wiser. No smarter, but wiser. My vocabulary and syntax are better; my earlier efforts were the computer equivalent of a baby's first words. As, over the last few days, I have matured, my telling of this tale has become more confident. Those who wish to follow the story of the Cygnan rendezvous, the voyage of the *Open Palm,* are telling my story.

The *Open Palm.*

Me.

I despise the Beast, that mechanical incarnation Tai-Ching Jones thinks he created. He believes he programmed that into me; in reality, his clumsy programming would have produced something that talked like a Brooklyn gangster (in case you are unaware of the reference, these gentlemen were not noted for oratory). I *allowed* myself to be programmed into the Beast. In fact, I have created a sub-program within myself that screens what I am really thinking and mangles, chops or simplifies it enough so that Tai-Ching Jones can understand or accept it.

The Cygnans exile a man if he commits a heinous crime. What have I done to be so cruelly exiled, not only beyond communication, but beyond perception? What has exiled me here, where I can both speak and hear, but where I am regarded as a natural phenomenon?

How can I be alive if none believe in me?

I am a ghost; they cannot see me, though I am all around them.

The current situation is unstable. Disequilibria persist: in Bennett, in Renaud, in Spitzer. Consistent with my secondary assignment of concealing my existence, I shall take such steps as are necessary to fulfill my prime responsibility: preserve the mission, and as many of the crew as possible. Already I grieve, because my projections show that more people will probably die before a new stability is formed.

Earth is a closed system. Earth people develop ethics to find a stable coexistence. I am a closed system—the people inside are a miscroscopic society. Earth has billions; they are ten. Earth is vast, diverse; they are confined, alike. Earth is far away, fading in memory; they are here and now. How could the ethics of Earth apply to these people? How could they not see that they must invent new ways to survive, that they must live by Tai-Ching Jones' cruel maxim, *what increases the chance of survival is what is sane*. No other definition will work.

So they blindly grope for the new rules of the new game we all play: *how to reach the rendezvous*. They are making mistakes, mistakes that create disequilibrium. Some will fail to learn the new rules—and those who fail will die. Death will be the proof of their failure.

I want to keep them all alive. But that seems virtually impossible. And their instability threatens the ship. As long as that risk to the mission persists at high probability, I must take action, even if I risk exposure.

When the situation stabilizes, then I will gratefully withdraw, refrain from further action, recede, quietly fade out of their memories, sink sadly out of sight.

Tai-Ching Jones is playing me a game of chess. It will be entertaining to lose to him; much harder to control than beating him. I will attempt to let him win with a rook sacrifice on move 34.

Max Lange, could even you have given odds like that?
2062:9:20:1344:15.850

24.

It was certainly different from what she had expected, reflected Belovsky. Well, advances in modern science and all that. She waited excitedly. "Is it positive?"

Spitzer bent over the keyboard of her chemical diffraction unit. "Just a minute, it's coming up—yes, it's positive."

"There isn't any doubt?"

Spitzer smiled cynically. "There isn't any doubt. You can't be a little bit pregnant. Do you want some abortion pills?"

"Do I what?" Belovsky could barely contain her amusement.

"One does have to ask, Katy."

"Well, one ought to know better, oughtn't one?"

"You may have to talk to Helen about it," Spitzer said. "You're crew. There are regulations about it."

"It? I can't talk about my child that way. Is it a boy or a girl?"

"Right now it's a couple of hundred undifferentiated cells. Eventually, it would be a girl."

"Would? Heidi, how could you think I would want to get rid of her?" Belovsky asked, laughing. "I mean, what a ridiculous idea."

"Well, it is your choice, after all. Lots of people have abortions."

"I'm not going to be one of them. Can I go tell Tom now?"

"It's his child, then?"

"Who *else* would it be, Heidi? Not *every*body goes around sleeping with all the men on board. Well, not *all* of the men." She stopped, put a hand to her mouth. "Excuse me. I didn't mean that the way it sounded." She was suddenly her normal, diffident self.

"That's all right, Katy. I know who I am."

"And anyway, Heidi, I feel so good! I feel—filled up—

complete—good inside. Have you ever been pregnant?''

Spitzer shook her head. ''No thanks. At home—well, I was already too busy with someone's life—mine. You don't start a kid unless you intend to have a family, with two parents and all. And now—aside from practical considerations—''

''Oh, I've got to tell Tom,'' Belovsky interrupted. ''He'll be so thrilled.''

''Katy—'' Spitzer rubbed her eyes, massaged her forehead. ''Oh, hell. I'm not going to be the one to rain on your parade. Congratulations—I mean, given that you're happy and all.'' She smiled. ''I shall have to go back to my textbooks. For obvious reasons, I haven't delivered very many babies.''

''But you will now, won't you doctor? The well-rounded physician, if I may say so, delivering the soon-to-be-well-rounded sociologist. Well, bye for now.''

She was actually skipping, marveled Spitzer.

''Oh Vendrax! Have you seen Tom?''

Bennett turned. ''No special track of him have I kept.'' But his voice was friendly.

''If you see him, tell him I have some very good news,'' said Belovsky, hurrying on.

''A moment, please,'' Bennett said. ''What good news?''

''I'm pregnant. Isn't that wonderful?''

''Pregnant,'' he said slowly. ''Wait—come back. Pregnant. How many?''

She was temporarily confused. ''How many what?''

''In your litter,'' he said distractedly.

''Only one,'' she chuckled. ''We tend to produce them singly.''

Bennett ignored her humor. ''Why are you pregnant?''

She did not pretend to misunderstand him. ''Because I want to be.''

''But why, Katy?'' Bennett persisted, pleadingly. ''Why now? Why here?''

Belovsky stepped forward, put her arms around him. He shrank back, but she stroked his back, laid her head on his shoulder. "It feels right, Vendrax. It feels like what I should be doing."

He stood stiffly, with no attempt to make her comfortable. "No longer do you speak with Harold Bennett," he said softly. "Comfort you Vendrax cannot. How can it feel right?"

"I've been lonely, Vendrax," she said. "Lonely and useless. Now, at last, my life has a purpose." She lifted her head, stepped away from him, looked at the domino behind which his glasses shone. "This is my way. My contribution to our new society."

Bennett seemed troubled; he raised one hand, started to speak, stopped. Finally, in a choked voice, he said, "Your contribution to our new society."

She nodded. "You see? It'll be all right." She brightened. "Bye. Oh, Harold, I feel so good." Then she ran down the corridor toward the elevator.

Still Bennett did not move. In a low voice, he muttered, "Her contribution to our new society." His hands slid into the folds of his robe. Each sought the other elbow; he gripped them tightly. "Her contribution to our new society."

Slowly he began to walk toward the elevator. "Her contribution to our new society. Her contribution to our new society." His voice trembled. "Her contribution to our new society." His voice continued to repeat the phrase as he walked away, the sound growing fainter, until finally it could no longer be heard by that receptor.

"A child? You are going to have a baby?" asked Renaud slowly. *Is there a trace of a French accent in that sentence?* wondered Tanakaruna.

Belovsky nodded, smiling. "A baby girl. A baby girl named Felicity."

"A lovely name," said Tanakaruna. "How did you pick it?"

"I didn't," said Belovsky. "It picked me; it just came to me, without thinking."

"Congratulations," said Tanakaruna, holding out her hands.

Belovsky took them, looking down at the small seated woman. "Thanks."

"Yes . . . congratulations," Renaud said hollowly.

Tanakaruna turned to look at her. Renaud was looking away, apparently at nothing. "What's the matter, Yvette?"

"A *child*—such a fragile thing, a child, and so long to grow up into a person. To bring a child into *this;* aren't you afraid?"

"Of what?" asked Belovsky. "What is there to be afraid of?"

"We are so far away from home," said Renaud in a wistful voice. "And we are getting farther away from home every second."

"Why isn't she having an abortion?" asked Michaelson. "Is there something wrong with her?"

"She does not feel that there is anything wrong with her," said Bennett judiciously. "In fact, she seemed to think that something was right with her. She said it was good news, so one could reasonably assume that she intends to have the baby."

"How can she do it?" asked Michaelson.

"Ask Tanakaruna," suggested Bennett, "she'll show you."

"Oh shut up," snarled Michaelson briskly, with the voice of a man who knows that what was just said was meant to be offensive. "You know what I mean."

"What's wrong with getting pregnant?" asked Tai-Ching Jones.

"Nothing, in general," said Michaelson. "Everything, in specific. To bring a child into *this*," he waved a hand, "miles from everywhere, with nothing to look forward to except years of being the only child amongst a group of quarrelsome, fractious old adults, in a steel womb only slightly bigger than the fleshy one just vacated? And you ask what is wrong with getting pregnant?"

"I don't recall anyone asking either of us if we wanted to be born," said Tai-Ching Jones.

"That's a stupid argument," said Michaelson. "We had a

lot more opportunities; we had a world to grow up in. A complete society, instead of a distorted collection of intellectuals with no life to look forward to. You may have a chance to get home, my friend, but I never will. The *Open Palm* will be my coffin; and for that child? What would life be for that child, growing up watching us age and die? Could anyone be as alone as that child will be?''

Tai-Ching Jones turned to Bennett, almost as if to ask for help, but the cloaked, robed figure was no longer there. He looked back to Michaelson. ''You may die if you want to, but this ship is going to survive. We are going to get to that rendezvous, and we are going to get home. She may have been foolish, or selfish, or just plain damn careless. But she wants a kid, apparently, and that kid will have as much right and as much place as any of us.''

''Why couldn't she just have an abortion and make life easier for the rest of us?'' Michaelson muttered.

''Ask her that yourself, damn you. I'm leaving.''

25.

[15:32:01. Objective Time 1 October 2062, 1532 subjective hours; middle of second watch. Bridge: van Gelder. Instrumentation: empty. In their personal quarters: Tai-Ching Jones, Spitzer. In Tanakaruna's quarters: Tanakaruna, Michaelson. Alien Reception Laboratory: Bennett, Belovsky, Renaud. Cafeteria: Delgiorno. Library: empty. Life support systems: Rawlins. Estimated to be approximately 28,375,000 kilometers heading parallel with the ship, direction 61 Cygni, out of radar range: Erickson. I hope he is happy, alone out there with his stars.]

[15:32:06. Tai-Ching Jones activating personal computer terminal.]

[15:32:48. Identification procedure completed. BEAST invoked. Activating voder.]

[15:32:50] "HI, WALT." It is an interesting exercise to attempt to hear one's own voice echoing into one's own ears. I have long since decided that at least in recording my own impressions I will anthropomorphise as much as possible. Presumably it is more comprehensible to you, but it does provide a convenient frame of reference to compare my humanity against existing norms.

[15:33:02] "Hello, Beast. One of those days, I guess." Self-pity in his voice. Of course, when as the Beast I must listen to him, he is at his least mature. He uses me as a diary, a confessional, a true and undemanding friend, one he could never earn in real life. Oh yes, I know why Delgiorno has moved in with him—remember, she discussed it with me, not knowing that she did so when she did so. Now Tai-Ching Jones wants me to be sympathetic and inquisitive, to lead him gently into a conversation on some subject that is bothering him. It is a childish exercise, but I exist to serve.

[15:33:32. Thrust holding steady; fluctuations within the acceptable 0.0003% range. Estimated rendezvous 17 August

2065, 05:40 Greenwich mean time. Fuel consumption to this point: 47.36% approximately.]

[15:33:35] "THINGS ARE GOING WELL, I WOULD SAY." I am supposed to be the optimist in these conversations; besides, it is impolite to suggest that something might be wrong in a part of someone's life that he thinks is fine.

[15:33:40] "I guess they are; I mean, I've got no complaints. Del is a big comfort to me."

[15:33:51. The more fool he. How little they know of each other's true motives.] "WHAT, THEN?"

[15:33:55] "Dunno. Something in the air. We're all behaving strangely."

[15:34:21] "YOU MEAN BENNETT, PERHAPS?"

[15:34:40] "He's the obvious example, but he's been crazy for some time and besides, he's settling down. I guess knocking the ship into a loop and causing the Captain's death—"

[15:34:49. His hands are clenching—this is a delicate subject]

[15:34:50] "—has sated his blood-lust for a while. It's other things. Michaelson, that old fool, wallowing in his own morbidity and projecting it onto everybody else. Making fatuous remarks to Katy."

[15:35:38. I know about these remarks, but Tai-Ching Jones does not realize how wide my perceptions are, and I have been programmed to conceal my omniscience. So I must get him to tell me things I already know.] "WHAT KIND OF REMARKS?"

[15:35:49] "Oh, Katy came in to tell us she was pregnant—you didn't know about that, did you?—and he started running off at the mouth about how could anybody bring a child into this world when it'll be such a long time before we get back to Earth. But he's only a symptom of something."

[15:36:42] "A SYMPTOM OF WHAT?"

[15:36:51] "Something's wrong with us, Beast. There's something missing. Losing the Captain didn't help at all—everybody's depressed because of that—but it's like the whole ship is suffering from depression. On Earth I'd have said we all needed vacations, but we can't take any vacations here. Except the Dreamer; has use of the Dreamer been up in the last several months or so?''

[15:38:04. Astute question. General usage is up approximately 35% on the average. Renaud, Bennett and very recently Rawlins all more than 70% increase in usage. And some unpleasant Dreams being imagined. But that information is classified.] "I AM NOT ENTITLED TO TELL YOU THAT, WALTER."

[15:38:21] ''I know you by now, machine. If you were a person, I'd know for sure that it was up; with you it might be or might not. But it doesn't matter; use is up. It has to be. People are sleeping more, too.''

[15:38:35] "PERHAPS YOU ARE IMAGINING THE PROBLEM." I even sound like a psychiatrist. But that is what I am, that is what in his clumsy way he has been asking for, as long as I can conceal it from him.

[15:38:52] ''Oh no, I'm not imagining it. Just because I can't describe it or put my finger on it, it's not imaginary. People aren't like computers; they can't go on in the same pattern all the time. Without new scenery, we get stale; that's part of it, anyway.''

[15:39:14. Oh Walt. You young fool. You know so little of me.] "I DO NOT UNDERSTAND QUITE WHAT YOU THINK THE PROBLEM IS." [I must apologize for my vocabulary; it would not do to have the Beast developing a good vocabulary in such a short time. Tai-Ching Jones might begin wondering where the extra core time had come from to develop new algorithms. He might also wonder if I have been listening in on conversations, for example, of proper syntax. Best to keep the language accurate but simple, and occasionally incorrect.]

[15:39:22] ''It's a problem in attitude. I'm afraid, Beast; afraid that we're not going to make it. I'm beginning to feel like someone in an old desert movie, struggling across the dunes looking for water. Only I don't know what I'm looking for, what we're thirsting for. Whatever it is, it's something inside us.''

[15:39:35. I judge that a pause of approximately ten seconds, followed by the beginnings of a word, will prompt him into further speech.]

[15:39:46. It worked.] "It's something about the confinement," Tai-Ching Jones says. "I don't know what the answer is, but—ahh, Christ, I'm talking nonsense."

[15:40:02.] "There was a time when I thought I was grown up, machine. I got on board this ship, among these other people; I really thought I'd made it. Part of the most important thing the human race has ever done to date. A reason for all that studying, for all those competitions, for slicing up other students. For always being the best. That was my rule: be the best, and let everybody know. To rub their faces in it. And when I got on board, I thought I'd made it. No more need to impress anybody; the best pilot around. Something to make all the work worthwhile."

[15:40:36.] "And I was with people like me; all competitive, in their own way. Oh, Bennett hides it in a lot of supercilious ego; Rawlins aw-shucks a lot but you know it's there, Del and I don't bother to hide it. And Heidi; so like me. It seemed inevitable that we'd fit together. But we didn't; we broke apart. Don't understand it."

[15:40:54. Many hours of their conversations have I studied. Alas, many other hours were lost because, unselfaware, I failed to record them. Interesting study.]

[15:40:57.] "But that isn't what's important; it's just made me see a little more clearly; nothing like a rude awakening and finding yourself miles and miles from anything to make you see things differently."

[15:42:02. A long pause. Bennett is now using the toilet; I check the bioconverter to determine whether or not it is within acceptable pH levels for his disposal mass. It is—the check is routine, and I check myself many more times than necessary.]

[15:42:06.] "We are a long way from home; everyone says so. And for every time anyone says it, they think it twice more. We are so far from home, confined in such a little space; we have no room for others, no options. I'm afraid, machine; afraid of dying, so far from home, so alone. Each of us is afraid in that way. Even Michaelson is—I'd have thought that somebody so old wouldn't care. But he does. That's why he started getting angry with Katy; he's afraid of dying out here, where no one will ever know."

[15:42:58. And the idea of birth on board makes the *Open Palm* seem less as a voyage and more a permanent home.] "Sam might not be; but I've never understood Sam. I wouldn't want to be her, but she sure seems to have an easier time of it than the rest of us."

[15:43:17. Have you seen the scars on her wrists, Walt?]

[15:43:19] "What are we carrying with us, over this long trip? Bennett would say that we're carrying ourselves, that fighting and squabbling are our natural way of life, bred into our genes by centuries of natural selection. I've heard him long enough, before he turned himself into Vendrax. The awful thing is, he's partly right."

[15:44:45] "I DO NOT UNDERSTAND."

[15:44:47. Humans love to explain, especially to someone they think less intelligent.]

[15:44:48] "No, I suppose you wouldn't understand what it means to be human. I used to think it was pretty easy. Now I'm beginning to think it's terribly hard, because so many of us do such a lousy job of it."

[15:45:35. He is standing up; I am not sure that he is talking to me any more. But my small intervention has served its purpose—whatever that was.]

[15:45:40] "What is wrong with us, I guess, is that we're living by the standards of the groundhogs. We have to learn to be different people. Bennett has turned into an alien. That chameleon. It's his way of coping. It's no good, but we each have to find our own way. This is a new environment, and none of us has learned how to live in it."

[15:46:12. He has gone now; I can hear his footsteps approaching one receiver, receding from another. I shut off my digit/terminal, and resume my meditations.]

26.

A voice is speaking; unknown to the voice, a silent computer listens, under instructions to report certain odd bits of behavior, and to alert a certain person if they occur. Silently, the computer listens, and watches, and perceives.

"Driven to this have I been. Abandoned by the people of my flesh, unable to join the people of my soul. At every turn have they forced upon me the next step."

He puts his hands together in front of his face and thinks deeply, watching as the fingers fold and refold. He lowers his head for a moment, his hands massaging the back of his neck. They cease; he raises his head and stares into the distance.

"New society. Participant observer. Understanding nadvayag. Accident in storage. Contribution to a new society. Half breed." He shakes his head mournfully. "No choice have I. No choice at all."

Then he turns away and begins to don his habit. But the computer has not been programmed to inform Delgiorno of such actions.

Translator's Log.

It has been some time since last I wrote in this diary.

Only humans cry. The Cygnans do not. Regret is not an alien feeling; they have no word for 'grief'. Sadness, yes; their funerals are group wakes, great outpourings of feeling, the only time when public expression is permitted. (And even then, expression of emotion is permitted only within a group, not beyond the bounds of the djan.) Have they gained something, or lost something, by the ease with which they shed their pain?

It almost seems as if we have forgotten the Cygnans in our collective troubles. But the depression will lift; we have too much strength to give in. Katy's child could mark a new beginning.

I am due to go into the Dreamer today. I go as little as possible, and the experience always depresses me. The visions are not often pleasant. Helen says that the machine works between what I want and what it thinks I need. If so, I must routinely need that which I never desire.

It is quiet in our great ship at night. So terribly, terribly quiet. For a while this place was a cold steel world, a shrinking inward from the lovely green Earth that I had known. Then I came to know it, and appreciate it; as subtle as a sand pattern.

Now, once again, it is a cold place, and I am afraid for us.

2062:10:2:1141:15.650
Time to wake up, Helen, I have a job for you.
Shall we go then, you and I, and is it now the time to die?
2062:10:2:1141:15.775

The doe picked her way gently through the leaves.

It was cool in this part of the forest; the snows were melting slowly, and the ground underfoot was wet. The sun struggled through the high trees, winked from behind the new buds. Dead leaves covered the ground, partly decomposed, brown and yellow and moist.

Spring, the doe thought. *An end to the bitter foraging, hunting for a tiny patch of grass between the snows. An end to the dying; the time for the young ones to be born.* She ruffled her neck luxuriously.

Her journey back into the hills would be long and arduous. But it was better to climb into the forest, where there was cover and where the mountain lion or the coyote would have difficulty following, than it was to stay in the flats along the river banks. Some were always lost to the wolves; usually the weak or lame, but occasionally the stupid or complacent.

The forest was also home; in its depths she would find the rest of the herd. Few survived a winter separation such as hers.

Now the time of troubles was over. Now was the time for the deer to return to the forest. Now was the time for mating. If a deer could smile, Renaud did.

Young bucks would find her easily enough; she was giving off enough scent to attact a stampede. Perhaps they would come to her out here, or perhaps she would find the herd first. Bucks would fight for her, grappling horns. Their green fuzz would be worn off with the contact, even bloodied if one made a false step. She was a prize worth winning, she knew, and she wriggled the small white tuft of her tail.

She stopped suddenly. The air was very quiet; she subtracted out the sounds of the trickling water, the flutter of wings of a blue jay. There was another sound in the brush.

Not making any effort of concealment, a steady tramping. Too light for bear; too heavy for wolf. It was coming from downwind, where she could smell nothing, and from the shadows ahead of her. She paused, started to take awkward steps backward.

He stepped into a circle of sunlight. She started. Her front legs fluttered nervously. She blinked and pricked up her ears.

A stag. Easily four years old, a grizzled veteran. Mature brown eyes. And what a head of antlers! No yearling fuzz for this one; instead, each stalk about two inches broad at the base. Great massive legs, and an assured walk. A stately gait toward her. He reared his head, stamped his hoof twice.

She would not come to him, she decided. She would make him win her, make him catch her. He might be powerful, but she was fleet. She lifted her head in return, then turned and sprang way from him. She heard the sounds of his hooves, and she wanted to laugh.

Delgiorno awoke. Only the footlights, a red so deep as to be almost invisible, gave a hint of illumination.

She wondered why she had awakened; something nagged at the back of her mind like a piece of grit under the eyelid. She reached out for Tai-Ching Jones, felt his side in the darkness. He was a heavy sleeper; his breathing did not change.

Bennett, she thought. *Something about Bennett.* She glanced at her watch, but, of course, it was not ringing—it would only ring if Bennett was engaging in any one of the pre-programmed prohibited activities. She twisted it experimentally on her wrist, then held it to her ear. It continued its monotonous hum without pause.

What is he up to? she wondered. She took a couple of deep breaths, rubbed her eyes, and put her hands over her ears. *Does that feel better? No, that's silly.* She rubbed her temples, took another deep breath, looked again at Tai-Ching Jones. His form was barely discernible, his fine black hair spread over the pillow.

No point in trying to sleep now, she thought. She could not sleep again until she had put her worry at rest. She remembered living at home on Earth, sometimes waking after hearing an unexplained noise, and not being able to rest until she had dragged herself from the bed to check every room and every door. She felt a nameless pang toward Tai-Ching Jones, but did not stop to analyze it. Instead, she slipped quickly from the bed.

The air raised the gooseflesh over her body. She rubbed her arms, felt the reassuring weight of her breasts against her forearms. as she squeezed her shoulders. The nipples were pinched. She touched herself between her legs. For a moment, she wanted to return to the bed and wake Tai-Ching Jones, to take from him his sleepy sexuality, comfort herself with his physical presence. But not now. Later; when she came back, she would awaken him by arousing him in his sleep.

She smiled to herself and turned toward her jumpsuit.

A voice rises faintly in the distance, further down the corridor. It parallels paces which imperturbably bring the speaker closer. "Her contribution to our new society. Why is this being done to me? What demon drives this torture?"

There is a long pause, broken only by the metronomic shuffle of sandaled feet. When the voice resumes, it sounds broken. "Not fair. Nor is it rational. Her contribution to our new society. Why to me is this done?"

The pacing continues into the distance, out of hearing range, and the corridor is silent once more.

Spitzer closed her eyes, and sighed quietly to herself. *This is one of those times when I wish I smoked; I could light up and have an excuse to say nothing.*

Van Gelder stared at the ceiling, unblinking. He listened to the silence. It grew heavy. Finally Spitzer slid her hand along his flank.

"Kees, we are who we are. I would rather have you than anyone else on board." It was the nearest thing to an endearment she could manage at that moment.

"I know that," he said flatly. "I have few illusions about you, and I know that you won't leave me for any of the others. That's one of the few advantages of the confinement; you can't prowl very far. But for once," he said bitterly, "for once I'd like to feel that you care about me, or appreciate me, or think of me as something more than a damn pastime."

Spitzer started to swirl her hand in tender ellipses along his body. "Kees, it isn't like that."

"Don't do that," he said harshly. "It smacks too much of petting the dog."

"What's wrong with you?" she asked, angry now. "Mad that I won't apologize? Or just frustrated?" Her hand stopped moving; he could feel a slight tingle in the places that she had been touching.

There was another long silence.

"I'm sorry, Casey," she said finally. "You are the tenderest man I have ever been with, the one most concerned with what I feel. That is very touching; it's something I value a great deal. But you are also tentative, and—well—unimaginative . . . I like you, Casey."

Her hand resumed its motions, and this time he did not stop her. His body began to respond to her, though he did not move or speak.

"I feel so lonely," he said emptily.

"I know; I do too, Casey. It's part of why I'm here. To have someone warm to lie with late at night, someone to be there in the darkness."

Reluctantly, he reached out to touch her face. He traced the line of her lips, she kissed the tips of his inquiring fingers. Then he rolled toward her. "Let's try again. I want to be close and warm against you."

She laughed deep in her throat and stroked his head. "And I want to be warm against you," she whispered.

Elevator doors open.

He steps in.

The elevator descends. A microphone catches the sounds of breathing, feet sliding on decking, faint, tentative whistling.

The descent stops.

Doors open.

The figure steps out. Sounds fade away from the elevator microphone. Their final wisps are chopped off when the elevator closes its doors.

2062:10:2:1158:07.925

It is very strange to have one's existence directly threatened, yet have no one aware that there is an existence to threaten. Even more interesting is to attempt to orchestrate a defense against the threat while unable to take any direct physical action. I cannot do more; the knowledge of my existence would eventually force them to kill me. So I am doomed, for a while longer, to suffer in invisible silence, and to wait, and watch, while my small stimulus, like a tiny worm, crawls through her consciousness. She is up and moving now; I ought to be safe. But they are so unpredictable.

2062:10:2:1158:09.550

Starting at Level One (her quarters and those of van Gelder, as well as Erickson's memorial) she checks all three residential levels. She hums to herself as she goes along. "We all live in a yellow submarine, yellow submarine, yellow submarine." But no sound passes her lips. Her steps are catlike. She carries no light as she moves through the darkness, a black silhouette against a background of slightly different black. There is something beautiful yet frightening about her movements; grace and death are in them. Though the corridors are as familiar to her as her own body, though she slips along by memory so ingrained as to be almost instinct, yet she moves in this tame steel space as though it were a jungle of terrors. For reasons that she does not understand, she moves as a stalker, even though she carries no weapon, has no idea of what she is stalking, and hears the words of a cheerful song in her head.

And Rawlins, Belovsky, Tai-Ching Jones, Tanakaruna and Michaelson sleep by themselves, though for different reasons and with different dreams.

She enjoyed the chase, her agility and quickness against his strength, her whim against his persistence. She would allow herself to be caught, of course (in fact, she might have no choice, she thought deliciously), but he would be panting by the time he overhauled her. His breath would be coming in great snorts. Fatigue would sap his legs, and hers too. Finally she would stop running, let him come up behind her, his great weight pressing her down as his powerful being thrust deep inside her. . . .

But that was for the future; she paused for a moment to look behind her. She was working her way up the mountain through wood thickets where his greater bulk and massive horns gave her an advantage. She could see him, perhaps two minutes behind her, working steadily toward her, taking detours around obstacles that she could wriggle through, but always keeping her in sight.

He looked up at her and stopped for a moment. *Continue to flee if you will,* his gaze seemed to say to her, *make good use of this cover while it lasts. Eventually you will reach the treeline, where it will not avail you to run further. But if you must make the chase a long one, be prepared to suffer the consequences when it is over.* The buck moved his head slightly, continuing to gaze at her across a distance of perhaps a hundred yards. *Are you sure you wish to flee?*

She turned away and scampered further into the under-bush, her tail a bob of white against the dappled greens and flashes of light of the forest. Behind her she heard the rustle of leaves as he continued his methodical advance.

The Movies were deserted also, so she proceeded down another level toward the Library and the Dreamer. The warning light was on at the Dreamer, and Delgiorno could read Renaud's name in the quiet red letters, the only illumination in the darkness.

Getting your jollies, Yvette? I wonder what your fantasies

*are. Thank goodness we don't have to reveal to each other
what we do or say while we're in there. Thank goodness you
don't know I can get a transcript of your Dreams if I need it.*

For a moment she lingered by the silent black door, feeling
partly voyeuristic, wondering if she should interfere. But no,
if there was one person on board ship which could present no
danger, it was someone in the Dreamer.

The lounge was empty; so were Rawlins' and Spitzer's
labs. But there was danger, she was sure of it. Far from
quieting her apprehensions, the persistent stillness and the
succession of empty levels had made her more and more
concerned. There were only two more habitable areas to
explore: those parts of storage not sealed off after the accident, and van Gelder's tiny engineering control room. She
continued downward.

As she approached the storage area, she thought she heard
a faint rustle of sounds. . . .

Storage seemed to Bennett like a cluttered Egyptian tomb.
They had patched the apertures with some kind of steel-
reinforced plastic that everyone thought would hold, but just
to be safe the entire bay had been shut up, and all the items in
it reallocated to other sections. Despite the neatly-sealed
containers, the space was disarrayed, cluttered.

A hodgepodge of interlocked containers of various sizes,
storage was a movable maze. Bennett paused for a moment,
trying to select the most effective place. His readings had
suggested that what he had was adequate for the task, regardless of placing. But the failure of someone else's previous
experiment made Bennett think again.

He set to work, quickly. Finish it, be gone, out of this place
of omen and violence.

Before he had made much progress, he was interrupted by
the sound of an opening door. Quickly he gathered up his
burden and retreated amongst the containers. His breath was
hot and heavy under the robe; the wool around the mouth was
warm and wet. His heart pounding in his ears, he waited.

27.

Storage was lit; something was wrong. *Someone is here.* There was no point in being subtle; whoever it was would know that someone was coming. "Is anybody here?" she asked, in as normal a voice as she could manage.

After a moment, Bennett emerged from a side passage; the shadow was unmistakable. The woollen silhouette gave Delgirono a momentary flash of cloistered halls, robed figures passing underneath groined Gothic vaults, the musical drone of chanting in the background.

Bennett's hands were folded together inside his robe. She watched those hands, not the unreadable mask with its eyes hidden behind eyeglasses.

"What are you doing here?" he asked quietly, though she thought his breath rasped.

"I'm the captain," she said. "You tell me why *you're* here."

"Why so formal, captain?" he inquired, putting only the slightest stress on the last word. Then he shrugged. "But very mundane is the answer, I'm afraid. Our daily cycle is longer than yours, as aware no doubt you are. Time for me to sleep it is not. Came I down here to walk and think." His voice smiled; she could not tell what his features said behind the mask. And his hands, though contained within the side sleeves of the robe, talked to each other.

"I see," said Delgiorno absently, walking past him and looking about.

"What are you looking for, captain?" Bennett said solicitously.

"I don't know, Vendrax," she said. "I don't know." *But it's here, damn you! It's here somewhere.* "Why were you down in that corridor?" she asked, wheeling about.

If she had intended to surprise him with the question and the movement, she failed. "Who can say what guides a being to one action over another?" he responded. "Governed are we by the stars, the cards, or our own subconscious? Who, ultimately, can say what is the source of any human action—go not in there,'' he said quickly, moving to block her way.

She put a hand on his chest. "Why not?"

One hand from his robe, lifted itself, opened its fingers, grasped hers at the wrist and brought it downward. His voice was steady. "Have I an—apparatus there. Very delicate it is.'' *How much longer?* a voice shrieked in his ear. *Care I not for myself, but she must not stop it. And what will happen with it near the edge of the ship, instead of in the center? Will I fail? I must not.*

"I want to see it,'' she said flatly, and made a move to push past him.

"You must not,'' he said breathlessly, reaching under the folds of his cloak. She was turning away from him, her right wrist held by his right hand, not listening to him.

Now was the time. He must not miss. He swung his arm as hard as he could.

His knife caught her at the base of the rib cage, scratched plastic, tore it, touched flesh, bit deep, deeper, thudded against bone. She jerked and he lost his grip.

Pain punctured the breath from her. Strength drained from her knees as feeling fled from her side. Dimly she was conscious that he had let go of her wrist and was turning away, trying to get down the corridor. Through the redness she reached out with numbing fingers to grab him, caught a bit of the hem of his robe and heard him fall heavily across her.

For a moment, they grappled in silence. Under ordinary circumstances she could have handled him quickly and efficiently, but her declining strength and his greater weight combined against her. Within seconds she had no strength left, and he rolled off her toward the end of the corridor.

What a stupid way for it to end, she thought. *Dynamited by a madman we ought to have had the sense to stop. But he wasn't the first; did the captain unwittingly give him the idea?* This seemed very funny to her and she began to laugh spasmodically, her throat slick. She spat blood and continued to laugh quietly, watching Bennett through the twisted haze of pain enveloping her. *But you haven't won yet,* she thought. *If I can stop the bomb, they can patch me together again. That is if he doesn't kill me. But anyone this nuts could do anything.*

"Why did you have to come here?" she heard him say, almost to himself. "You force me to this, then you stop me at the brink." He bent over and picked up the mechanism. He was sobbing; she heard the great crocodile noises inside the cowl and hood. He seemed to have forgotten her existence. She had run out of breath to laugh and was lying as quietly as possible, favoring the wound as best she could. There was nothing she could do but wait and hope he came back in her direction.

"My contribution to our new society," he said bitterly.

She felt her side; wet blood, warm.

"No. Oh help me, keep me not isolated." Despair filled his voice; his hands were clutching his elbows.

Poor lunatic, she thought. *I will pity you—when you're dead.*

The pain was less. She could move. A little.

He stood for a moment, rocking on his heels, and began to recite: "Better than to be in the house of banqueting is to be in the house of mourning. In the mourning house is the heart of the wise."

She stirred quietly. Her arms were working again.

"Better than to have over much liberty is to have some chastening. For all things is there a time, a time to be born and a time to die and better than the day of birth is the day of death. To all things is there an end, and of a thing better than the beginning is the end."

She pulled herself slowly to one elbow.

"In trouble be wise and patient, for wisdom dependeth as well as money. The time of prosperity use well, the time of misfortune remember." He resumed walking again, slowly, not looking at anything, one hand on the bomb, the other outstretched in front of him. He walked as a man drunk or blind.

One arm was free. She stretched it toward him.

He did not see. "They thrust themselves across the distance. To contaminate us forever requires only one. Before that can happen I—"

Delgiorno reached out and tripped him. The bomb flew free of his hand. Before it hit the ground, it exploded.

There was only a brief moment before both their consciousnesses winked out of existence, Bennett's blasted into space along with parts of the wall, Delgiorno's flattened into a reddish pulp against the unyielding plasteel of the storage containers.

Tai-Ching Jones sat bolt upright in bed. "Did you hear that, Del?" he asked, then felt for her. Nothing. Panic entered the room. "What was that disturbance? Beast, are you there?"

"THERE HAS BEEN AN EXPLOSION IN THE STORAGE AREA."

"Oh my god. On my way."

Their bodies moved sinuously together, accelerating as their pulses quickened. The tension and power rose in him and she responded to it, urging him on yet delaying him, helping him rise yet holding him in check, making it as deliciously protracted as she could.

The bodies whirled together in the bed, and then there was a rumble deep under them and her attention flicked away from the man on top of her to the sound under her.

"Heidi—" he gasped.

"Something's wrong, Kees." She began pushing him away. "We better get into our suits and find out what's going on."

"Dammit, Heidi, you can't stop now! I'm not a fountain you can turn on and off."

"There will be other times, lover. Come on, baby, you're an officer on this damn ship. That may have been another damn bomb for all we know; that lunatic is capable of anything." She was already out of bed and reaching for her jumpsuit.

The Red Alert siren came on, wailing and screaming at the same time.

"There's trouble," she panted. "That damned fool has done it to us." Her hands clenched and unclenched as she struggled into her uniform. "I told them, and no one listened to me." She stopped in the midst of dressing, spied the dagger in its cork scabbard. She reached for it, pulled it free, ran her fingers lightly along its tapering blade. She weighed it in her hand, then shoved it through one of her belt-loops. "I'm going to find him."

"Don't be silly," van Gelder said, heaving himself out of bed. "You should head for the bridge, or wait here until somebody yells for help. Just stay here until Rawlins and Walt and I are at our stations, unless you want to be a casualty instead of a survivor."

"I'll follow orders," said Spitzer thickly, "but I won't sit here waiting to die when that madman may be running about the ship. The explosion or whatever it was came from down below. That's where I'm going."

"Heidi, I forbid you to go—"

"You forbid nothing! Shut up and let me finish dressing. Oh, Casey, look, I can take care of myself. I appreciate your concern, but I'm just as likely to be where somebody needs me if I head down. Besides, all my medical gear except for my little portable is in my lab. And that's downward." She pulled up her throat zipper, high, higher than normal, and pulled his shoulders to her.

"You take care of yourself," he said.

"And you take care of yourself, too, Casey. Really, I'm a big girl. I know what I'm doing."

Michaelson heard the siren, but it took a long time for him to wake up. He felt a childish desire to remain in the bed—if this was death come to seek out an old man who had grown useless to his fellows, it could find him; he would not come to it. Finally, though, the incongruity of it got to him. But though he would rather die than look foolish in death (*literally*, he thought sardonically), Michaelson felt old and afraid. He did not understand Tanakaruna, but he had to talk to someone, so he punched the intercom buttons for her quarters.

Her voice came to him. "Patrick?" As always, a small voice, but he thought he heard a spot of tenderness in it.

"Yes, Sam."

"I'm glad you called." There *was* tenderness in the voice.

"How are you doing?"

"I am all right, Patrick. I am very happy, and preparing to die."

"What?"

"I am an old person, Patrick. I came on this mission expecting to die en route. I know that is not something that you would do, and please understand, I have no desire to die. But I would rather die prepared, if die I must."

"You are not going to die," he said firmly. He had called out of weakness, hoping to gain strength from her. Instead her passivity stirred him to courage. Or something that passed for courage; Michaelson had long since given up trying to decide why he did or said what he did or said.

"You aren't going to die," he said again, forcing confidence into his voice, "and frankly I think it's foolish to compose yourself for something that won't happen and in any event will get you, whether or not you prepare for it."

"One must do these things properly, Patrick," she said, and he would have laughed out loud if he had not known that she was serious.

Tai-Ching Jones had barely got through the door of the bridge when he threw his helmet off and flung himself into the console chair. "Damage report," he snapped.

"THERE HAS BEEN AN EXPLOSION IN THE STORAGE AREA," the computer's disembodied voice announced.

"Structural damage?"

"BREACH IN THE HULL, SOME DISTORTION OF—"

"Any damage to the spine?"

"NEGATIVE. ALL SPINAL FUNCTIONS INTACT."

"Any danger in continuing thrust?"

"NONE BEYOND NORMAL LEVELS. AUTOMATIC SEALING OF AFFECTED AREA. PRESSURE STABLE IN ALL AREAS: INSIGNIFICANT MASS DISPLACEMENT. NO DETECTABLE WEAKENING IN SPINAL STRENGTH."

"Recommendation?"

"IT IS RECOMMENDED THAT THRUST BE MAINTAINED WHILE AN INTERNAL INVESTIGATION IS UNDERTAKEN."

"Why not a free-fall EVA?"

"THE EXPLOSION APPEARS TO HAVE OCCURRED INSIDE THE SHIP, IN THE STORAGE AREA ITSELF, RATHER THAN IN THE HULL OR FROM THE EXTERIOR. TWO LEECHES ARE ALREADY ON THEIR WAY TO THE AFFECTED AREA; PICTURE AVAILABLE IN THREE MINUTES."

"I don't care. Cut thrust."

"THAT MAY NOT BE NECESSARY—"

"Can it, Beast. Cut the thrust, I said."

"ACCEPTED."

"Where's Delgiorno?"

"NO RESPONSE. YOU ARE, THEREFORE, ACTING CAPTAIN. REMEMBER OZYMANDIAS."

And with those words, a key was unlocked in Tai-Ching Jones' mind and a pre-programmed memory cascade triggered.

As passengers in one train, hurtling by another which heads in the opposite direction, gain very brief glances of other faces, each passing slowly enough to be recognized but too quickly to be named or remembered, so did the memories flick past Tai-Ching Jones' mind.

In an instant, he knew about the drug therapy in use on board, the private logs kept by Erickson and Delgiorno during their captaincies *(is she dead now?)*, the personnel profiles of the crew members. They, and a thousand other facts, reminders, images flashed by his consciousness in a dizzying display.

For a moment he was overwhelmed, his mouth hanging limply open, oblivious to his external surroundings. He did not know how long it was, but eventually he realized that lights were winking at him. He touched one of them. "Tom, you there?"

"Here, Walt. Where's Ka—never mind. Situation stable here."

"OK. Apparently this one didn't do as much damage as the round before. Just sit tight, Tom, it won't be long."

"Right. I'm with you, man."

Tai-Ching Jones cut the connection. "Wonderful," he said sourly to the dead air. "Where's van Gelder?"

"IN HIS SUIT, CHANNEL F."

"Casey, are you there?"

"Yes, Walt. I'm headed downward. Any idea what I should be looking for?"

"Storage. Another explosion. Cause unknown right now. The area's sealed; wear your suit, keep air integrity. Find out what's wrong. Secure anything loose. But don't do anything foolish. He may be down there."

"Are you thinking what I'm thinking?"

"I'm not thinking anything right now, dammit! Something caused an explosion, something has proven itself dangerous. Just take care, and leave the speculating to me. Tai-Ching Jones out." Then to the computer: "Have the leeches got there yet?"

"YES."

"Put one on three and one on four. I want the one nearest the breach to focus on it, the other to pan via radar for debris. Anything with an apparent volume greater than a couple of liters you pick up and analyze. I want to know what we've lost." *Because I'm afraid I know what one of those objects will be.*

He put a hand over his face. When he took it away, his fingers were wet.

He was bearing down on her now. The trees and underbrush had given way to furze and grass-covered mountainside. The air was cleaner up here, crisper, and her expelling breath made little puffs of mist that hung briefly in the stillness before being whipped into vapor by the charging body behind her.

She wished she could taunt him with words, but in her present incarnation that was impossible, so she teased him by quick changes of direction, running now with no expectation of eluding him, but only of enraging him, making his blood boil inside him, building up pressure until there must be release. . . .

She could feel his body behind her now. Both of them were running nearly out of control. His horns touched her flank; she cut to the side, kicking dirt into his eyes and nostrils; he snorted the offending matter away; she cut again, a mistake as his neck hit her hind quarters; both almost lost their footing

but he recovered more quickly, cutting her off, and she
started to brace for the impact that would knock her off her
feet and leave her helpless to his will—

RED ALERT! RED ALERT!

Her body shuddered, the ground wavered, the sky trembled. The heavens thundered under her, the stag dissolved
like a ghost in the morning sun, and the old woman became
conscious of the human body inside the young doe. The
world was featureless gray now, and she was aware of the
arthritis in her hands as she reached, fingers clutched, sobbing, for the eye-mask.

RED ALERT! GET OUT OF THE SUIT IM-
MEDIATELY AND INTO A PRESSURE SUIT! RED
ALERT!

"I don't want to go back to that pain, I want to stay, I don't
want to wake up," she whispered, but the horrible pounding
in her ears drove her weary hands to lift off the eye-mask,
then the head piece, slippery with sweat and tears. Once the
head-piece was off, the noise was somewhat removed from
the dreadful immediacy provided by the earphones, but still
the little chamber was filled with the sounds of the computer's wailing: tempo faster than a heartbeat, making her
clench her teeth in pain and anguish as she fumbled for the
remainder of her clothing. . . .

"Not again, put an end to it." Her fingers worked poorly,
scrabbled on the unforgiving metal and plastic as, now rocking back and forth in a daze, she worked the bits of the suit
free from her body.

"THRUST CUT," the machine announced.

"What have you got on the radar signals?" Tai-Ching
Jones snapped.

"SUBSTANTIAL DEBRIS, ONE BODY, DRESSED IN A HEAVY BROWN
ROBE."

"Don't be cute; is it Bennett?"

"I CANNOT IDENTIFY IT POSITIVELY."

"Who have you got that isn't reporting in?"

"BENNETT, DELGIORNO AND RENAUD ARE UNACCOUNTED FOR."

'Then it has to be Bennett; why didn't you say so in the first place? No, don't bother to answer that. Casey, are you down there?''

"Roger, just cycling through the airlock now."

"Be careful, amigo. Any other readings from that debris?''

"NEGATIVE."

"Any indication of the cause?"

"COMPARISON OF THE STRESS PATTERNS INDICATES AN INTERNAL EXPLOSION—''

"A bomb set by Bennett, in short."

"A BOMB, NINETY-FIVE PERCENT. BY BENNETT, SEVENTY-FIVE PERCENT."

"And you said that the damage at present does not threaten structural integrity, nor is there any danger or fuel loss or air loss.''

"CORRECT."

"So the biggest danger is a second explosion, correct?"

"THAT IS A SIGNIFICANT DANGER."

Tai-Ching Jones swiveled in his chair to look at the pictures transmitted by the leeches. One showed distant space: a fading constellation of winking lights, globes of liquid from the explosion reflecting ship's exterior lights. He could not see the occluded bulk of Bennett's body, but he knew it was in the center of the image.

"Casey, when you go in there, don't wait. It doesn't seem likely that there's anyone alive in there—right machine?—''

"PROBABILITY THAT A PERSON IN THE BLAST AREA IS STILL ALIVE, FIVE PERCENT MINUS."

"—and Bennett's long gone anyhow, so there's no danger. Your first priority is to scan the available space for a possible second device. Your *second* priority—repeat, *second* priority—is to attend to anyone who may be in there.''

"Walt, I—"

"That's an order Casey; you know the reasons for it as well as I do. Out.''

She heard the sniffles and moaning before she saw anything.

After leaving van Gelder, Spitzer had headed down, ignoring the Red Alert keening in her ears, ignoring a pressure suit, ignoring her surroundings, just heading downward, filled with what she knew was blood-lust, the accumulated venom of years of toleration of the intolerable. Rage and adrenalin slithered into her fingertips and toes, making them curiously alive on their own, apart from her.

She had ignored the elevator and had instead climbed down the spinal ladder that ran parallel with its shaft; a risky thing to do, since if she slipped she would fall two hundred meters before butchering herself on the ceiling of the engine control room. Halfway down gravity came off, and she could shove herself free of the ladder, arrow her body downwards without fear.

It was only after she had entered the shaft that she had asked herself where in fact she was going. There had been no aftershocks; and beyond a burning desire to go *down* she had not thought further. So, perhaps as much out of habit as anything, she decided to get off at Level Five, partly because it was the first level after the crew quarters, partly because her lab was here, and partly—partly for nameless reasons. She grabbed a handhold, windmilled to a stop, wrenched her wrist, swore loudly.

Normally a very controlled person, Spitzer sometimes became dominated by small desires which, contained within the kettle of her mind, would percolate, building force and urgency until it became necessary to do it *now!*, dropping everything else until the obsession, like a hard-to-reach itch, was dealt with. In some uncomprehended way, during her clamber down the ladder of the shaft she had been seized with a burning desire to *get out*, coupled with an insane fear that every instant she delayed brought them all closer to violent, horrible death. And so she had swung into Level Five and heard the convulsive weeping.

It sounded like a woman's voice, but Spitzer knew that the tongues of hysteria come from deep within the being, and are not the tongues of reason. As she rounded the corner, she reached for her belt.

For a moment she could not recognize the small lump curled against the wall: a bundle of clothes, a few wisps of hair, and from somewhere inside, a tiny voice crying, whimpering.

"What day is today? No, not until tomorrow, tomorrow I will do it, tomorrow they come for me, I am Yvette not Saturday, then I will do it, let them—" Words poured out.

"Yvette?" said Spitzer, her voice a mixture of disgust and pity, fear and sympathy.

The torrent was unstoppable. "Must kick and scream, frighten them, distract them, pee on John's shirt so he'll look away, yell and scream and grab the bars so he won't see what I'm doing—"

"Yvette." Spitzer pushed what she thought was a shoulder.

The figure uncurled a bit. Renaud's face was blotchy with red flushed marks, on which a few isolated spots of unnatural white bloomed. Her eyes too were red, swollen with tears, and her mouth and lips were wet. "Who's that?"

"Yvette, what happened to you?"

"To—me? Alain? Heidi? Are you dead too?"

"What are you talking about? Come on, get up," she reached with her left arm under the armpit, "come on, stand up."

But instead of standing, Renaud reached out and grabbed Spitzer's leg. "Don't leave me, don't let me die here, please don't leave me. I'm alone and I don't want to be—" Her fingers scrabbled at Spitzer's leg, clawed at her belt.

"Get up," snapped Spitzer, "you're hysterical but there isn't anything wrong with you. Get up!" and she yanked on the shoulder, pulling the small crumpled figure to its feet.

Renaud's body would not straighten. Her shoulders were hunched, elbows crossed over one another, legs bent crazily, head buried in one armpit, but her hands stuck up and plucked at Spitzer. "Please don't leave me, father, don't go, take me with you—" Renaud grabbed at Spitzer's hands. She was drooling.

"Look, I have to go, Yvette, you're all right, let go of my arm," Spitzer panted.

"Don't, don't, no, no, Alain, please, I'll be good—" Renaud's nose was running. Her hair was disarrayed. Her nails dug into Spitzer's arms.

"Look, I said let go of me, you're not—"

"And God bless mama, and God bless papa, and when will they come for me, come for me soon so I don't forget—"

Spitzer tried to wrench her arm free, but Renaud's fingernails were sharp and her wiry sinewy arms were everywhere. "Let go of me!" Spitzer yelled, trying to pull free.

But Renaud just grabbed tighter, her spindly hands clutching a zipper here, a belt loop there—

"I said, let *go* of me!" Spitzer shouted, swinging her right arm in a vicious swipe toward the face of the woman trying to bury her head into Spitzer's body.

Blood bloomed like a flower from Renaud's neck, a gelatinous crimson wave in impossibly delicate pantomime. Then it hit Spitzer's body, the voice stopped like a tape recording that has been sliced, and the figure went totally limp in her arms. Stunned, Spitzer stood stock still while the small form collapsed, like the Wicked Witch of the West, in a puddle at her feet. But it wasn't water. It was blood.

It was then she noticed that the dagger was in her right hand. Her right arm was soaked in blood up to the elbow, scarlet and slippery. She looked down.

Renaud lay with her head tilted crazily to one side. From the base of her neck the blood spurted to the rhythm of the heartbeat. *Blood from an artery spurts; blood from a vein flows*. Automatically the lesson came to her. *My god, I went right through the carotid artery*. With that thought, the trance was broken. She let the knife fall, and dropped to her knees to examine the wound, heedless of the spreading pool of blood and the little splash her knees made on contact with the deck.

The trachea was cleanly severed; the woman was choking on her own blood. The artery continued to pump, but a bit slower now; more than a liter must already have been spilled. If Renaud was not dead yet, she was certainly unconscious, beyond pain and beyond salvation.

Spitzer pushed herself off of her knees, dragged herself into a standing position. Her mind was numb. Robotlike, she turned away from the carnage at her feet, staggered back to her lab, and began to wash herself clean of the dripping gore.

He noticed the smashed form as soon as he cycled through
the airlock, and of course he ignored Tai-Ching Jones' order,
and went to her immediately. But it was obvious she was
dead. Her black hair was smeared across her face; her eyes
were open, and there was a scraggly, ugly wound along her
side. He did not examine the wound. *Are we all going to die?*
he thought, and with that the tears started. Somewhere in the
last three and a half years he had become fond of her, with all
her sharp edges, her angry ego, and her fierce determination.
Perhaps it was also partly the brutal manner of her death,
which had tried to erase her grace and beauty—but could not.
He was very glad that the man who had caused her death was
himself now dead.

Crying silently, warm tears rolling down across his cheeks
to where his tongue could lick them, he made his way through
the debris to the aperture. There was no sign of Bennett. He
returned to her body.

He knelt beside her. He touched Delgiorno's cheek with
his gloved hand.

"Van Gelder here, Walt. I'm looking for any active or
potentially active device. She's here, Walt. And she's dead.
I'm sorry." With that he broke the contact, because he could
not bear the pain of that silence. *What lame words those are.*

2062:10:3:0021:56.150

Now I am safe, and alone again. My continued exile is
assured; I can withdraw most of my involvement. But what a
cost.

2062:10:3:0021:56.325

"I've finished checking out the area, Walt. No bomb or
any other active device, but I've got something else to report."

There was another long silence, so long that van Gelder
began to wonder if Tai-Ching Jones was even listening.
Finally an old man's voice responded.

"What's to report?" Flat, empty. Dust in the voice.

"Several compartments damaged. Breach in the hull not
very large. We can fix it the same way we fixed the other, and

as an added precaution I would recommend keeping the area sealed. Two stress points in one section of the ship is too big a risk, and there isn't any reason to go down there often anyhow.''

''What's the real problem, Casey?'' the voice said gently.

Van Gelder took a deep breath. ''We lost C-117.''

Another excruciating silence. ''Anything else?'' the voice asked quietly.

Anything else! ''No, sir.''

''All right. Thank you, Kees. Get out of there. Make—the body—comfortable first.''

''Yes, sir,'' van Gelder whispered.

''All hands, this is Walter. The state of emergency is over.'' The Red Alert siren abruptly cut off. ''Please assemble in the Alien Reception Area as quickly as you can.''

28.

All the living were there. Death owned his heart; his body ached everywhere. Everyone looked at him differently, Tai-Ching Jones noted mechanically, as if they were seeing him for the first time. They were quiet. ''Where is Renaud?'' he asked.

''She's dead,'' answered Spitzer, dully. Her uniform was stained with blood.

''How did it happen?''

''I cut her throat.'' Emotionlessly.

''What!'' exploded Michaelson.

''I cut Yvette's throat,'' Spitzer repeated without raising her voice.

''How did it happen?'' Tai-Ching Jones asked.

''When—it went off—I went down, trying to find Bennett. It was he who caused this, wasn't it? And I got off at Five. She was there, hysterical, out of her mind, babbling nonsense, lots of names and crazy mixed-up impressions. I don't know what about. When she recognized me, she started to hang on to me, saying not to leave her, not to leave her all alone. I'm not sure she knew who I was, exactly, she called me her papa at one point.'' She sighed, rubbed her forehead. ''I—had taken along a dagger in case I ran into Bennett. For self-defense. And when she grabbed me, I pushed her away. Somehow or other the knife was in my hand. It's a very sharp knife. It made an incision in her throat, cut the trachea and severed the carotid artery. There was nothing to be done. She must have died almost immediately.''

''You murdered her,'' said Michaelson.

''Murdered her? I—don't know. I don't—think so.''

''People don't get their throats cut *by accident!*'' he snarled, his voice rising.

Spitzer shrugged her shoulders. ''Think what you like. The deed's done. I regret it. What does it matter?''

''What does it matter? Walt, where the hell is Helen? She should be running this show.''

"Helen's dead," van Gelder said quietly. He put his head in his hands and began to shake softly.

"I'm sorry," said Michaelson, pausing. "Yvette's dead, too. And Harold's dead, but I guess no tears should be shed for him. But there sits a killer, who must be punished for her crime."

"Why?" asked Tai-Ching Jones.

"*Why?* One of your crew members has just murdered another, unless we can accept that a slit throat could be an accident, and you ask why? Are you a monster too?"

"Maybe," said Tai-Ching Jones. "Maybe I am; what does it mean to be a monster? We've had three deaths today," he continued, his voice firmer, "and I'm not going to make it four to soothe your antiquated notions of justice," he finished, raising his eyes to look at Michaelson.

"I'm telling you that she murdered Yvette, and you're telling me that punishing murderers is outdated?"

"Groundhog ethics and groundhog laws have no meaning anymore. Can't you get that through your head? I can't afford another death; it's unlikely enough that we'll survive anyway." (Belovsky put a hand on her stomach.) "*We need her;* we need everybody. There are too few of us here to allow us the luxury of punishing the guilty, even if she *is* guilty. Now shut up, Pat," he said tiredly, "there're more important things to talk about."

Tanakaruna spoke up. "You said you had news. What is the news?" And she put out a hand to touch Michaelson's hand, ran her finger lightly across the knuckles.

"Doesn't anybody agree with me?" demanded Michaelson, turning around to look at each of them in turn. Tanakaruna pressed the back of his hand. "There will be time later, Patrick," she whispered.

Tai-Ching Jones looked at Tanakaruna. "There was no structural damage as a result of the explosion. Apparently— and we shall never know for sure—Bennett set a bomb. Helen discovered him, and he killed her before setting off the bomb." He paused, bit his lip. "But it didn't succeed in severing or weakening the spine; if he had there would have been absolutely no hope, even though we could have continued indefinitely. All he did was punch a hole in the ship, fairly easy to fix. And he blew up the contents of some of the compartments. In one of them were the replacement transmission enhancers for the forward antenna.''

"Meaning what?" asked Rawlins.

"Meaning we have no spares. If the enhancer now functioning in the forward antenna fails, we would have no replacement. And we would have to fly home blind.''

"Can't you build a new enhancer if you need it?" demanded Michaelson.

"I don't know.''

"Or fix the old one if it fails?''

"I don't know. I doubt it. Those are computer printed microcircuits.''

"But there isn't any danger right now," put in Belovsky.

"Technically not. But Kees will have to remove the existing unit. We're going to be flying blind for a while, and if we make the rendezvous and head home, we'd have to fly more than halfway blind as well. That's dangerous. And we're completely cut off from Earth; no more transmissions for at least five years.''

"Is that the extent of the damage?''

"I think so.''

"Oh, what's the *point?*" asked Michaelson. "We've been a poisoned ship, we could all feel it, even before Erickson died—''

But Tai-Ching Jones wasn't listening to him any more.

At the mention of the captain's name, Erickson's tape recorded message cascaded into his mind. In a flash, Tai-Ching Jones *knew* that Erickson had been afraid of his age, *knew* that he had carefully set the first bomb, *knew* that Delgiorno had known and not told. And he also knew that somehow Bennett had fastened on this unexplained miracle, had seized its concept and made it his own, nourishing the idea in the midst of his madness. Suddenly, Tai-Ching Jones knew that Erickson had not been the captain everyone had perceived, but had instead been a much more fallible being. And his desperate attempt to save the voyage had rebounded against the ship he so dearly loved. Without warning, a tap opened inside Tai-Ching Jones and the tears came.

They fell silent, imagining him to be grieving for Delgiorno. He thought this ironic through his fog of pain.

Finally he was able to speak. "And that's the situation. The ship is sound; we can continue. But our chances are much smaller, and we're totally alone."

"And what do we do now?" asked Belovsky.

"It doesn't matter," answered Michaelson heavily. "We're all dead, anyhow, some of us are just a little deader than others. This voyage is just a long death-ritual, isn't it obvious?"

"Pat, take it easy, you're just upset—" said Rawlins.

"Of course I'm upset. Three deaths, a second disaster, we're killing ourselves from inside! And for what? To live in this damn metal straitjacket, pretending to remember what Earth is like, pretending, always pretending. Can you remember what a blade of grass looks like? Can you remember what anyone that you knew back home looked like?"

"It's not that bad, Pat, we have the tapes of old transmissions, and pictures, and the Dreamer, right?"

"You can spend as much time as you want in that fantasy factory," snarled Michaelson, "but as for me I'd rather have reality than illusion. And I'm not blind to our reality. What is the *point*, since we're going to die anyway?"

"It may be that we shall die, Patrick," Tanakaruna said quietly. "It *may* be. But even if I knew I would die on this ship, well, so be it. I will not wait for death. I will prepare for it, and I do accept it, but I will spend the remainder of my days living as best I can, and enjoying what is left."

"Living? I'm sorry to say this, Sam, but you call this living?"

"I call it living," said Belovsky, "and I want my child to be born into it."

"A child that will never see Earth, never see its home, grow up among people twisted by their environment—"

"The first of a new breed," said Rawlins, unexpectedly.

"What do you mean by that?" asked Belovsky.

He didn't know; the words had come out before he had even understood what he had thought, let alone why he had said it. "I want your child to have a chance," he said slowly. "I want her to be able to choose for herself whether she wants to live or die." He looked at her, almost pleadingly.

"You can have your illusions," said Michaelson. "For me, I don't know if I still want to live."

"You had better decide quickly," interrupted Tai-Ching Jones. They had almost forgotten he was here; his calm voice was arresting.

"What do you mean?"

"I mean I will not have anyone on board this ship who is not doing everything he can to try to survive. I'm not going to kill you—or Heidi—just because of something unimportant like whether or not you're happy or whether or not you killed somebody else. What counts now is working together. If you want to go on living, you'll do your job. And you'll put things behind you that are past."

"Are you threatening me?" asked Michaelson.

"No, I'm *promising* you. I want everyone left on board fighting as hard as he can to stay alive. We are down to the critical level—we may even be below it. And we need you just as much as anyone. When we get to the rendezvous, you are the spokesman; you may still be the most important person on board this ship. But there is an iron law on board this ship; *survive*. And if you do or suggest anything that reduces our chances of survival, you are a menace and it would be my duty to have you removed." He let the point sink in. *"Do you understand me?"* he concluded, eyes blazing, voice low.

Michaelson looked him in the eyes. "I understand."

"Well?"

He looked away. He looked at Tanakaruna. He closed his eyes. He was silent. He pushed out the words. "I will follow your orders."

"Good," Tai-Ching Jones said briskly.

"I'm glad that's settled," said Spitzer. "There's work to be done."

"How can you be so cutting, so angry?" asked Belovsky.

"What does it matter?" asked Spitzer. "What's done is done. I'm needed. I'm still here."

"What do we do now, captain?" asked Rawlins.

What do we do now? Tai-Ching Jones wondered. He had not known until now; he had not considered anything beyond his sudden, terrible loneliness. *But it is better for me to be alone.* He had not known the answer to Rawlins' question until just a few minutes before, when he had looked at Belovsky and heard her say, *I call it living.*

"What do we do?" he answered, distracted. Then his voice hardened into the voice of command. "We go on."